SHARDS OF THE SUN

BOOK THREE OF

THE REALM OF AREON

R.T. COLE

DEDICATION

Harry and Andy – The 'Thasus' and 'Andemar' to my 'Rudimere'.
The two best brothers and friends that anyone could ever ask for.

Special Thanks to members of my Udder Madness crew:
Lauren, Troy, and Vivian,
the inspiration for Loreena, Ornell, and Valentyne.

CONTENTS

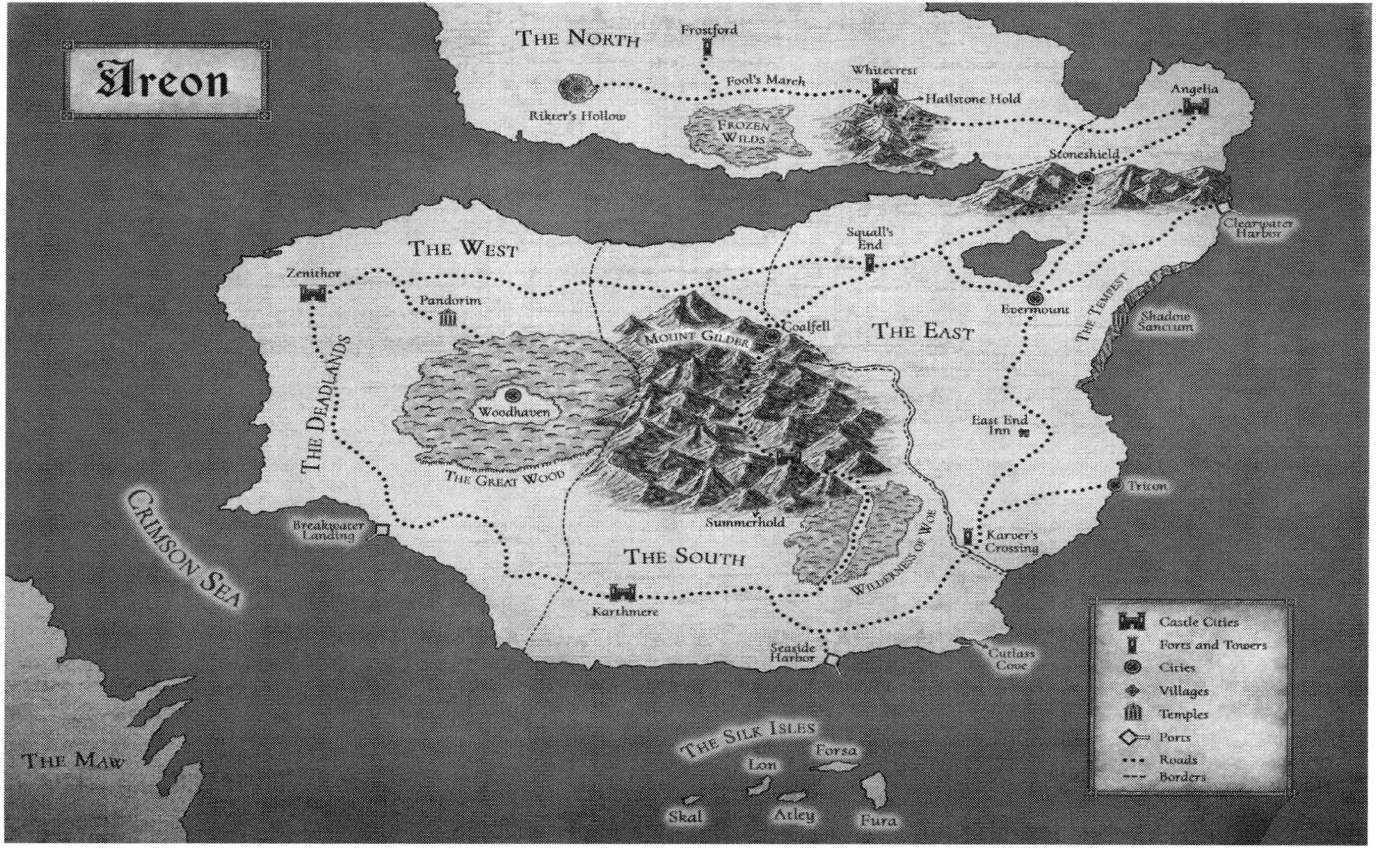
Areon
The North
Frostford
Fool's March
Whitecrest
Hailstone Hold
Angelia
Rikter's Hollow
Frozen Wilds
Stoneshield
Clearwater Harbor
The West
Squall's End
Zenithor
Pandorim
Evermount
The Tempest
Shadow Sanctum
Coalfell
Mount Gilder
The East
Woodhaven
East End Inn
The Deadlands
The Great Wood
Triton
Breakwater Landing
Summerhold
Karver's Crossing
Crimson Sea
The South
Wilderness of Woe
Karthmere
Seaside Harbor
Cutlass Cove
Castle Cities
Forts and Towers
Cities
Villages
Temples
Ports
Roads
Borders
The Silk Isles
Forsa
Lon
The Maw
Skal
Atley
Fura

Chapter 1

A DISGRACE TO THE NAME

He slept peacefully next to the woman that despised him. The Lords of Areon did not always have it easy when it came to arranged marriages. In that regard, the recent marriage to someone so strong-willed had left the Lord of the Frostford exhausted – in mind and not so much body. While he had not yet consummated the union, he considered it only a matter of time before Kaya Gargan – now Kaya *Brock* – accepted her new role as his wife. Still, the wedding had paled in comparison to the events that had taken place recently.

Four days ago, Cale Brock had met with the North King and his entourage at the crossroads of the Fool's March to discuss the king's surrender. But things did not turn out as Lord Brock had intended. King Cyrus, Lord Bowlin, and Prince Thasus had convinced him to set aside their differences until the threat of West King Kelbain had been dealt with. Cale did not want to settle anything with King Cyrus, as he believed that the Nortons' time on the throne was over. The truth of the matter was that Cale's alliance with Oswall Gargan, of Rikter's Hollow, was contingent upon the removal of House Norton. Cyrus had seen through Cale's veiled threats, claiming that Cale only meant to put Lord Gargan on the throne instead. Refusing to admit his loyalty to Oswall, Cale – along with Grenna Gargan, who spoke on her father's behalf – agreed to King Cyrus's offer of peace. To appease Lord Gargan, it was stated that King Cyrus would also take one of Oswall's daughters as his wife, effectively making her the new North Queen. With a new treaty formed between the Northern houses, Cale suggested that they all celebrate the historic occasion at the capital of Whitecrest.

It was a night that had not been seen in almost a century. All of the North was represented at one table, and though they did not love one another in the traditional sense, a small part of Cale considered it an honor to take part in such a moment. He and his men were feasting and drinking into the night, but when most of the guests had gone to bed, Lord Brock was sure to leave his people in good spirits.

"I'm off to join my *loving* wife!" he exclaimed in a mocking tone. Earlier, at the start of the feast, when Kaya stormed off angrily in front of everyone, Cale had made a similar remark to mask his inner annoyance with the reluctant bride. It was not so much the behavior she exhibited that vexed him, but those who witnessed such an outburst. Cale did not like King Cyrus, regardless of any peace established between them for the time being. Nor did he have any respect for the Lord of Stoneshield, Marc Bowlin. But it was his animosity toward Thasus Palidor that plagued his thoughts. Cale had attempted to kill the Prince of Angelia at least twice in a matter of a month, yet the man continued to escape death. Though a part of him still wished for Thasus's demise, he could not help but keep his end of the bargain when honor called for it.

As his men raised their pints of ale, laughing along with their lord, Cale walked out of the great hall almost triumphantly. The corridors were brisk with cool winds, and the moon lit up each corner of the passageway in an almost majestic aura. He was not sure that it was any better than the Frostford, though his home was entirely made up of ice and was exceedingly frigid in comparison.

Perhaps I'll move south one day and spend time in the warmth, he considered. He assumed that the weather in the Silk Isles would provide more comfort than the bed he would occupy momentarily. His expectations were confirmed when he entered the room where Kaya was already sleeping. As Cale approached, he put one foot into the bed, only to notice Kaya turn over and slide closer to the edge – presumably to get as far away from him as possible. It did not bother him, though. Cale was growing curious about how the alliance with Cyrus and Oswall would play out in the coming months, so he fell asleep with relative ease.

While he continued to rest peacefully, a sudden noise jerked him from his slumber. His eyes opened in surprise, and he found himself sitting up with haste.

"What is going on out there?" he asked aloud. He had not expected an answer from his wife, though he knew that she had awoken as well. After he spoke, he noticed that she had remained silent and adjusted herself, if only slightly.

The noises grew louder, and after a moment, Cale realized that he heard footsteps – they sounded as if they were getting closer with each passing moment. A sudden sense of awareness crept into his chest, pulling at every ounce of courage that he possessed. The running footsteps were deafening now.

"We have to leave," he said directly to Kaya. "Now."

Kaya stirred and sighed. "Why? What have you done?" she asked casually.

"I've done *nothing*," he hissed. "Pack your things. You and I are heading back to the Frostford." A feeling of dread washed over him like a blanket of snow during a winter blizzard.

Kaya jumped out of the bed as if the God of Death had chased her out of it. She quickly adjusted the furs that enveloped her body. She had, no doubt, wrapped them around her while she slept in an attempt to avoid any contact with Cale.

"I am *not* going anywhere with *you!*" she said in a hushed tone of defiance.

"Woman, this is not the time. Something is happening out there."

Suddenly, the door to the bedchamber flung open, and before Cale could get in a word, soldiers in the dark grabbed him by the arms and dragged him into the hall.

"What is the meaning of this?! I am Cale Brock, Lord of the Frostford! Let go of me!"

He assumed that Kaya had been taken as well, as he heard her cursing the armored abductors. Cale noticed that the passage was a bit cooler than when he left the feast, as he was only in a light tunic this time. Through the darkness, he could not tell where he was being taken, and the more questions he asked of the soldiers, the faster they dragged his feet across the floor.

Finally, Cale and Kaya were brought into another room – one that was much larger than the hallways they had just been carried through. Allowing his eyes to adapt to the dimly-lit area, Cale recognized the great hall surrounding them, clean and arranged as if there had not been a bustling feast hours before. To see more clearly, he jerked his head backward, tossing his dark blonde hair out of the way, as his hands were bound by the men standing behind him. With a quick look to his right, Kaya stood a few feet away, a look of panic spread across her face. She, too, had been held against her will.

"Cale Brock," a voice called from up ahead. "You have been arrested this morning on the charges of murder and treason."

Staring at the man in front of him, Cale narrowed his eyes when he caught a glimpse of that awful-looking golden crown.

"Why have I been brought here, Your Grace?" Cale asked in an annoyed tone. "You interrupted a very comfortable sleep."

"You are speaking to your king," a woman said as she crept out from the king's right side of the throne. "You would do well to take this matter seriously."

Cale looked upon King Cyrus and his mother, Celia. Hatred and realization rushed through him. "So…I take it our alliance has already come to an end. Tell me, Cyrus: Was this your plan all along?"

"This is *your* doing, Lord Brock," Cyrus stated. "We all believed that you would hold to your word when Prince Thasus killed your best fighter. To secure the peace between us, I even agreed to marry one of Oswall's daughters – or have you forgotten? By the gods, the alliance was an important achievement for the North…but you went ahead and threw that all away." A hint of disappointment rang in Cyrus's words.

"I have done nothing to betray the treaty!" Cale shouted. "What is it you think I've done?!"

Cyrus and Celia looked to one another and, as Celia nodded, Cyrus stood from his throne. The king took a heavy breath before he spoke.

"Lord Cale Brock, of the Frostford. You have been charged with the murder of Lord Marc Bowlin, of Stoneshield. You have also been charged with treason. Do you deny the charges brought against you?"

Bowlin is dead? Why is this fool of a king pointing the blame at me? "This is madness," Cale said breathlessly. "Complete madness."

"There was an attempt on my life in the middle of the night," Cyrus started to explain. "A man tried to murder me in my own bedchamber before Lord Bowlin attempted to subdue him at the behest of my mother. Instead, Marc Bowlin was murdered for his efforts. The murderer was one of *your men*, Lord Brock." Noticing the display of shock on the face of Cale, Cyrus asked again, "Do you deny the charges?"

Cale merely shook his head in disbelief. "I deny *all* of the charges," he said with conviction. Then, after a moment of contemplation, he asked Cyrus, "Where is the assailant?" He thought it was suspicious that the supposed murderer's whereabouts had not been mentioned until now.

"He is no longer of this world," Celia replied. "We moved his body from my son's chambers and threw him to the snow outside. He will *not* be given a proper burial and will *not* be given passage to Volsi," she said scornfully.

"After Lord Bowlin was killed," King Cyrus continued, "I took the life of the attacker with my own dagger." He presented the blade in front of all who stood within the great hall, presumably to provide them with proof of Lord Brock's treachery.

Cale's eyes became slits. "Of course you did," he said bluntly. In an attempt to reason with the king, Cale proclaimed, "We all know how things began at the crossroads. If I wanted you dead, I would have done so in the tent where we all met."

The guards that stood to either side of King Cyrus drew their weapons, reacting to Cale's underhanded threat.

"So you'd have me believe," Cyrus retorted. "But the better plan would be to suggest that we all come here to the capital, where you'd try to assassinate and supplant me."

Cale frowned. He had almost forgotten that it was *his* idea to have the celebration at Whitecrest. Things were not looking in his favor. That much was clear. Cale was still not convinced that anybody within his army would be stupid enough to try and murder the North King. Something was amiss, though he could not figure out what. He only knew that King Cyrus was hiding something.

Suddenly, a door to the right side of the great hall opened up to reveal Thasus Palidor. The man wore his full suit of armor, as if ready to do battle right then and there, though his scarred face showed signs of confusion.

"I heard raised voices, Your Grace. What has happened?"

Cyrus's eyes met the floor. He took a moment to compose himself before looking at his friend. "I am sorry, Thasus…"

The Prince's brows lowered in further bewilderment as he searched the room. He caught a glance of Cale Brock, bound from the back by Whitecrest soldiers. King Cyrus started to speak again, but Thasus could not hear him, as he quickly became worried.

"Where's my uncle?" he asked Cyrus. When his gaze was met with one of sadness, his heart skipped a beat, and his stomach felt weak. "Cyrus...Where is he?"

The North King sighed. "He's dead, Thasus...I'm sorry."

"No..." Thasus said, refusing to believe Cyrus. "I-I just spoke to him. *We* just spoke during the feast."

"He was murdered in the night," King Cyrus began to say, "protecting *me*. There was an assassin in my bedchamber. My mother heard the struggle and called on Marc to defend me...He *did*." Cyrus said with a shudder in his voice.

Thasus listened intently. Though he found it hard to believe that his uncle would ever come to Cyrus's defense, he knew that Celia would have been the only one to convince Marc to do so.

"After Marc fell," Cyrus continued, "I stabbed the murderer and avenged your uncle."

"Lies!"

Cyrus, Thasus, and all of the attendees turned toward Cale Brock after the man's outburst.

"The man who killed your uncle," Cyrus said to Thasus as he stared at Cale, "was a soldier from the Frostford. Lord Brock has been charged with Marc's murder and treason."

Thasus saw nothing in that instant except rage. He lunged at Cale faster than anyone could have anticipated, tearing him from the grip of the king's men and inflicting his pain on the Lord of the Frostford's face.

"Guards!" King Cyrus yelled.

Whitecrest soldiers grabbed hold of Thasus and pulled him off the prisoner, though it took four men to do so.

"Unhand me! *I* will avenge my uncle myself!" Thasus roared throughout the great hall.

To everyone's surprise, Cale, blood pouring from his mouth, had to be held back from retaliating against Thasus. "I should have killed you when I had the chance!" Cale shouted at the Prince of Angelia. "My men will have your *head* for this! I promise you that!"

"I think we've seen enough, Your Grace," Celia said calmly to her son, but loud enough for all to hear.

King Cyrus then raised his hand into the air, signaling all to stop and listen. Cale still struggled, but Thasus stopped, and the soldiers released him.

"There is sufficient evidence to find you guilty, Lord Brock," Cyrus declared.

"I did *not* kill Lord Bowlin!" Cale screamed, though his words fell on deaf ears.

"*Therefore,*" King Cyrus emphasized the word, for all to pay attention, "you will hang on this day."

***

Dawn had come and gone. The people of Whitecrest gathered in the town square to find out what had transpired in the night, though the rumors had already reached their ears. Lord Cale Brock was to be executed for murdering Marc Bowlin, of Stoneshield, and for betraying the trust of all Northerners.

Soldiers emptied from the great hall, walking beside their prisoner. King Cyrus, his mother, and Thasus the Mighty followed from the rear. The men from the Frostford, who had accompanied Cale Brock to the capital, shouted from the crowd, demanding to know the truth behind their lord's imprisonment.

Cyrus expected the angry mob of men to be loyal to Lord Brock but planned to address them soon enough. He felt unimaginable guilt for lying to his friend, Thasus, however. He did not mean to kill Marc…He was only trying to defend his mother from harm. *Too late*, he thought. *We must all try and move on from here.* He may not have liked Marc, but for the sake of his friendship with Thasus, and the sake of his people, he was willing to lie if it would help their cause.

The entourage finally arrived at their destination. As the guards led Cale up the steps toward the noose, King Cyrus stood before the crowd and spoke loudly.

"People of the North! We are here today to witness the sentencing of a traitor!" The last statement was met with disapproval from the soldiers of the Frostford. "My friends," he spoke more softly to them in particular, "you must listen to what I have to say."

After giving his account of the night's tragic events, Cyrus compounded his lies by appealing to the people's honor. "You are all Northmen, as am I. Have we not strived to be civil with one another, even in times of stubbornness?" He then turned and pointed directly at Cale. "*He* broke the pact that we had all fought so hard to accomplish – even after Thasus the Mighty defeated the Frostford's best fighter!" Cyrus observed the hesitation to defend their lord on the faces of those below him. He was winning them over, and so he continued. "So the fact remains: Lord Brock committed treason. He has shown his true nature, and with that, I ask you all one thing…Men of the Frostford, will you join me and continue to stand for a unified North?"

Cale Brock displayed an obvious smirk on his lips at the thought of his own men betraying him. But, to his utter shock, his people cheered for King Cyrus and broke their pledge to him right before his very eyes.

"You are all fools!" Cale scoffed, mocking his people. "This has been a wonderful charade, that's clear. But, you would all betray *me* and follow this spineless man?" He looked at King Cyrus when he spoke and then spat at his feet. "You can all burn in Mistif." After his remark, he saw Cyrus nod to a man hidden in the corner. The man in the black hood brought a wooden stool in his direction and placed it down in front of him. The executioner then lowered the noose and tied it around Cale's neck, securing it in place. Internally, Cale exhibited great fear at that moment, knowing well enough that he was about to die.

As Thasus stood to the side, watching his uncle's murderer prepare to be hanged, he noticed that Kaya Brock was brought out, hands bound in the front, to watch her husband's sentencing take place. By that point, Cyrus had joined him, ready to witness the execution. Without thinking twice, Thasus leaned in and whispered to the king, "What was *her* part in the assassination attempt?" He did not fully believe that she had anything to do with it, given her outburst toward Brock at the feast, but he had to be sure.

"We cannot be certain of her role in that," Cyrus replied after a brief pause. "For now, she will remain in our dungeons until we can determine our next course of action." That seemed to be enough for Thasus for the time being.

Thasus continued to watch as the executioner and a couple of guards lifted Cale onto the wooden stool. Knowing that Cale's time was almost at an end, he could not help but speak up. "Wait!" he shouted. King Cyrus turned to him, puzzled. "It must be *me*." Before Cyrus could interject, Thasus waved him off. "I know what you would say, Your Grace…but Marc was my uncle. I *must* see this through." Cyrus nodded gravely, but Thasus considered the reaction to be one of understanding.

Thasus walked slowly, but with purpose, up the steps to the platform where Cale Brock stood atop the stool. He stopped in front of the man who had tried to kill him on different occasions – the same man who was responsible for his broken heart – and said nothing. He stared into the killer's eyes, unflinchingly. Cale glared at him in return but did not speak a word.

"This is it," Thasus broke the silence. "No funeral pyre. No Hall of Legends. Just a quick trip to meet Saurius…God of Death…Lord of Mistif. Whichever you prefer, I assume you'll know each other well while you're burning for all eternity."

"You say many things, *Mighty* Thasus," Cale chuckled. "Do you even believe your own words? Think!" he pleaded. "You once asked me to live up to my name. I did so when I agreed to the treaty."

"You're a disgrace to the name," Thasus shot back. "Son of *Baldric*. Grandson of *Maven*. These are men worthy of the Brock surname. But you? You've single-handedly led your family's legacy to ruin."

"Trust me, Prince Thasus. When Oswall Gargan is done with you all, the North will be a burial ground for Nortons and Palidors alike." As he watched the look on Thasus's face change to a mix of hatred and curiosity, he continued with his attempt at securing a release. "But with *my* help, we can push back against the Gargans before they lay waste to all of your armies."

Thasus let the information sink in before he gave Cale his reply. "Even if Grenna and Jorga fail to convince Oswall to keep the peace, do you truly believe that the Gargans can survive against Whitecrest? Against the Frostford?" Thasus knew that by mentioning Cale's home, it would remind the man of his men's betrayal. As he stepped back, he looked upon Cale Brock's contorted expression and asked, "Any final words, Lord Brock?"

Cale shook his head in defiance and addressed the crowd instead.

"I am Cale Brock, Lord of the Frostford! Rightful heir to the Northern throne! Descendant of Rikter! I am the *last* living Brock! If you kill me, you destroy a legacy that has lasted in Areon for centuries! You can't do th—"

Thasus had heard enough. The force of his kick had splintered the wood from the stool as it fell to the ground and off the platform. Kicking it out from under Cale Brock felt satisfying, but, at the same time, it saddened him. Brock's death would not bring back his Uncle Marc. That particular light in the world had gone out. If anything at all, Thasus was glad to be rid of the man who had troubled him since he left Angelia and come to the North.

It took longer than expected, but Cale hung from the rope until his death rattle could be heard amongst the silent crowd. As Thasus stood there in front of Cale's lifeless body, he gazed toward Kaya once more, noting the emotionless expression that she presented. He surmised that either she was good at masking her genuine feelings, or she truly hated her late husband. *Either way,* Thasus thought, *I'll find out with certainty.*

Chapter 2

THAT NIGHT AT REDBERRY

The dream was always the same. The young boy and his mother walked outside their home, intent on picking fruit from the garden. It all seemed so real. It *was* real, but it had become a distant memory. These days, the memory turned into a nightmare.

"Do you want to pick them today?" the boy's mother had asked him.

Please, no...

The fruit had ripened to the point where the boy knew exactly how delicious they would taste. Though the selection was vast, he centered on the small tree in the middle of the garden. Reaching up to one of the lowest branches, he plucked a green apple and smiled in wonderment.

"Does this look like a good one, Mother?" the boy inquired.

Not again…

"It's perfect," his mother replied. "But there's plenty more to choose from. How about some blueberries?"

The boy smirked. "Can I just pick the apples today? I love apples: the green ones, the red ones. Please, Mother," he pleaded playfully.

His mother knew that there was no arguing with him when it came time to apple picking. The tasty fruit had been the boy's favorite since he was old enough to try one.

"Alright, Mika. But fill the whole basket this time. I'm going to make us a nice pie later," she said as she nudged him, returning the playful banter. "I'll fill this one with berries and grapes and then take them to your father."

By the gods…Why must I go through this again?

The dream would always take the same course. After Mika and his mother picked fruit from the garden, time moved directly to another moment – the moment where *he* arrived.

"Is this it?" the young commander from Woodhaven asked his soldiers. After one of the men nodded, the Commander looked at Mika and his parents with intensity. "Your village burns to the ground. Your people are dead, and you are all that remains." Taking a moment to let the statement sink in, he asked, "Do you know why I've done this?"

Young Mika could not help but look up at his parents, hoping that they would have an answer. They merely shook their heads in fear and confusion.

"To send a message," the man stated. "Redberry was one of the last remaining villages in the Deadlands," he said as he pointed out the devastation that engulfed the homes nearby. "Woodhaven will *never* bow to Zenithor. It is time that the son of the Demon Sorcerer learns that."

Mika's mother sobbed and curled up into her husband's arms. "Please, Commander...spare our son," she begged. "Our Mika..."

"I have no intention of killing any of you," the commander revealed, speaking directly to the small family. "You will be sent to Lord Kelbain's castle to tell him what has transpired here."

Mika's father tilted his head. "But...then we will die *anyway*," he said earnestly.

"Yes. I expect you will. But that's between you and your Lord of Zenithor," the commander replied with no sympathy. "I am allowing you and your family to walk away freely. Surely, you are thankful for my leniency?"

Mika's father darted his eyes around in a panicked state. In an instant, he pushed his wife to the side and grabbed a sword from the belt of a soldier standing to his left.

Please, Father...Don't!

"Run! Take Mika and go!" Mika's father charged toward the commander from Woodhaven and swung with all of his might. As

his opponent simply raised a hand in defense, the steel connected –
but to his horror, the blade broke in his clenched fists, shattering
against the palm of his enemy.

Young Mika and his mother stood in shock at the revelation of
the commander's power. The man was an Evolutionary: a rare type
of Sage in the realm of Areon.

Without flinching, Mika's father recovered and connected his
fist with the commander's jaw, knocking him to the ground.
Woodhaven soldiers restrained him as his family looked on and
shouted. The commander then rose to his feet, his eyes filled with
anger.

"Fool," he said quietly. "You may have lived after delivering
my message to Kelbain…but now you've struck me." His eyes
narrowed. "*That* cannot go unpunished."

The soldiers proceeded to kick their captive in the back of his
knees, lowering him to the dirt. As Mika watched, unblinking, his
mother screamed for her husband.

"Hold him," the commander addressed his men.

Father…No!

It was the moment. The one that Mika had forever wished he
could change. But every time he dreamt of that horrible night, he
could do nothing except yell into the darkness, his voice a silent
breath. The familiar event began to unfold in front of him once
more.

The sound of steel scraping against the inside of the commander's scabbard rang in the night as the man drew his sword. Holding on to the pommel, he placed the blade straight down into the ground in front of him and spoke. "Any final words?"

Mika's father was allowed to raise his head to address his family. It saddened him to see them so scared and full of grief.

"My darling," he said to his wife, "live for our son. He will need you now, more than ever." His eyes reached his son's. "Mika...my son...don't be afraid." The man bravely turned his gaze toward the ground, ready to face the inevitable.

"I, Draven Darkwood, Commander of the forces of Woodhaven, sentence you to die," said the would-be executioner. Without delay, Draven swung his sword downward, beheading the poor man in front of his wife and child.

Mika's mother, yelling in anguish in the direction of Commander Darkwood, suddenly found herself with a sword through her back. While she became silent, staring at the blade that had come out through her belly, young Mika cried into the night.

Make it stop...Let me wake...

Draven stared at the woman in confusion but then noticed one of his soldiers standing behind her as the man pulled his blade out of her back. Commander Darkwood shut his eyes for a moment before approaching the impatient young man.

"Sh-She was going to attack you. I thought I s-saw her take a step toward you," the soldier mumbled in defense of his actions.

Draven quickly removed a dagger from his belt and introduced it to the young man's throat. Sighing, he knelt beside the dying woman on the ground, paying no mind to the dead soldier.

"I would truly have let you all go free," he said sorrowfully. As the woman began to cough up blood, Draven told her, "You are in terrible pain. Allow me to grant you this small mercy." He pressed the end of his dagger to her chest and plunged it deep into her heart. Within moments, she was gone.

Draven stood up and turned to face the young boy who witnessed the death of his parents. "What is your name?"

"Mika," the boy replied in a state of disbelief. His eyes were fixed on his mother and father. "Mika Gainhart."

"Well, Mika, you're the last survivor of this village. Are *you* going to try something stupid as well?"

I'm going to find you...

"No, ser."

I'm going to kill you...

"Good," Draven said. "I'd hate to have you meet your parents so soon..." Underneath his green armor, Draven then used the cloth end of his tunic to clean the blood from his sword and dagger. "Go now, Mika. Deliver my message to Zenithor...and pray that we never meet again."

The hatred inside Mika burned for years after that night. He was 10 when Draven Darkwood murdered his parents. He had to wait patiently before he could seek his revenge.

As the nightmare came to an end, Mika's memories started to pour in unexpectedly. On his 14th birthday, he joined the army of Zenithor, under the direct command of Lamia, a young Illusionist who was fiercely loyal to Lord Kelbain. For many years, serving Kelbain seemed to be the easiest way that he could battle Woodhaven's forces, in hopes of confronting Draven someday.

When Mika was 19, he participated in the Battle of Grimdor – where Woodhaven attacked the last city in the Deadlands – and confronted Draven for the first time since they met in Redberry. Fighting with all of his anger and frustration, Mika knew that he would not have beaten Draven that day, though he never found out for sure. The city of Grimdor was brought down by an Earth Elemental, causing a chaotic amount of retreating on the part of both armies. No one ever found out which army gave the order to decimate the city, but Mika did not care. His chance of getting his revenge was gone.

Flashes began to flood in Mika's mind. After the fall of Grimdor, Mika had many encounters with Lamia's sister, Dirce, as the woman made her usual rounds within the encampments. Shortly after, Mika heard rumors that Darkwood was banished from Woodhaven, so he deserted the army of Zenithor to track down his parents' killer.

"*You told your friends that you disagreed with Kelbain's methods,*" a voice called out.

The memories stopped for a moment, and Mika addressed the unknown person.

"I did *disagree with him…but I needed to find Draven…Who* are *you?*"

More of Mika's memories rose to the surface. A year ago, Mika fought in Single Combat against Baldric Brock, which ended in the Lord of the Frostford's death and the ascension of his son, Cale. After the duel was over, Mika picked up Baldric's axe, the Brock family heirloom, and left.

This isn't my dream…Who's doing this? he wondered.

Deeper and deeper, the memories appeared: The battle at Squall's End. Merroc's death at Draven's hands – a twinge of guilt and sadness struck Mika at the time of this forced memory.

Stop it…

The fight with Draven in The Great Wood, followed by Jasian's capture. Mika's battle with the Lekuzza under Mount Gilder and the surprising conversation with…

"*Aman?!*" the voice said loudly in shock.

The sudden sound was thunderous in Mika's ears. The recovering Sageslayer awoke in a feather bed, surrounded by a well-lit room with open windows and the sun shining through. The wind was calm and brought a small feeling of comfort until Mika found a young man sitting in a chair next to him.

"You actually *spoke* to Aman?" the voice from outside Mika's dreams asked.

Mika jumped back and sat up. "Who are you?! What am I doing here?!"

"Remain calm, Mika, please. You arrived on our steps two days ago, badly wounded. Your friends brought you in, and we've cared for you since then."

Mika stared at the man, though he was sure that the 'man' was still just a *boy*. Gaining a better sense of his situation, he took another look around and noticed that the walls and ceiling were bright gold, with blue and red drapes by the windows.

"Did I make it?" Mika asked, almost lost for words. "Am I in Summerhold?"

"Yes," the young man said, smiling. "You're safe now. I am Prince Tomis, son of King Wilfred. It's nice to finally meet you, Mika. Your friends have been worried sick."

Mika let everything sink in while Tomis explained more. It was reassuring to find out that Rudimere, Paxton, and Ashra had kept true to their word and headed to the Southern capital. Though, a feeling of dread washed over him. He knew that he would have to explain what happened to Jasian in The Great Wood.

"I have to see them," Mika began to say as he slowly brought his feet out of bed and onto the floor.

"Wait," Tomis said as Mika grunted in pain. He rushed to the wounded man's side and helped him get back into the bed. "You are in no condition to leave just yet."

"I must tell them about Jasian," Mika insisted.

"They already know."

Mika blinked, trying to be sure that he heard the boy correctly. "How?" he asked.

"When you collapsed on our steps, you were murmuring about something. Lady Ashra was determined to find out about Jasian, and you told her that he was in Woodhaven."

Mika shut his eyes for a moment and sighed. Then, he looked at Tomis and asked, "Will you bring them to me? I must speak with them at once."

"Hello, my friend," a kind voice spoke from the doorway.

Mika turned and saw a man, brown-haired and blue-eyed, leaning against the wall and smiling. He could not help but smile back.

"Hello, Rudimere," he addressed the East Prince.

Rudimere approached Mika's bedside and extended his arm in friendship and respect. Mika returned the gesture.

"It is good to see you," Rudi said. "We were unsure if you'd ever wake. Your wounds were truly grievous."

"It will take more than a *giant owl* to kill me," Mika laughed in between coughs. Rudi cocked his head and stared blankly. Tomis mirrored the same expression. "I'll explain later," Mika chuckled.

Looking in the direction of the young man in the room, Mika said, "Thank you for watching over me, Prince Tomis. I would speak to your father and tell him of your kindness." The South Prince bowed humbly in response to Mika's words.

"He's done more than that," Rudi said, as he put a hand on Tomis's shoulder. "He's worked with the city healers to help treat your wounds. Without him, you may have been sleeping much longer than two days."

Mika's smile disappeared. Tomis was a prince and not likely to be one of the healers that Rudi spoke of. Suddenly, he became fully aware of what Tomis was, as he remembered someone speaking to him in his dreams.

"What are you?" he asked Tomis in a disgusted tone.

Tomis and Rudimere looked at one another in confusion.

"Sorry?" Tomis asked.

Leaning toward the edge of the bed and grabbing Tomis by the collar, he said, "You're a Reader. You were in my *head*."

"Mika!" Rudi shouted.

"Apologies," Tomis replied in fear. "I-I've done you no harm. Diving into your mind helped you cope with your losses. Your mind began to heal, so your body healed faster because of it." Tomis winced as Mika grunted in frustration.

"That's enough, Mika!" Rudi yelled at his friend again. "The boy only wanted to help you."

The Sageslayer looked away and shook his head. After he released the South Prince, he said, "Stay out of my head. I don't *need* your help."

Surprised by the man's response, Tomis gave a slight bow and then left the room in a hurry, shutting the door behind him.

"Mika..." Rudi sounded disappointed.

"I do not need one of *them* in here, Rudi. I certainly do not want one inside my mind," Mika declared. His hatred of Sages still lingered, even after his encounter with the mysterious Aman.

Rudi sighed. If there was a better time to reveal his secret, he did not know it.

"I'm an Evolutionary," he blurted out, "just like Draven Darkwood." Noticing the look of astonishment on Mika's face, he gave rise to the question, "Will you no longer count me amongst your friends?"

"How?" It was the only possible question that Mika could bring himself to ask.

Rudi went on to tell the story of how his mother, a Kindler, gave him his power before he left Angelia, though he was unaware of his mother's secret and the ability she had gifted to him at the time. He then told Mika of the moment that he figured out his first immunity. During the battle at Squall's End, an arrow was fired at his chest...but then it shattered, much to his and Ashra's surprise. Rudi then reminded Mika of the *first* arrow that he had come into contact with – the one that the bandits were responsible for – and that Mika had helped with when they first met.

Mike let out a half-chuckle under his breath. "You healed fast from that arrow. I thought it was my skill of healing herbs…" The smile at the corner of his mouth then turned into a frown. "Your mother should not have cursed you with such an ability," he said with sadness.

"If she had *not*," Rudi countered, "I would have been dead, along with many others. King Wilfred's daughters…Paxton…Ashra…"

Mika's eyes met the floor. Nodding, he seemed to accept the answer for the time being but wished to learn more later. *I've only just awoken*, Mika thought to himself. *What else have I missed?*

The clang of the door latch sounded, and the door itself opened with a low creak. Peeking inside, a head full of blonde curls appeared to be making their way in at a slow pace.

"Ah, you're awake!" Ashra said, regarding the happy surprise. She walked over to Mika and embraced him tightly.

"I was about to inform him of our time at the Temple of Aman," Rudi said to Ashra.

Mika looked bewildered. "The Temple of—?"

"We'll tell you on the way," Ashra interrupted. "King Wilfred wishes to see us in the throne room."

Chapter 3

THE FOUR

The hall stood a bright example of the glory of Summerhold. Some considered it to be Areon's version of Volsi – a true 'Hall of Legends'. In another time, the great Gilder Orthane sat on the throne of the South, planning his attack on Woodhaven, where he would eventually defeat the young Kelbain in battle. Almost single-handedly, he turned the tide during the Sorcerer's War and gave hope to those who had none. While he may not have been a god from the realm of Volsi, he became a legend in his own right. His son, however, still yearned to live up to the Orthane name.

King Wilfred Orthane was a good man. He respected his father's renown, took care of his people, and loved his children unconditionally. But he was never prepared for war. Peace had lasted for so long in Areon; many had never imagined that they would see anything like the Demon Sorcerer in their time. Yet, that time had come.

The king gathered those closest to him, as well as his new allies, for an important meeting: his wife, Queen Kayla, and their surviving children: Mora, Saris, and Tomis; the Chancellor of Summerhold, Gale Lambin; the recovering Sageslayer and former soldier from Zenithor, Mika Gainhart; Ser Paxton Korba, knight of Angelia; Lady Ashra Argon, of Triton; and East Prince Rudimere Palidor, of Angelia.

"Thank you for coming," King Wilfred addressed all in attendance. He was the only one seated, while the others all stood around him, listening closely. "The last few days have been...difficult to endure, to say the least."

The others all knew that he spoke of the death of his son, Willard. Allying himself with the false Patriarch, Oreus, Willard had plotted to overthrow his father and rule the South, while Oreus would have gone ahead with his own plans for Areon. Once their scheme had been discovered, a battle took place inside the Temple of Aman, where Willard's own sister, Saris, had killed him. Oreus himself had been buried underneath the rubble when the temple burned to the ground. Understandably so, Willard's death had taken its toll on both the king and queen.

"While my wife and I share the grief of losing our son," the king said as he grasped Kayla's hand, "we must continue to prepare for the immediate threat. With the Wilderness of Woe burnt down, the armies of Zenithor and Karthmere will march on us soon."

"We are at the top of a mountain, Father," Saris spoke up, unconvinced of the danger. "We have the position. We have the numbers. It would be foolish to overestimate the enemy."

Paxton stood to the side, admiring Saris and her dark brown curls that draped onto her shoulders. He attempted to pay attention to the actual conversation but found it troublesome when looking at her. Feeling a sudden prod to his side, Paxton snapped out of his trance and noticed his friend Ashra as the one behind the interruption. She gave him a serious look.

"Pay attention," she gestured to him, using just her eyes. Paxton stood upright and focused from then on.

"It would also be foolish to *underestimate* them," Mika called out from beside his friends. "I fought for Kelbain many years ago, and his strategy is not one to make light of."

"Forgive us, but perhaps we do not *want* the advice of a former Zenithorian," Queen Kayla said curtly, her green eyes piercing through Mika like daggers.

At the sight of Mika's face — one that was filled with regret — Rudimere stepped forward and addressed the king and queen. "Mika Gainhart is our ally," he said. "After fighting the mercenary, Draven Darkwood, he made his way here, despite all of his injuries. Your own son can attest to this man's loyalty to a friend and companion."

Mika shot Tomis a scathing look. Rudimere had been referring to the young man's sessions of peering into Mika's memories. Mika was still attempting to push past the intrusions.

"Tomis learned a great deal while Reading him," Rudi continued. "My cousin, Jasian, was captured, as you all know…" He gazed at Ashra, who had lowered her head in sadness.

"Tomis mentioned something else," a soft voice made its way into the air. Mora Orthane stepped away from her siblings and walked toward Mika. She took note of the look that Rudi was giving her – it was the same look of wonderment she had noticed when he watched her perform her wind dance at the Temple of Aman only days ago. As she stopped in front of Mika, she asked, "Is it true? You *spoke* with Aman?"

Mika raised his eyes to meet hers, then looked to Rudi, Ashra, and Pax, who were all brimmed with confusion. Turning back to Mora, he nodded. "Yes. I spoke with the Mystic."

From there, he told the tale of his journey underneath Mount Gilder. The rumors of the terrifying creature that turned out to be true, the battle with the Lekuzza itself, and the shock of finding out that it was Aman all along. He had spoken to her spirit and learned that she had been murdered by the townspeople of Summerhold a lifetime ago when they no longer accepted her. Afterward, she became a vengeful wraith that preyed upon the travelers within the hidden passage below. However, when Mika defeated the Lekuzza, he had set her free, and she left this world peacefully.

"It must have been truly inspiring to stand in her presence," Mora said quietly after Mika concluded his story. She had previously denied all rumors of Aman's vengeful spirit, but if the past few days had taught her anything, it was that some things are never what they seem. Even after the revelation that the Convergence had been a lie, she was still fascinated by the Mystics and their history.

"She was beautiful," Mika found himself uttering until he turned a shade of red in embarrassment. "Though, I was mostly trying to stay conscious," he joked, referring to how he could barely stand after his duel with the Lekuzza.

"She saved your life," Saris pointed out to him. "That satchel of apples she had given you. They must've had some magic to them."

Mika let out a small chuckle. Begrudgingly, he agreed with her. "I suppose she did."

"Did she also mention how she gave birth to an evil Sorcerer?" Rudi asked Mika with a hint of sarcasm. During the battle at the temple, Rudi and his friends had discovered that Oreus, the Patriarch of the Convergence, was none other than the son of Magor and Aman, born over 200 years ago. Rudi had stood toe-to-toe with the self-proclaimed 'true' Mystic and learned things about himself that he had not known before. Being an Evolutionary had its advantages, but Oreus had shown him that physical attacks could injure him. A simple punch could weaken him enough for an attacker to behead him and end his life for good. It was a lesson he was sure not to forget.

"She failed to mention that part," Mika replied in amusement. While they made their way to the great hall earlier, Rudi and Ashra had informed Mika of everything that transpired within the temple before its collapse. "I heard rumblings of this group during my travels," Mika said, speaking of the Convergence, "but I had assumed that they were an insignificant cult."

"You weren't the only one," Paxton stated in earshot of Rudi and Ashra. He enjoyed reminding them that he had been right about the Convergence all along.

"Nevertheless," Chancellor Lambin interjected, "with Oreus dead, it is one less dark Sage to worry about in the coming conflict." His proclamation had prompted the king to agree with a nod.

Rudimere took note of the comment and began to think back on Oreus's claim of being a 'true' Mystic. *It didn't help him in the end*, Rudi thought to himself. Then, another curious notion entered his mind: Oreus was the son of two Mystics, but the other two were mostly shrouded in mystery. After arriving in Summerhold, Mora proved that the South had much more knowledge on the topic than in the East. He needed further details.

"Mora," he addressed the woman whom he cared for. She turned and stared at him, affectionately. "You know everything about The Four. In the East, these things are not shared with us entirely – at least, not to my knowledge. Can you tell us more about them?"

"Of course," she said with a smile. "Hundreds of years ago, The Four arrived in Areon. Their names were Magor, Aman, Rikter, and Garis. They possessed *incredible* magical powers – more than the Magians of old. It is believed that they came to us to show us all the truth: our people have the innate ability to wield the same powers that they do. This is why Sages now exist. The Mystics showed us that it was within ourselves to possess such gifts." Glancing at the many faces of disbelief and shock, she continued. "But it wasn't easy…As benevolent as they were, they could not simply coexist with us equally. Sometime after their arrival, they built the place that we refer to as the Ironforge. There, they each created a relic that would enhance their powers. Of course, they continued with their mission of truth, teaching us all to wield our latent abilities with purpose, but even *that* did not last long. You see, as much as it is not so today, *all* of the Mystics were Kindlers. While Aman, Rikter, and Garis began to *give* the people their powers, rather than teach them any longer, Magor started to feel that he was above such generosity. He distanced himself from the others and moved west, where he built the castle of Zenithor and enslaved the people in the region."

A look of acceptance washed over Rudi and the others as they took in the entirety of Mora's tale. It was all beginning to make sense.

"After that," Mora spoke further, "Garis headed east, Rikter relocated to the north, and Aman made her way here. We all know what happened next: Magor betrayed them all when he started a war that lasted through the ages. We know every bit of this history because Aman passed it down to the people of the South after The Four split up. Of course…I have already shared with you the tragedy of Aman," she said with sorrow.

When Rudi and his friends first came to Summerhold, Mora told them how her people murdered Aman. Mora had surmised many things as to the reason why Aman was killed: Either Magor's actions prompted the townsfolk into action, they were distraught when Aman's Kindling did not work on some of them, or they were angry at her for creating so many Sages throughout Areon. The result was still the same, however.

"What happened to the others?" Paxton asked abruptly. "Garis and Rikter?"

"No one truly knows," Mora responded. "The curious thing is that Rikter was the only Mystic to take a surname – and it is one that has lasted for generations."

Mika thought for a moment and became instantly aware of what she would say next. He asked the question anyway.

"What was the name?" he inquired.

"Brock."

Mika sighed deeply. The memory of his Single Combat with Baldric Brock came rushing back, as did the memory of the prize that he walked away with that day.

"The axe," he said. "*My* axe – the one that I took from Baldric Brock. The one that Draven took from *me*," he lamented. "It is a Mystical Artifact." He had always assumed that the weapon was made at the Ironforge, but he could never have imagined the truth. Yet, the reaction that Cale Brock demonstrated when Mika took the axe, along with Mora's tale, provided enough confirmation for Mika to make the connection. He had been holding onto one of the most powerful relics in all of Areon…*and it is now in the hands of a murderer*, he regretted.

Mora and the others looked at him in astonishment. "You are full of surprises," Mora declared. "You've held Harbinger?"

He had never known its true name before but thought to himself that it was well-suited. "Yes, but as I said, it is now far beyond our reach."

Thinking of what Draven could do with Harbinger, Mora expressed great concern. "This is unfortunate…The power that he now possesses…It is unheard of."

"I had the axe for over a year," Mika countered in denial. "I wielded no such power. It was a superb weapon, but it held no 'magical abilities'."

"Even so," Mora said, "Harbinger *must* be retrieved at once. It cannot stay in the wrong hands."

Rudi had waited long enough to speak. After hearing all that he needed to hear, his mind was made up.

"That is why I will be heading to Woodhaven," he announced. Everyone in the room turned to look in his direction, all with raised eyebrows and looks of distress spread across their faces. "I will rescue my cousin, Jasian. I will retrieve Mika's axe. And if the gods will it, we will keep any of the other Artifacts from falling into the hands of the enemy." Out of all the trials he had faced on the road alongside his friends, Rudimere always doubted his leadership capabilities. He had wondered when his true test would come – when he would face a decision that would risk the lives of those closest to him. *Jasian followed me on this journey*, he thought. *It's my duty to save him now.*

"It's suicide," Saris said bluntly. Her sister glared in her direction, but her face was unwavering. "Apologies, but that is what I feel. Darkwood has an army, Rudimere. He has *Harbinger*. What hope could you possibly have?"

"Like Draven, I am also an Evolutionary," Rudi replied. "If there's anyone who has a chance at ending him, it's me."

"You will not be alone," Ashra made her voice known throughout the hall.

Rudi turned to his friend, wide-eyed. "Ash, you cannot—"

"Cannot go?" Ashra shot back. "I'm sorry, Rudi, but I've waited long enough to be reunited with Jasian...I'm done waiting. You know, more than anyone, that I would do anything in my power to get back to him." She stared at Rudi for a moment, hoping that her friend would understand, but the man merely looked back at her with a worried expression. "I will *not* leave him to die," she said decisively. "Like it or not, I'm going to Woodhaven."

From the side of the room, Mika limped forward. "Jasian and I chose to hunt down Draven *together*. I owe it to him to see this through to the end," he stated as he looked to the others in earnest.

Walking over to Mika, Rudi put a hand on the man's shoulder. "I would gladly have you at my side in battle again, my friend. But we both know that you cannot make the trip," he said gently.

Mika shifted his gaze toward the floor in disappointment. He knew that Rudi was right. Though, while he spoke the truth about his responsibility toward Jasian, a part of him was a bit bothered that Darkwood could be killed when he would not be able to bear witness. It was a problem that he had no control over, however.

By that point, Ashra had approached Mika from his other side and put a hand on his shoulder in a reassuring manner.

"We will find Jasian," she started to say, "and we will find Draven Darkwood." Ashra was sure to remind Mika that she and Rudi would be going to Woodhaven for more than just a rescue mission. "After all, we will need to retrieve this 'Harbinger'."

Mika looked up and acknowledged the two of them. "For Jasian, then."

"Yes, and for your parents as well," Rudi added with determination.

Mika smiled. "Thank you, my friends."

Suddenly aware that they had been having a conversation all their own, they turned to face the South King.

"Your Grace," Rudimere addressed King Wilfred, "it seems that we will be leaving a bit sooner than expected."

Sadness and dismay swept over the king's face. "Yes, it is regretful, indeed...after you had made a promise to stay and help defend our city," he explained with a hint of inflicting guilt.

"Father," Mora spoke up, "you must understand their reasons. I have seen their capabilities up close," she said, referring to the battle at the Temple of Aman. "If Rudi and his friends wish to go to Woodhaven, then I'm sure that they will return to aid us in our time of need." As she made her last declaration, she glanced over at Rudi, silently giving him her support, though she remained in distress. Summerhold had a great army, but she worried about their chances against the two joint forces of Zenithor and Karthmere.

Out of nowhere, Paxton stepped forward and into the center of the great hall. He had stood by and watched his friends make their plans – which he encouraged, as he knew that Jasian would not survive long in Darkwood's hands. Then, after hearing what Mora had just said, he chose to speak up and correct her.

"Forgive me, Your Grace," Paxton addressed King Wilfred with respect. "As a knight of Angelia, I am bound by honor to serve the Palidors." Dropping to one knee, he continued, "But that also means serving their interests. In the name of King Vandal, I will stay here and represent our alliance with House Orthane, and provide any aid that is within my power."

"Thank you, Ser Paxton," King Wilfred said. "This brings joy to my heart – as I am sure it does for others in attendance as well," he added with a long grin.

Glancing over at Saris, Paxton saw her face light up in delight, but it faded as soon as she saw that he had been looking in her direction. He assumed, though the king was a Reader and could easily read the minds of anyone in the room, that Saris did not display such happiness too often. Paxton smiled and could not help but turn a shade of red.

A moment later, as the king engaged in casual conversation with his son and daughters, Ashra and Rudimere approached Paxton.

"Thank you, Pax," Rudi said. "You honor House Palidor."

Paxton's eyes grew large. "Of course. And while that is *definitely* my intent," he muttered as his eyes ventured toward the Orthanes, "now I can spend more time with Princess Saris."

"*There* it is," Ashra commented as she shook her head and smirked.

Chapter 4

A QUESTION OF FATE

There was a cool breeze within the morning air. With the shadows looming over the town between the mountains, it was not unheard of for the weather to be brisk. Of course, men of the East never minded such a thing.

Prince Andemar arrived at Stoneshield, eager to continue onward to Evermount. His father, King Vandal, had given him leave to pursue one of the Mystical Artifacts, supposedly hidden in a dark place called the Shadow Sanctum. As the Sanctum was located near Evermount, Andemar planned on learning all that he could about the dangerous place from Lord Drudorn Varian. *Though Lord Varian's illness could cause a delay*, Andemar had pondered on the road as he rode his horse with speed. *Lady Varian already denied Rudi the assistance we needed for the war effort. Who knows if she'll have anything to say about the Shadow Sanctum?*

However, he reminded himself that Evermount was a part of the Eastern kingdom. King Vandal had even mentioned that Lady Varian would have trouble denying a request from Prince Andemar in person. It may have been an underhanded tactic, but it was a necessary one.

Pushing aside thoughts of his overall mission, for the time being, Andemar took in the sights of the familiar town of Stoneshield. He was elated to be back there, as it had been a very long time since his last visit. The stone wall was still as battered and worn as he remembered, though the battlements seemed to be lower – Andemar had grown late in his teenage years, which most likely explained the difference from his point of view.

"Who goes there?" a man shouted from the top of the wall, to Andemar's surprise.

Removing his helmet and allowing his short, dark brown hair to breathe, he shouted back, "Prince Andemar, of Angelia!"

Without a word, the armor-clad soldier grew wide-eyed and left his post, leaving Andemar to stand in the dirt without a reply. Cocking an eyebrow, the Prince wondered what had just happened.

Not long after that, the gates opened up to reveal a line of men and women on either side of the open area within the walls. In a more standardized formation, a small amount of Stoneshield soldiers stood in front of the townsfolk, awaiting Andemar's entry.

Accepting the formal invitation, Andemar, still atop his horse, passed through the gates, as all who surrounded him bowed in reverence. A short way into the town, he was met by a woman accompanied by soldiers in shining white armor. The middle-aged woman stood smiling, her light brown hair, along with her simple dress, blowing in the wind. Andemar stopped and descended from his horse.

"Aunt Hana," he said with a big smile. "It has been too long."

"*Far* too long, Andemar," Hana said as she embraced her nephew lovingly. "Thank you again for sending reinforcements from the capital," she mentioned as she pointed to the soldiers that stood at her side. "Marc took much of our own forces with him to Whitecrest, as you know."

"Of course," Andemar said with a courteous nod. "It was our duty to do so. Besides, we're family."

Family...Saying the word caused him to think of his late cousin and how he should have begun the conversation with his Aunt Hana more respectfully.

"I am...sorry about what happened to Merroc," Andemar spoke with regret. "He was a great man."

Somberly, Hana responded, "Thank you, Andemar. I only hope that he has found peace in Volsi with our ancestors. Perhaps Vulcan Palidor himself will regale Merroc with tales of the old world." The thought brought her some comfort.

As Andemar and Hana walked to the hall of Stoneshield, Hana confided in her nephew of her recent worries. "Andemar…I am fearful of what your uncle will do when he finds out about Merroc…" Hana had sent her husband a letter detailing the events that took place at Squall's End. Andemar let her know that he and King Vandal had also sent a letter to Whitecrest with the same information.

"It will be hard for him, but my brother is there as well. He and Uncle Marc have always been close. I *know* that Thasus will persuade him to stay the course and fight in your son's honor," Andemar stated with confidence. He noted Hana's look of content and knew that he had eased her mind — it made the next question harder for him to ask. "Have you had any word from Jasian?"

Hana shook her head. "Nothing yet," she replied. "I only know what *you* know — that he is still chasing down this 'Draven Darkwood' alongside some mercenary."

"Draven is the mercenary, from what I understand," he corrected his aunt. "Mika Gainhart is a travel companion of Rudi and Jasian's."

"Whatever the case may be, I do hope that they find that man…"

Andemar could tell that Hana wished death upon Draven for murdering her son. Though she attempted to hide such a feeling, he could see it as clear as day because it was the same feeling that *he* had too. Andemar was no stranger to disliking Sages, but with everything that he had found out about his own family recently, his views had become more blurry. *Draven is different*, Andemar thought. *He deserves to die for what he did.*

"So, Andemar, what are you doing down here?" Hana attempted to change the subject. "Last I heard, you were made the new master-at-arms of Angelia."

"A lot has happened..." Andemar began to say. He then explained everything about what the Foreseer told him, the mission that he had set upon, the Mystical Artifact, and his role in saving Areon. The one thing that he left out of the story was Magor's curse on the Palidor bloodline. Withholding the truth from Hana was, from Andemar's point of view, not about trust, but shame and embarrassment. He did not want to share the humiliation of his family being tied to the former Demon Sorcerer.

Hana's eyes bulged after Andemar had finished telling her of the recent occurrences. "Mystical Artifact, you say?"

"Yes," he replied with hesitation. Andemar tried to understand what his aunt was thinking but eventually came to one conclusion. "You *know* of it, don't you?"

Hana let out a small laugh. "It is the Varian family legend," she said amusingly. "Growing up in Evermount, it was something that would only be uttered in whispers amongst the people. As children, Drudorn and I were very close, and we remain so to this day," she went on to explain. "When Dru was still a boy, he shared something with me that I'm sure he was meant *not* to, though I

47

believe he was trying to impress me at the time." Hana's face grew more serious. "You see, being a Varian, he knew things that others did not when it came to such legends as the Mystical Artifacts. Over the years, I started to believe the stories…"

"But you are a Varian too," Andemar pointed out.

"Right, but Dru was in the direct line to sit on the seat of Evermount someday. Being that close to a lordship, he was privy to a *lot* more than I was."

Circling back to her newfound belief in the existence of the Artifacts, Andemar asked, "What changed your mind? Why did you begin to believe?"

"I have met many Sages in my life – more than I can keep track of. If they could wield such 'magic', then there has to be some truth to these Artifacts," she admitted. Observing her nephew's demeanor, she wondered if he had left Angelia prematurely, as he seemed to contain a look of skepticism. "Do you believe in fate?" she asked Andemar randomly.

"No," he answered back quickly. "We are all in control of our own destiny." Andemar was unsure if he agreed with his own words, especially after everything that happened lately, but a part of him was still in disbelief.

"That Foreseer, Horus, saw your role in the fate of Areon," Hana reminded him.

"A Sage's power has little to do with fate," he retorted, "but more of an unfortunate circumstance brought about by the Mystics. Though, I'm still unconvinced of *their* existence either."

"Well, I *do* believe in fate," Hana declared. "When your brother, Rudi, came through here, I told him one of the secrets that Drudorn had shared with me when we were children. Now, *you're* here," she stated emphatically, "searching for an Artifact that only my cousin and I have knowledge of. To you, this may have only been a stop on the road, but you were meant to be here – to find out what I know."

Andemar hung on her every word, thinking for a moment how he had been such a fool. Before he left Angelia, his mother, Serena, and Horus had done all they could to convince him of his destiny. But somewhere along the way, Andemar had grown in denial once more. Speaking to Hana had reinvigorated his enthusiasm for his quest.

Leaning into Andemar's side, Hana whispered in his ear, "A storm rises from the shadows." She had uttered the phrase to Rudimere as well but knew with certainty that the message would reach its destination this time. "Go and speak to Drudorn," she urged Andemar. "Tell him those words and that *I* shared them with you. But remember, they are for *his* ears only. Share them with no one else."

"I promise," Andemar swore. A part of him was reminded of his grandfather and the conversation that they had – the one that set Andemar upon the path that he was on. Many phrases had been presented to him since then. Between the secret that he had just learned from his aunt and the 'tainted blood' that his grandfather mentioned, Andemar was used to the riddles by now. Though, his grandfather's *final* words still eluded his understanding, as he was no closer to finding out what 'will of Ragnarok' meant. *Perhaps one day*, he thought, but he chose not to dwell on it.

Taken by surprise at all that had transpired on his journey so far – and he had only traveled to the next town – he was sure that things would only get more complicated from then on.

Chapter 5

LORD WALLIS

The newly appointed lord strutted through the great hall proudly. His loyal subjects stood to either side of the room, there to bear witness while Harlan Wallis took his place on the seat of Karthmere. House Duke ruled the city before him until he and King Kelbain murdered Rayburn and Dalton, the last Dukes in the line.

Years ago, Harlan had also taken part in the original coup of Karthmere, when he helped Rayburn – Captain of the Castle Guard at the time – usurp the lordship from the Weylands, killing their entire family in the process. Harlan himself had dealt the fatal blow to Lord Samus Weyland, ensuring the success of Captain Duke's plan. With Rayburn as Lord of Karthmere, Harlan rose to become captain of a new, elite group of soldiers called the Viper Legion.

It was only recently that Harlan and Kelbain discovered one of the members of House Weyland, alive and well, in the Wilderness of Woe. For many years, Rayburn had lied to Harlan and the rest of his people, telling them that he had personally slain Jaris, the last of the Weyland children. But once Harlan and Kelbain found Jaris, it was revealed that Rayburn had been hiding the fact that he never found the boy at all. Years of lies and ineptitude are what turned Harlan against his liege lord.

The old man deserved what came to him, Harlan thought darkly, ready to accept Karthmere for his own. The hall's green flames illuminated the room with a unique hue, giving Harlan's blonde hair an unusual look, though he failed to notice. Abandoning his armor for a change and dressed in the garb of one with nobility, his old post as Captain of the Viper Legion was soon to be a thing of the past.

As he approached the stone chair at the end of the hall, he pictured the moment of Rayburn's demise. The West King, Kelbain, had used his power to manipulate the earth to open a hole beneath Rayburn's seat. It had swallowed Lord Duke and was then shut forever, leaving the 'Lord of Lies' to scream in vain from beneath the floor. Rayburn's son, Dalton Duke, had been tortured and then killed shortly after when Harlan pierced the man's back with his sword. In the morning, his body was thrown into the kennels, where he was summarily ripped apart by hungry dogs – this was done with the utmost disrespect, as it was believed he would be denied passage to Volsi without a proper funeral pyre. Kelbain and Harlan made sure to have the soldiers watch, issuing a lesson in what would happen to cowards who ran from battle as Dalton did.

Back in the lord's hall, Harlan finally reached his destination, admiring the new seat that Kelbain had created and placed over Rayburn's tomb. Before Harlan could take his rightful place, he bowed to the man standing before him.

"Harlan Wallis," Kelbain said loudly so all could hear. "As West King of Areon, I grant you lordship over the city of Karthmere." The West King glanced at the people in the hall for a moment, noting the look of hesitation and shock on their faces. He smiled and continued. "In the sight of the denizens of this city, and in the eyes of your loyal army, do you accept?"

"I do," Harlan replied in an equally loud voice.

"Then arise," Kelbain said as he drew his sword, Hyperion, from its scabbard. "Arise, Lord Harlan Wallis, of Karthmere." The announcement drew slow but steady applause from the people in the great hall.

Once Harlan stood in front of Kelbain again, he turned around to look upon all of the attendees. Kelbain then removed Harlan's cloak by unclasping the silver serpent that held it on. The particular cloak and medallion had been a symbol of Harlan's rank for so long; he felt almost naked without them. The feeling dissipated when Kelbain placed a new cloak over Harlan's shoulders. The cloth was black with green trim around the edges and was fastened with two emerald serpents. Lord Wallis was already beginning to enjoy the power of his position.

Holding a hand up to silence the clapping, Harlan spoke to the people. "Thank you. As you all now know, the *Lord of Lies*, Rayburn Duke, forced this change upon us. He deceived us for too long – *too long* into making us believe that he was the true ruler of this great city. With his death, and the death of his foolish son, *I* will take us into a new age for Karthmere!" he boomed with pride. "And as my first act with this authority, in the spirit of the alliance that was already formed with West King Kelbain, I hereby renounce Wilfred Orthane as our king. We must make room for a South King that will bring prosperity to our lands." Taking a breath and listening to the gasps and murmurs amongst the crowd, Harlan added, "All those who would swear fealty to me, here and now, please step forward." His smile was more prominent than before.

The first to approach Lord Wallis was a woman of average height, dark brown hair, and wearing the armor of Karthmere. She knelt in front of Harlan and spoke clearly.

"Lord Wallis, I am Loreena Stenwulf, a soldier of the Viper Legion. I have served under you since I could wield a sword. I swear fealty to you, now and always."

The new Lord of Karthmere was more than familiar with the name. The Stenwulfs were one of the oldest families in Karthmere, dating back to a time before the Weylands took the seat in the great hall – a long time ago, back when the Karthans first ruled the city. Moved by the woman's respectful oath, Harlan reached a hand out to King Kelbain, motioning towards his old cloak. With the dark cloak in his hands, he draped it over Stenwulf's shoulders, clasped it shut with the familiar serpent medallion, and unsheathed his sword.

"Your loyalty and worthiness stand out amongst the rest, Loreena." Suddenly, Harlan used his power as a Water Elemental to cover his sword in ice – the edge of the blade enveloped in a cold tinge of bluish-white. Slowly, he touched Loreena's right shoulder with the flat side of his sword, leaving a small but noticeable trace of frost behind. "I name you: Captain of the Viper Legion," he declared as he moved his sword over to the woman's left shoulder. "I expect you'll continue to serve me well," Harlan added. The accolade had left a special mark – one that Harlan had only gifted to the new captain of his former legion. One by one, the rest of the Vipers followed, each one swearing allegiance to Lord Wallis. The citizens of Karthmere acknowledged their new ruler as well, much to the pleasure of both Harlan and Kelbain.

Later, after the coronation was over and the attendees had all left the hall, an unexpected event occurred. King Kelbain collapsed to the ground, grunting in pain. Harlan was at his side immediately.

"Your Grace! Are you alright?"

Kelbain pushed Harlan's hand aside. "I'm fine!" he said rudely as he stood back up. "I used too much of my power…It's the reason why I tend to use only fire when displaying my abilities," he divulged. In response to Harlan's look of confusion, Kelbain explained further. "Elementals who can wield *all* of the elements can grow weak for a time if they use too many of their powers. I was…*compelled* to make an exception when it came time to deal with the Dukes," he said with frustration. "Rayburn should never have mentioned Dirce in such a way." Of course, he was referring to the moment that Rayburn revealed the truth about Dirce's demise.

"What about the spear?" Harlan pointed out. Kelbain had retrieved the legendary weapon from the vault beneath the great hall, using the key that he stole from Jaris Weyland. Harlan knew that, by obtaining the Mystical Artifact known as Nightfall, Kelbain had grown in unprecedented power.

"That is a *new* sensation," the West King admitted. "The transformation does take its toll." Once again, Harlan exhibited a perplexed look, but Kelbain waved off the topic to avoid revealing exactly what Nightfall had done to him. "Moving onward, let us speak about the next phase. Are you sure that you can handle the attack while I'm away?"

"I will have no trouble taking Summerhold, Your Grace," Harlan responded. "Preparations will take a few more days, but we will be ready soon enough." A feeling of worry suddenly came over him like an unstable wave in the ocean. "Your Grace, if I may," he began hesitantly, "why are you willing to risk all to attack Woodhaven? You said you had grown tired of the woods." It was a phrase that Kelbain had uttered when speaking of heading into the Wilderness of Woe a few days prior.

"Draven must pay for Dirce's murder," Kelbain replied in a more serious tone.

Although she had betrayed him by conspiring with his son, Zane, Kelbain had truly loved Dirce. He sometimes regretted his decision to lock her in a cell for her transgression but knew that she would have come to her senses one day. Their history together was complicated, however.

Half a century ago, a married couple from Zenithor had approached Kelbain, swearing that they were the most devout followers of Kelbain's father, Magor. It was not the first time he had met such extreme fanatics, but it *was* the first time someone offered to prove their loyalty. The man and woman were so eager to demonstrate their faithfulness; they swore to gift their unborn children to Kelbain's cause when the time came. It was an oath that Kelbain was more than happy to take advantage of many years later. The couple's firstborn, Lamia, entered into Kelbain's service at the age of 14, and to his surprise, she rose through the ranks rather quickly. Lamia's younger sister, Dirce, was expected to join the army of Zenithor a couple of years later, but Kelbain had received word that she rebelled against her parents' will and was cast out from her home as a result. It was an unexpected development, but one that did not plague Kelbain's thoughts, as he had yet to meet the girl.

Around a decade later, after Lamia had become one of Kelbain's most trusted generals, he kindled her into an Illusionist and also gave her the gift of long life. Shortly after, Lamia had requested that her sister Dirce be given a spot in Kelbain's inner circle, as she was a 'cunning and resourceful woman' – from what Kelbain recalled – though he knew that Lamia merely had a soft spot for her sister. He permitted Dirce to make her way into his fortress for their first meeting. As she walked toward him, Kelbain became immediately enamored with her. Her dark hair, pale skin, and brown eyes pierced through him as no one had before – not even his former love, Zane's mother. He knew that Lamia wanted her sister to be placed into a leadership position within the army, but Kelbain felt that he had a better proposition. Instead, he declared Dirce to be his betrothed, where she would hold a new position of 'Queen of the West' in due time. Knowing that the decision would be met with a little hesitation, he even offered to kindle Dirce and give her longevity like her sister.

After the bargain had been struck, Lamia had her sister within the same walls, Dirce had a position of power, as well as an extended lifespan – even her eyes had changed from brown to a color that resembled the sun – and Kelbain had a beautiful woman that would soon become his queen. It was all so perfect.

Kelbain's mind then forced itself to remember the events of late. Dirce's betrayal – not just with Zane, but her hidden powers as an Illusionist that were unknowingly kindled by Kelbain – her escape from the castle, Draven's vow to find her…and now the news of her death. To him, the blame rested solely on Draven's shoulders.

"He may not have done the deed, but he is the one responsible," Kelbain continued to explain to Harlan. "The man has also taken Woodhaven from me. It is *mine*, and I will take it back, along with his head." Before he ventured into a more anger-filled tirade regarding Draven Darkwood, Kelbain added, "I don't plan on rushing into Woodhaven without a plan, Lord Wallis. I have already sent word to my men at Zenithor. General Soros and a host of soldiers now march toward Pandorim."

"Pandorim?" Harlan blurted out in surprise.

"That is correct, Lord Wallis. That is where I will meet them, and from there, we will head to Woodhaven and retake the city. I expect to leave within the next day or two."

Not a moment later, the doors to the hall slammed open as a simple messenger strode in. Kelbain and Harlan both looked into the young man's direction with a face full of contempt. The young man knelt in front of the two of them and anxiously began to speak. "Forgive the intrusion, my Lords."

"What news?" Lord Wallis asked.

"I bring a sealed letter for King Kelbain," the young man stated nervously.

Harlan looked to Kelbain and noticed a perturbed expression on the king's face. Kelbain had reached out and grabbed the letter in seconds, opened it, and started to read its contents. Studying the words on the page, Kelbain's manner became serious, and then almost fearful.

After he finished reading the letter, Kelbain addressed Harlan. "I must leave for Pandorim at once." Without so much as a second look, Kelbain was moving down the hall with haste.

Suspicious of this turn of events, Harlan called out to Kelbain, "Your Grace, I thought you were leaving for Pandorim in the next couple of *days*."

"Plans have changed!" Kelbain yelled to the other side of the hall without turning around. Suddenly, he stopped in his tracks, and this time he turned to face Harlan. "By the way, Lord Wallis…Do not fail me at Summerhold," he said threateningly before heading out through the doors.

Chapter 6

A LESSON IN TRADITION

The day began to look brighter as it approached midday. Staring out into the sky, Jasian Bowlin remained a prisoner at Woodhaven, but the young man knew that his time would come soon. Whether that meant his death or liberation, he was not sure. The future was still in motion. Running his fingers across his face, he felt the surprise appearance of stubble, which told him the number of days that he had spent inside of a cell. Though, in another surprising moment, he chuckled to himself as he remembered his captor's recent generosity.

Almost a week ago, after Lord Draven Darkwood had learned of Jasian's true name, two guards had come to Jasian's cell to move him to better quarters. He scoffed at the men, believing their tale to be nothing more than a cruel joke on the part of Lord Darkwood. But as it turned out, Draven felt that the young Bowlin should be kept somewhere with a window, away from the blackness of his old cell. Truthfully, Jasian was glad to be rid of that awful dripping noise that kept him awake most nights.

Do not fall for it, he continued to tell himself. *He killed your brother.* In his heart, he knew that Draven was merely keeping him comfortable and sane, only to crush his spirit with the supposed trial that was to come. *Soon*, he repeated in his mind. *The time will come. Merroc will be avenged.* Jasian's quest for vengeance had come to a halt when he and Mika lost their battle to Draven in The Great Wood, resulting in his capture and separation from his travel companion. It was bad enough that he had failed to kill his brother's murderer, but Mika's axe had been stolen as well. Besides beheading the Evolutionary, that axe seemed to be the only weapon that could harm Draven. Then, after learning a great deal about Lord Darkwood from the man himself, Jasian steadied himself and vowed to wait for the right opportunity. He'd accept the new cell with the window. He'd graciously thank his captor for being so accommodating. But he would *not* forget his true purpose.

Suddenly, Jasian trembled. While he had focused on killing Draven – even in the knowledge that he'd be cut down by Woodhaven soldiers afterward – he struggled with a single thought: It was likely that he'd never see Ashra again. He began to imagine her as if she were there in the stone room with him – her golden curls moving in the wind, her eyes a replica of the sky, and the softness of her lips against his.

"Gods, I miss her," he said aloud to the lonely space around him. Time and time again, he almost regretted saying farewell to Ashra at Squall's End. Then, he'd curse himself for living with doubt. He decided to follow Mika and chase after Darkwood, and Ashra reluctantly accepted it. But he wondered if either of them had known that it would be the last time they'd see each other. He hated to disappoint her again, especially since they had just recently reconciled...but Merroc needed to be avenged.

Peeling his eyes away from the sky for a moment, Jasian took a long, slow look at the room he was in. Turning back to peer outside once more, he whispered, "I *will* see you again, Ash. In *this* life or the halls of Volsi." A single tear fell down his cheek.

A loud noise came from the entryway to Jasian's dungeon cell, startling him. Noticing the latch on his door change positions, he took a deep breath. If it was time for the trial, he was prepared – ready to die if need be. He saw a familiar face walk through the door, though he did not care to act surprised.

"Lord Darkwood," Jasian feigned a courteous greeting. "To what do I owe the pleasure?"

Draven's head cocked sideways. "Good day to you too, Jasian." His face contorted into that arrogant smirk that Jasian came to despise. "I'm here to speak about the upcoming trial. Now, as you know, you will be facing six of Woodhaven's greatest warriors."

"What's left of them, anyway," Jasian pointed out. "Surely, there can't be *that* many warriors remaining?" Referencing Kelbain's takeover of Woodhaven, and its people's subsequent massacre, was probably not a great idea.

"Watch it, boy," Draven warned. "Woodhaven is a city of honor and a peaceful way of life. I explain the rules of the trial to you because duty requires me to." He took a step towards Jasian's cell door. "Speak ill of my people again, and perhaps a tragic accident will befall you before the trial begins, eh?"

Their eyes locked. Jasian understood the threat well enough. "Fine," he said through his teeth. "Do continue."

"You'll face six warriors," Lord Darkwood repeated, "but not at the same time, and not on the same day."

This surprised Jasian. He had assumed that Draven would use any means to kill him, but perhaps the former mercenary had a more elaborate plan.

"You'll fight three on the first day. Then, if you survive, you will fight the other participants three days later."

"Why give me that much time in between battles?" Jasian asked, utterly perplexed.

"We're not savages," Draven said incredulously. "Make no mistake: Every single warrior will be fighting you to the death. But even those on trial need to rest before engaging in more bloodshed."

"Kill three warriors. Rest for three days." Jasian mocked as he made an imaginary list. "Anything else I should know?"

Ignoring the insolent tone, Draven added, "And there will be *no* Sages." He took note of the Young Bear's shocked expression. "The way I see it, since you don't have any Sage abilities, it would be unjust to put you on trial against those who would defeat you in a matter of seconds."

"I can handle myself," Jasian stated defiantly.

"I *know* you can. But this is our way. Sages or not, you'll have some challenges to overcome, I think."

Jasian chuckled and shook his head.

"What amuses you?" Draven inquired.

"I'm a bit relieved, to be honest. Fighting another Illusionist such as Dirce would not have been pleasant."

It was Draven's turn to laugh, though he had done so lightly. "Yes, she was quite powerful," he said. "Completely mad as well. I passed by the village of Coalfell after she burned it to the ground…"

Both of them had stopped laughing, recognizing the devastation that Dirce was responsible for.

"She was a unique individual," Draven said with a hint of admiration.

Jasian's face turned to disbelief. "She was a murderer. Just like you."

"Why do you think that is? Was she born that way? Was she in her right mind? Sometimes, things happen to a person that causes them to act differently."

"I suppose you knew her so well," Jasian said sarcastically.

"I did not. But her betrothed shared things with me that he cared not to share with many others. You see, I met Kelbain *before* I made my grand entrance at Zenithor for the first time. In the eyes of Dirce and Prince Zane, I was a simple mercenary that had come at the behest of King Kelbain. While that was true, Kelbain and I had discussed Dirce at great length beforehand. I was there to get information out of her, and I was willing to do anything to achieve my goal. The stories that Kelbain told me were tragic. Dirce and her sister were practically promised to serve Kelbain from birth. Their parents were bad people, you see – devoted supporters of Magor."

Jasian's eyebrows raised. His reaction was not because of Draven's tale so far, but because it seemed that the Lord of Woodhaven did *not* consider himself a 'bad person'.

"Anyway," Draven continued, "while Lamia fulfilled the wishes of her parents, becoming another servant of Kelbain, Dirce refused. She was then cast out of her home for her disobedience. It was at that point that I learned the most important aspect of her dreadful story," he said as he strolled through the room casually. "She went on to become a whore."

Jasian narrowed his eyes. He was not sure what relevance that held, though he did remember Mika mentioning such a thing to Dirce when they saw her at the tower of Squall's End.

"Laying with numerous men in the encampment, she became well-known throughout Zenithor. If it wasn't for her sister, she might have done that sort of thing for the rest of her life. Dirce eventually made her way into Kelbain's arms, that much was clear, but the West King clearly had suspicions that she held a secret. That is where I put my talents to good use." Draven grabbed a wooden chair from the opposite corner of the room and dragged it right in front of Jasian's cell, sitting down to finish his story. "I laid with her one night and learned a great deal. She used her powers as a Reader to coerce me into divulging my true intentions. But I'm an Evolutionary. I became resistant to her power and shared everything with Kelbain the following morning."

"What did she tell you?" Jasian was intrigued and wanted to hear more.

"Well here's the thing: The West King had no knowledge of her power as a Reader – and certainly not her power as a Changer, which I found out later, unfortunately. Kelbain had kindled her with long life but did not comprehend that he may have given her something more…What a fool," Draven said, shaking his head. "But here we are. Dirce planned to assassinate Kelbain with the help of her lover, Prince Zane – I revealed their plot to the king, all for a great amount of gold – and Kelbain, though spurned by his betrothed, wanted her back home to marry her anyway."

Jasian sighed. "What is the point of all this?"

"My *point*, boy, is that we are who we are. I said earlier that Dirce was completely mad. But look what led her to become such a thing. If she had stayed with Kelbain, she would have been forced to do his bidding for the rest of her life. Yet, she chose to live another way. A *better* way."

"And the people of Coalfell? Do you think their spirits share your opinion of Dirce?" Jasian fumed.

Draven considered him for a second. "True. She had reached a breaking point when she escaped Kelbain's clutches. By the gods, she even sought out a Mystical Artifact to become even more powerful – all because she did not want to bow to anyone. She and I are alike in many ways." He stood up and shrugged, putting the wooden chair where he found it. "Ah well, best to leave the past in the past." Turning toward Jasian, he said, "You have three days until the trial begins, young Bowlin. Until then, you will have full use of the arena so you can practice. You'll be under supervision, of course."

The Young Bear attempted to digest everything that he had just learned – about Dirce, Kelbain's treacherous ways, the extent of Draven's powers – but was taken aback when he found that he would be able to leave his cell for the next few days. Draven must have noticed the look on his face.

"Go on, you can say it."

With pure disgust, Jasian said, "Thank you."

"You are very welcome, Jasian." The smug expression returned, and before Jasian could get in another word, Lord Darkwood had left him to his thoughts.

Chapter 7

DEPARTING FOR WOODHAVEN

"Why are we here?" Rudi asked his friend.

"You *know* why," Ashra replied. "We may be heading to our deaths. Don't you want their blessing?"

Rudi rolled his eyes. After the events at the Temple of Aman, he wanted nothing more to do with prayers and ancient deities. Though, somehow, Ashra had convinced him to pray to the gods before their journey. The city of Summerhold worshipped only Aman for so long that King Wilfred had decreed the people should put their faith in the gods rather than the Mystics – if they chose to.

As the old temples had opened up once more, Ashra thought it was a good time to take Rudimere to one of them and pray for safe travels to Woodhaven. The temple she had chosen was, in her eyes, perfect, as all six of the Gods of Volsi could be paid tribute there. Ashra was glad that the original seventh god had no presence at the temple. *No one in all of their senses would ever pray to Saurius,* she thought. Saurius, after all, was the God of Death and Lord of Mistif, cast out from Volsi a lifetime ago – or so the stories said.

"It has been a long time since I did any praying," Rudi said, "but I'll do my best."

Ashra smiled at her friend before the two of them made their way around the square, statued room, kneeling in front of each representation of the gods. Ashra knelt first in front of Vestor, the God of Wisdom. She prayed for the knowledge to defeat their enemies and to find Jasian with no trouble. After she stood up, she noticed that Rudi lingered in front of one of the statues with a look of curiosity.

"What is it?" she asked him.

Every stone figure displayed the form of a man or a woman, and each one also had a specific bird on their shoulders. It was common knowledge that the gods would sometimes take the form of a bird when they wanted to deliver messages and provide a symbol of warning – or hope, depending on how one would read the signs. Rudimere stared at the statue of Nira, the Goddess of War.

"Do you remember the old tales, Ash? Nira would appear to mortals as an owl when war was about to begin..." Rudi spoke without taking his eyes off of the statue, almost as if he were under a spell.

Ashra made her way to Rudi's side, where she gave him a sideways glance. "Have you seen any owls lately, Rudi?" she asked mockingly.

"No," he retorted, "but Mika has." Ashra seemed to understand, though she still formed a look of confusion. "When Mika fought the Lekuzza – or Aman – she took the form of an owl," he explained. "Dangerous premonition, is it not?"

"Rudi," she said gently, "we *are* at war. No owl is going to change that. Kelbain declared war before Mika encountered Aman. Besides," she waved her hand in dismissal, "Nira is a Goddess. Aman was a Mystic. They are *not* one and the same. It's just a coincidence."

Rudi turned to Ashra with worry. "I hope you're right," he said with gloom.

Eventually, both of them made their way to the statue at the back of the room. At the base of the stone, there was an inscription that was difficult to read at first. But after Rudi wiped it clean, he read it to himself.

For Tritus, forever the guardian of the sea
For Nira, always the architect of war
For Vestor, unfailing in his wisdom
For Reana, the bringer of perpetual harvest

For Vemaris, endlessly given life

I grant you these gifts

For I am Galdrafor. Then, now, and everlasting, the God of All Things

"Do you think he's watching over us?" Rudi asked Ashra.

"Galdrafor? Of course."

"No," Rudi corrected her, "I meant Merroc."

Ashra's face turned white. It was typical of Rudi to question certain things, but they were both there for Merroc's funeral. "You *know* that he is," she voiced her thoughts. "We sent him to Volsi as any warrior should be."

Rudi chuckled under his breath. "He's probably dining with Reana as we speak, asking her why Stoneshield lacks a consistent harvest." He laughed louder this time. "Ha! That man loved to argue!" Ashra laughed along with him, and the two of them smiled broader than they had in recent memory.

Suddenly, a loud noise sounded from the back of the room as another figure stepped foot through the temple entrance. Rudi and Ashra turned around to find Mora Orthane walking toward them, her dark hair flowing as she took each step.

Rudi could not help but compare her to Saris, as she resembled her sister quite a bit. He was still getting used to Mora's subtle but clinging garments, especially since they were an impressive change from a Convergence member's simple robes. He was not complaining, however. Rudimere and Mora had shared many moments since their first kiss outside the burning Temple of Aman but did not have the chance to speak about their feelings for one another. Time, he was afraid, was not on his side. He and Ashra were leaving soon, and he would have to confront Mora about his departure sooner rather than later.

"Hello, Rudimere," Mora said.

Her soft, innocent voice always got the better of Rudi, as it did the first time that he heard her speak. "Hello, Mora," he replied with a smile. "Ashra and I came to gather blessings from the gods."

"So you have," she said. Her own smile contained sadness behind it. "If I may, I'd like to speak with you."

Sooner, it is…Rudi thought to himself, almost wishing he could escape the upcoming conversation. He did not want to see Mora upset but knew that he must rescue Jasian at all costs. "Of course," he said. "Ashra, can we—"

"Say no more, Rudi," Ashra quickly responded. "I'll just finish my prayers to Galdrafor, and then I will wait outside."

Once Ashra knelt in front of Galdrafor's statue again, Rudi began speaking with Mora in a low voice. "Is everything alright?" he asked her as he took her by the hands.

Mora looked down with sorrow. She did not want him to leave, as she was only starting to get to know him, though she understood why he needed to go west. "I supported your decision in the throne room. I support you now," she stated as she lifted her head and looked into Rudi's blue eyes. She felt as if she could get

74

lost in them. "But I must know...Is there *any* way that I can talk you out of going? Are there any words that will make you stay?" Her voice began to break, and she held on tight to Rudimere's hands.

The East Prince felt regret for leaving Mora so soon after finding her but knew in his heart that he had to go. He then sighed before he spoke.

"I am responsible for my cousin's death," he divulged. It was a truth that he had been hanging onto since Squall's End. Out of the corner of his eye, he noticed Ashra flinch as he said the words. He was sure that she had heard him. "Merroc died because he was out there with me. He *followed* me...It's my fault – and because of that, his brother, Jasian, went after Draven Darkwood and proceeded to get captured. Now, another cousin of mine is in danger...all because of me." Mora started to shake her head, but Rudi continued. "You see, I *must* go after him. Killing Draven and retrieving Harbinger is vital to our mission. But Jasian? I need to find him and bring him home."

Mora loosened a hand from Rudi's grip and put it on his cheek. "I don't want you to make any promises, Rudimere. I *know* you'll come back to me," she said with conviction. "If that's what you want."

Rudi took note of the way she changed her tone of voice, as well as the way she recoiled timidly. Returning the gesture, he

placed his hand on her left cheek and said, "*You're* what I want –
and I *will* come back to you," he reassured her.

Later that day, Rudimere and Ashra said their final farewells in
the great hall of Summerhold. No one knew what would become
of the East Prince and the Lady of Triton, so each goodbye was as
emotional as one could imagine.

As Rudi embraced his best friend, Paxton, he observed Ashra
exchanging words with the members of House Orthane. He was
fully aware of Saris's respect for Ashra, knowing of the Princess's
wish to leave the city and go on an adventure one day.

"Don't die out there," Pax said to Rudi. "Remember what I
always say," he started to remark.

"No, no," Rudi waved his friend off with a laugh, "None of
your infamous words of encouragement, please."

Paxton laughed heartily. "That's quite alright. I have none at
the moment," he said with a smirk. Within a couple of seconds, his
face grew serious, and he pulled Rudi in for a hug. "Be safe, Rudi."
His friend replied optimistically, and then, before he knew it, Ashra
had made her way to say goodbye to him as well.

"Looks like this is it," Ashra said with a sigh.

"Must be," Pax replied casually.

Looking at each other grimly, they both ended the charade and
smiled, embracing fondly in friendship.

"Don't do anything stupid," Ashra said to Pax while they still
held on to one another.

"You know *me*," he said.

"That's what I'm afraid of," she countered.

Off to the side, Rudi found his way over to Mika, who was still on the mend. They grasped arms honorably before saying their own farewells.

"Good luck, my friend," Mika said. "I wish I could go with you. But I know that you have it in you to end Draven's rule and rescue Jasian."

Rudi nodded. "Thank you, Mika. I hope that Ashra and I can avenge Merroc, as well as your parents," he was sure to add. "I expect that it will bring you some measure of peace."

"It most certainly will," Mika stated. Though, truly, he was not entirely sure that it would. For years, he had longed to see Draven dead for what he did – he had gone so far as to seek vengeance on all Sages within Areon. But things were changing. After recently finding out that Rudimere was an Evolutionary, Mika began to doubt his own methods. His perception of Sages had already been challenged when he met the spirit of Aman, but with his friend counted amongst them now, Mika could start down a new path – one of acceptance.

After Rudi and Mika said their goodbyes, Rudi finally approached Mora. They had said all they needed to within the temple of the gods. Without saying a word, they embraced in a long, tender kiss, ignoring all things around them. By the time they had finished, Mora was crying. Rudimere held her tight against his chest.

"I *will* return," he whispered. As they separated, Mora nodded, believing his every word.

"Are you sure we cannot persuade you to take some of our men?" King Wilfred asked as he stepped into view.

Rudi bowed to the South King in appreciation of his offer. "Thank you, Your Grace. But Ashra and I would do well to travel light and without attracting too much attention."

"Horses, at least?" Saris spoke up as well.

Rudi formed a smile at the crack of his mouth. His loyal horse, Skymane, would serve them well on the trip to Woodhaven, but Rudi was unwilling to risk his safety on such a perilous mission.

"We will be alright, Saris," Rudi said. "Skymane will be in good hands." He glanced over at Paxton. They had spoken to each other earlier, and Rudi told Paxton that Skymane would be left in his care. "Besides, the hidden tunnel beneath the mountain is no place for horses, even if the Lekuzza is gone."

Throwing their small packs of gear over their shoulders, Rudimere and Ashra turned to leave Summerhold. In one final moment, Rudi reached down to his scabbard to be sure that he remembered his sword, Vulcan. Nodding with readiness, he and Lady Argon departed the golden hall, intent on reaching Jasian with haste.

Chapter 8

AWAKENING

He awoke with a start. His blue eyes, like most of his kin, pierced through the shadows of his bedchamber. Sitting up, Anden Palidor attempted to slow his breathing as he struggled to remember what woke him up in the first place.

"Another bad dream," he said softly as he shook his head. Running a hand through his unkempt, dark brown hair, the young Palidor sighed – he started to remember what it was that stirred him from his peaceful sleep. For days, he had been having the same dream, ever since he had displayed his powers in front of his grandmother. Like the Demon Sorcerer, Magor, he had the ability to summon the elements. So far, he had learned that he possessed fire and water abilities, but he assumed that he would be cursed with the other two elements at some point. A part of him thought that it was exciting to have such powers at his fingertips, but that was until he saw the look on his grandmother's face – that look of terror that she tried to hide. That was the first night the dream occurred.

There, Anden would find himself walking throughout Angelia as his city burned to the ground. Fear and shock gripped him during the devastation. He could only watch while an unknown army torched his home, transforming the White Jewel into a mass of reddened stone. After a while, he could no longer recognize the Eastern capital of Angelia. When all had seemed at its worst, Anden would look up only to find three figures standing a few feet away from him. One of them wore a robe, red as the sun, and flowing to the ground. Another had long black hair and carried a large spear. But it was the figure in the middle that scared him the most. It was a shadow, complete with a silhouette of features that Anden could not decipher, except for one: It had flames where its eyes should have been. The burning slits stared at the sky at first but would eventually make their way in Anden's direction, causing him to freeze in place.

As the cobblestone beneath him grew hotter and the burning buildings around him collapsed, the shadow advanced on him with haste, brandishing a weapon too small to see clearly. The darkened figure took hold of his shirt with one hand, and before Anden could find out what his fate would be…he would awaken.

The boy shuddered, his dream lingering as he got out of bed. *Father would want you to be brave*, he thought. Anden's father left the city days ago in search of a powerful weapon to use against the armies of Kelbain. While Anden knew that he should not fear for his father's safety, he could not help but let his mind slip in that direction. Secretly, he wished that there was a Pathfinder that he could speak with to track down his father's whereabouts. But ever since his father departed Angelia, Anden's mother grew quite protective – he and his sister, Ginny, were not allowed to leave the castle.

Pushing through all of the depressing thoughts, Anden decided it would be best to make it to his lesson on time for once, though he was unsure what his grandmother had planned for the day. He put on his clothes and opened the door.

"Ginny!" he yelped.

His sister stood outside the door, waiting for Anden. "Oh good, you're awake!" she feigned surprise.

Anden held a hand over his heart. "Are you *trying* to scare me to death?! What are you doing out here?"

"I heard you," she said. "You were moaning again."

"No!" Anden replied defensively. "Not at all. I have no idea what you think you heard, but—"

"Are you on your way to see Grandmother?" she asked her brother, ignoring his false excuse. "Maybe you should tell *her* about your *nightmares*."

Annoyed, Anden replied, "I *didn't* have a night—"

"Well, hurry along then! My lessons are right after yours!" she exclaimed. Catching the perturbed look on her brother's face, Ginny explained her sudden change of heart regarding her daily lessons. "Grandmother has begun teaching me about Vulcan Palidor," she said with a grin. "Today, she's going to tell me all about how he conquered the East!"

"You're *so* foolish sometimes," Anden shook his head in further agitation. "He didn't conquer our kingdom. He *formed* it. He brought the Eastern cities together and became their first king – but only after defeating an evil ruler," Anden pointed out, much to Ginny's delight.

"Now you *must* hurry," Ginny stated, her mouth still agape. "Go!"

Anden smirked, then hurried down the corridor. As much as he would grow vexed with his younger sister at times, he also knew how to make her happy. Ginny, though only eight years old, was quickly becoming an eager student of Areon's history. Anden almost envied her innocence, as she still did not quite understand the danger their father would be in when he reached his destination. While Ginny focused on her newfound love of history, Anden began to find out all he could about the mysterious Shadow Sanctum.

Before his father had left the city, Anden overheard his grandfather speak about the peril of the Sanctum. The East King mentioned the rumor of a demon inside. While Anden and the rest of his family had shown concern about that information, his father still left, brave enough to confront the possible evil within the Sanctum. It was just another reason why Anden thought so highly of his father and why he wanted to be just like him when he grew up.

"Family is the most important thing in this world, son."

His father had spoken those words to him in a private moment, in an attempt to make Anden feel at ease about his inevitable departure. While the words rang true and would most assuredly stick with Anden for the rest of his life...there was a part of him that wished his father would have stayed. Anden missed him dearly.

Approaching the room where he was supposed to meet with his grandmother for lessons, Anden pushed his worries and doubts to the back of his mind. He opened the door to the circular chamber and found his grandmother standing in the middle of the room. It was early enough in the day for the sun to be creeping in, lighting up the floor. It had the same effect on Serena's hair. Though there was only a trace of blonde left within most of her light brown hair, the sun revealed every hidden strand. Her attire consisted of a blue dress, glowing brightly, with white garments underneath, and the last thing that Anden noticed was his grandmother's green eyes, shining amidst the gleam in the chamber.

At times, he would pretend that his grandmother was one of the Goddesses of Volsi – perhaps Nira, the Goddess of War. He felt that if a deity could teach him the ways of a Sage, then having such abilities would not be a *bad* thing. It was sometimes difficult to escape the fear in his grandmother's eyes altogether, and the veil of the 'game' would be lifted.

"Hello, Anden."

"Hello, Grandmother," Anden replied dourly.

Queen Serena tilted her head. "What troubles you?"

A great many things, he wanted to blurt out. "I am…just nervous about today's lesson. Things are happening fast." Anden looked down at his hands as if he were staring at unrecognizable weapons of some kind. "I don't know what it all means," he admitted, as the words poured out of him.

Serena smiled at her grandson, knowingly. "Whatever is happening to you, we will face it together. Rest assured, I have not told anyone else about your Elemental abilities. That stays in this room."

Anden was not sure how to respond. If his powers were to be kept secret, then he wondered if he should be afraid. "Father and I spoke in the days before he left," Anden started to tell Serena. "He told me that there are 'good' Sages and 'bad' ones…Am I a bad one?"

The queen walked toward her grandson, a look of concern spread across her face. Gently laying her hands on his cheeks, she said, "You are *not* a bad one. You are one of the kindest, most noble men in all of Angelia – but you also have great power. Many will not understand the burden you now carry, and that is why we must continue to meet and have our lessons the way we have." Studying the boy's features, she ran her hand through his hair and smiled. "Don't worry, your grandfather and I will always protect you." This seemed to make Anden feel better, as he returned the happy expression.

From there, they began the lessons of the day. Within minutes, Anden produced flames from his fingertips with relative ease, though the water that revealed itself from time-to-time would douse the fire. He would get frustrated, but Serena told him, "Concentrate on one element, Anden. Tell yourself that the flames are stronger than the water, and you will succeed."

Anden nodded and tried again. This time, the flames enveloped his hands completely, but just as he began to celebrate his accomplishment, water rushed up both of his arms, and the fires disappeared once more. He grunted and cursed loudly.

"Anden…"

"Apologies, Grandmother. I'll try it again."

The next attempt was worse than the last two. The fire sizzled for a moment in his palm, until water, and then ice, encased his hands. He shouted as he slammed his hands to the floor, breaking the ice.

"You must control your emotions, Anden. The angrier you are—"

"How would *you* know?" Anden shot back accusingly. "Are *you* an Elemental? Can you create *this* with your hands?!" A blinding ball of flames appeared in his right palm. Before he could say another word, the fireball left his hand and propelled toward the wall, leaving a blackened scorch mark. Before either of them could react, Anden recoiled with the same hand and, suddenly, a mighty gust of wind formed between him and Serena. The sound was deafening. Anden shouted over the noise, "What is happening to me?!"

"You *must* calm down, Anden!" Serena attempted to alleviate the situation.

After a moment, Anden was able to put a stop to the winds in the circular chamber, creating an eerie silence. He held out his hands, staring down at them in disbelief. "Make it stop…" he whispered. Then, the same burning sensation he had been experiencing crept into his hands, and large amounts of fire emerged again. Before he and Serena could react, the blaze grew to become an uncontrollable inferno. "MAKE IT STOP!!"

Now cowering to avoid the danger, Serena yelled, "Anden! Please, you must regain control!"

Fire flung itself in all directions, burning the walls around them. Through the roaring of the flames, Anden was on his knees, screaming, as red and orange heat leaked from his hands. His grandmother remained in a corner, still attempting to escape the devastation somehow, coughing through the smoke.

Suddenly, the doors opened up, allowing a portion of the fire to make its way into the hall. But as fast as it had traveled down the corridor, it was immediately doused, even though there was no water to be found. A man made his way into the chamber, shouting Serena's name with a look of pure horror on his face. At the same time, with a wave of his hands, he seemed to make the flames disappear entirely, almost as if he had taken them into his own hands. Afterward, it was not until he caught sight of Anden, unconscious and drained, but with a small number of embers at his fingertips, that Vandal realized where the conflagration came from.

"By the gods..." King Vandal said into the silence. Peering down at his grandson, he had an intense feeling of fear come over him. *The curse has spread even further.* Shaking his head, he turned to find his wife hidden in the corner, recovering from the incident. Darting to her side, he knelt beside Serena and lifted her.

"Serena," he said shakily, "are you alright?" His wife nodded her head slowly. "What happened here?" He knew all too well what had occurred but wanted to hear it from the queen.

Serena began to sob quietly into her husband's arms. "I'm sorry, Vandal. I tried. I just wanted to help him..." Tears streamed down her cheeks as the king held her tight.

Sometime later, Anden awoke on the floor of the room he had almost destroyed. Sitting up, his eyes widened as he saw his mother and sister. His mother was yelling at his grandparents. Through the fog of his aching head, he heard his mother accuse the king and queen of keeping too many secrets.

"How dare you keep this from me! From Andemar!" Maryn shouted, her face seething with rage.

"Calm yourself, Maryn. You are with child," Serena pointed out.

"We should've been told," Maryn spoke through her teeth. "And not only is my son a Sage but now you tell me that there is a *curse* on the Palidor bloodline?"

A curse, Anden thought, shocked to his core. The boy felt betrayed, frightened, and angry all at once. His grandparents knew of this 'curse' but did not tell him. He was beginning to show the same powers as the Demon Sorcerer, but why? Was this the answer? Without warning, fire began to form slowly on his hands.

"No more…" Anden said aloud, finally gaining the attention of the others in the room.

The king spoke first. "Anden, remain calm. Let me show you—"

"I can't!" Anden screamed, the flames growing larger.

"You can!"

"You must!" Serena called out.

"Anden!" His mother shouted.

Nothing was helping him. Nothing would stop his powers from taking shape. Water ran up his arm as well, solidifying as it battled the fire. He looked up for a moment and saw the distress in everyone's faces, which made him feel even worse.

Out of nowhere, he saw his little sister approach. While the others yelled to her in a panic, Anden tried to recoil, but his powers were too strong – he was on his knees, shaking in terror and rooted to the ground. "Ginny, don't!" he pleaded with her. Still, his sister walked toward him, showing no sign of fear. As she closed in, Anden could do nothing but hold his hands outward in an attempt to keep Ginny as far away from the peril that awaited her. Slowly, Ginny knelt in front of Anden, and without saying a word, she reached around his body with her little arms, embracing her brother tightly.

Anden's breathing finally became steady while he watched the fire die down, and the water evaporate. A collective sigh could be heard throughout the room as the others looked on. With a whimper, Anden slumped into his sister's arms and began to weep.

Chapter 9

THE SKELETON IN THE CLOSET

Two days, he pondered. The man ran his fingers through his newly-formed beard, as his father would at times, reflecting on recent events. It had been two days since Lord Cale Brock's execution – since Prince Thasus figured out that he no longer wanted any part of the North.

His uncle was dead – murdered by an assassin sent by the late Lord Brock. Though Thasus was still vexed about the whole situation, he was glad that his Uncle Marc died saving King Cyrus. *A noble end. He'll have a fine feast alongside the gods in Volsi, as well as his son, Merroc*, Thasus thought, as he pictured his uncle's funeral pyre from the previous day. He only regretted that Marc's family members were not present for the ceremony. His mind shifted and focused on his hatred for Cale Brock. The man had given Thasus several reasons to want him dead, but murdering a member of his family stood out above all others. He thought of how good it felt to kick the stool beneath Cale's feet, watching as his body flailed about as the Lord of the Frostford hung for his crime. *I'd do it again in a heartbeat.*

Latching on to his personal feelings on the matter, he thought up a scenario in which he could lead his army, and that of the army of Stoneshield, against the rest of the Brocks. He wished he could obliterate them all, and he envisioned it happening as such – but he quickly remembered that the Brock army now pledged their loyalty to the Nortons. Marc's death was not their doing, and they made it known as such when they turned on their lord after his transgression came to light.

Tired of this line of thinking, Thasus decided to Pathfind his way to his brother, Andemar. He had already found Rudi earlier, still at Summerhold with his friends, as well as Mika Gainhart, but was curious about Andemar's current location after 'seeing' him leave Angelia recently. Closing his eyes, he focused on his brother, finding him fairly quickly. Pathfinding was becoming second-nature to Thasus, as he was able to find those he had searched for previously with a newfound mastery. Andemar was on the road to Evermount, having passed through Stoneshield already. Thasus was still confused about why his brother would have left the capital, though he surmised that Andemar was attempting to speak with Lord Varian. With Rudi in the South, it made all the more sense.

A sudden knock on his door broke his concentration, though he had 'found' what he wanted to anyway. "Come in," Thasus announced. A sturdy, gravelly-looking man entered, dressed in full armor. The man's chest plate displayed a black bear, and the gray armor itself was darkened with marks from previous battles. The man's hair was ashen and almost as long as Thasus's. His eyes, dark brown in color, told a story of legend and, at the same time, weariness. Thasus knew the man well – Ornell Balgon was the commander of Stoneshield's forces, and he had personally trained Merroc and Jasian since boyhood.

"Prince Thasus," Ornell addressed Thasus with a short bow.

"Commander Balgon. What can I do for you?" The Prince's mind raced with nostalgia. Whenever Thasus visited Stoneshield as a young man, he had made it a point to spar with Commander Balgon on occasion. Ornell had already been tough on the Bowlin boys and, even though Thasus came from royalty, his treatment by the grizzled veteran was no different. He had been knocked on his ass more times than he could count. *The enemy won't pour you wine after swinging a sword at you,"* Commander Balgon had told Thasus back then. It was a memory that continued to stick out, even to this day.

"I've come to offer you my sympathies," Ornell stated in a deep, rough voice. "Lord Bowlin was a great man. Eternally in

Volsi," he interrupted himself to say after mentioning the late Lord Bowlin's name.

"Eternally in Volsi," Thasus repeated, bowing his head slightly.

"I wanted to inform you, my Prince," Commander Balgon continued, "my men will now follow your orders until we return home." He stood tall, straightening himself in anticipation of his prince's command.

Recognizing the older man's desire to know what his next move was, Thasus responded with courteous haste. "Remain here at Whitecrest for now, Commander – at least, until I speak with King Cyrus. The North King needs to make a decision, now that he's taken in the remains of the Brock army." Of course, he was referring to the possible threat of Oswall Gargan, the Lord of Rikter's Hollow. No one was sure where his loyalty would lie, now that his allegiance with Cale Brock had come to an end. Thasus had a feeling that Lord Gargan would back down, especially since King Cyrus was set to wed Oswall's own daughter, Amasha. But there was also the problem of Cale's wife, Kaya – another of Oswall's daughters, and currently a prisoner in the dungeons of Whitecrest. Thasus was still unsure if she had anything to do with his uncle's murder, but it was too risky to let her out until they could find the truth.

"Yes, my Prince," Ornell said. He stood in front of Thasus, ready to follow any further instructions.

"Here," Thasus said, turning to grab something from his wooden desk. Opening the drawer, he pulled out a letter, which was sealed with the sigil of House Palidor. "I've written to my Aunt Hana. She deserves to hear the news from us before anyone else. Please see that this is sent directly to Stoneshield." Thasus handed the letter to Commander Balgon, then stood up to see the man off.

"At once, my Prince." Ornell bowed and turned to leave. Before he left, however, he rounded again to speak with Thasus once more. "If I may speak plainly…"

Thasus nodded. "By all means."

"Your uncle told me how you felt about your scars. Do not think of them as anything more than a symbol," he said simply.

"A symbol of what?" Thasus asked.

"Victory, mighty Thasus. Victory." Ornell, like everyone from the North to their homes in the East, had heard of Thasus's fight against the infamous Fenrok of the Frozen Wilds. He then took a step toward the Prince before speaking again. "And don't bother with what others think of you. If your scars vex them so much, to Mistif with them. You are Thasus Palidor, heir to the Eastern throne. You're not the boy that I kicked to the dirt a dozen times as a kid. *Are* you?"

Thasus smirked. "No, I am most certainly not." He held out his arm, expecting the commander to reach out and grasp his in friendship. The gesture was returned.

"He loved you, you know," Ornell said. "Like a son."

The comment was about Marc. Thasus knew that much. Still, he was taken aback. It was not until that moment that he truly felt the need to grieve, though he would wait until Ornell left the room before doing so. "Thank you, Ornell." Thasus watched as the older man left the room and then sat down to weep for his uncle.

Later, Thasus ventured to the North King's throne room. He found King Cyrus sitting atop his chair, the man's blonde-haired head adorned with the gaudy crown that Cyrus's mother made him wear. *He's a grown man*, Thasus thought, shaking his head with disappointment. Cyrus's attire was the same as usual – an all-white tunic, white pants, and the furs of local wildlife draped over his shoulders. The prince was fond of Cyrus but felt that the North King did not need to remind people that he was the ruler of a vastly snow-covered region.

"Ah! Thasus the Mighty!" Cyrus exclaimed. "Good of you to come. I want you to meet someone." The king motioned to the man standing in front of him. "This is Vyncent Reign. He's my oldest friend, and he's the commander of Hailstone Hold. The *former* commander, actually. Vyncent, here, will now be putting together a Royal Guard for House Norton. Long time coming, I'd say."

"It's still a bit strange, Cyrus," Vyncent spoke to the king casually. "Becoming a glorified bodyguard? Who will take up my post at Hailstone?"

"Don't worry, Vyncent. Someone worthy will be appointed," Cyrus assured his friend. "I need you *here* now. I'll admit, it was my mother's idea, of course – for me to have an entire Royal Guard – but she's right. If there are any other assassins, they will be easily thwarted now," the king joked half-heartedly.

The actual look on Cyrus's face was one of nervousness. *Perhaps he does fear another attempt on his life,* Thasus thought. It was probably a good idea to have the extra protection, though the East Prince was skeptical of Vyncent's battle prowess.

"Besides," Cyrus continued, "with my wedding in just a few days, the ceremony *should* be heavily guarded, don't you agree?"

Vyncent sighed. "Very well, Cyrus. I'll begin selecting members for the Guard immediately." The man's face showed anything but happiness as he obeyed his friend's command. While he turned to leave the king's hall, his black hair, evenly parted down the middle, seemed to bounce with every single step.

Even his walk is irksome, Thasus mused as he rolled his eyes. Though, he was glad to have the opportunity to speak with Cyrus alone. There were matters that he wanted to address with the North King.

"I knew he'd fight me on his new appointment – every step of the way," Cyrus remarked after Vyncent had left the room. "But I trust him with my life." Turning to the grim-looking East Prince, Cyrus changed topics. "What can I do for you, Thasus?"

"Your Grace," Thasus attempted to keep up with formalities, "I was wondering if you had a moment."

"Certainly," Cyrus replied.

"We need to send word, King Cyrus – of my uncle's murder and Cale's execution," Thasus asserted. "Brock's betrayal should be known throughout Areon."

"Agreed," Cyrus said with sincerity. "I apologize for not doing so already. I will have my fastest messengers deliver the letters to King Wilfred and King Vandal. You have my word."

Thasus nodded. "Thank you, Your Grace. Commander Balgon has been ordered to send one to Hana Bowlin as well. She deserved to hear it from *me*." His voice bordered on sadness.

"A wise decision," Cyrus said with a nod of his own. "If you like, I could send one to her as well."

"That won't be necessary. After losing both a son and her husband so close together, she may grow tired of being reminded of such dark times." Thasus, of course, had known about his cousin Merroc's death for a while, as he had learned about it through Pathfinding, but failed to tell his uncle before his untimely demise. Regrettably, Thasus had chosen to hide his power as a Sage for too long. Though in a way, he felt a bit of guilt had been lifted from his shoulders – in the hours that followed Marc's death, King Cyrus had informed Thasus that he had found two letters in Marc's room. Both of them had detailed accounts of Merroc's murder.

"He must have read them just before he came to my aid with the assassin," Cyrus had told Thasus.

While his uncle's murder was unexpected and tragic, Thasus was glad that Marc found out the truth about Merroc. He hoped that they would meet again in Volsi – in the Hall of Legends.

"As you wish," Cyrus replied, knowing that the ruse that he and his mother had conjured was working. He hated to deceive Thasus, but he was not sure of any other way to keep the peace. *What choice do I have?* He made many excuses to keep up with the lie, and he even found himself defending his actions from time to time. *What choice* did *I have? Marc put his hands on my mother…*It was always an eternal struggle. Though he felt justified for killing Marc, there was something in his mind that would make him remember what Marc said.

"Your mother is not what you think she is."

There had been many words flung between Celia and Marc that night, as Cyrus remembered it. Marc claimed that Celia tried to murder her and Marc's bastard sons, which Celia did not deny. Marc *also* insinuated that Celia was responsible for *Marcel's* death. That was a point that Cyrus questioned, as everyone had known his father was a drunk who fell from the tower. For the most part, the North King waved off Marc's accusation – but there was a part of him that kept the knowledge at the surface. Perhaps he did not want to know the truth, he would tell himself.

"Also," Thasus pressed on, "I have given orders to Commander Balgon to keep Stoneshield's soldiers here for now." He was cautious about his next choice of words. "May I ask what your plan is regarding Oswall Gargan?"

Cyrus's brows lifted. He was still figuring out what to do next but did not want to let his indecisiveness slip. "That depends on the Gargan woman's involvement in the assassination attempt," Cyrus replied.

"What *is* her involvement? Has anyone questioned her yet?" Thasus was letting his impatience get the better of him, as it did on occasion.

"I'm not entirely convinced that she is innocent, Prince Thasus," Cyrus snapped back. "No one has spoken to her yet, but she will remain in a dungeon until I deem it necessary to find out what she knows."

Thasus was taken aback. *Why the delay?* There was something odd about how the king clung to his belief that the Gargans were involved in the attempt on his life. He decided to push the matter further. "You *do* remember the feast, Your Grace? Kaya stood up and stormed out of this very hall – all after insulting her husband in front of the entire North."

The North King seemed to be getting irritated. "That may be," Cyrus almost floundered, "but while she is our prisoner, it will keep Lord Gargan in line." It was just another excuse to extend the lie and protect himself, along with his mother.

"*In line?*" Thasus retorted, losing all of the patience he had left. He only wanted to end the civil war in the North, so Cyrus's forces could assist in the true war with Kelbain.

"Enough," the king stated in a loud voice. "I have other matters to attend to. So if you would take your leave, I think that would be best."

Stunned, Thasus stood for a brief minute before nodding slowly. "Your Grace," he bowed slightly as he turned to leave the king's hall. His footsteps echoed throughout the room, leaving a cold silence between the two men.

Thasus found himself in the next corridor, straightening the furs around his shoulders, adjusting to the chill of the lengthy passageway. Coming to a fork, he remained rooted to the ground. Ahead, he would find himself back in his room. To the right, he would locate the dungeon. "Don't be foolish," he muttered. But he felt the pull of his usual rebellious nature. He turned right. In his gut, he was unconvinced of Kaya's part in Cale Brock's plot – he just needed to hear it from her on his own.

Strolling through the halls, he was careful to avoid any guards that were patrolling. It was a bit difficult due to his size and stature, but he was able to make it to the end and down the stairs without detection. Not only was it much darker down there, but even colder than up above in the main area of the castle. He wondered how the Gargan woman was able to survive in such a frigid climate.

Eventually, he found the cell that Kaya sat in – but before he spoke to her, he quickly used his ability to Pathfind around Whitecrest, searching for anyone who would be heading to his location. He focused specifically on King Cyrus and his lackey, Vyncent Reign. He found Cyrus, still sitting on his throne, but his mother was also there. She was standing above him as they discussed something unknown to Thasus. Shortly after, he saw Reign in the barracks, presumably to recruit others in his quest to form the Royal Guard. Thasus rolled his eyes at the thought of the man's attempt to put together an elite group such as that.

Returning to his body in the dungeon, Thasus approached Kaya's cell. Within, he caught sight of four torches that were lit on the walls. He assumed that they were the woman's only source of heat and comfort. "Hello," he announced to the silent room. Suddenly, he heard scattered noises of stone and dirt rustling together. Apparently, he startled the poor woman.

"Who's there?" Kaya called out fearfully.

"My name is Thasus Palidor, of Angelia."

Kaya took a torch from the wall and brought it to the cell door, illuminating the man in front of her. "I know who you are," she said through her teeth. "You're the one who couldn't keep his eyes away."

Caught off guard, Thasus almost chuckled despite his reason for being there. *Was I that obvious?* It was true: Thasus was, at first meeting, surprised at how much he stared in her direction. Her hair was brown, light, and simple – something not unexpected for a woman from Rikter's Hollow. But since Thasus admired *all* women, and he had already taken a liking to Northern women during his stay at Hailstone Hold, it was a natural thing for him to show an interest in Kaya Gargan. But now was not the time for such things, he reminded himself. *I need to find out what she knows about Uncle Marc's murder.*

Keeping his composure, he said, "I assure you, I meant no offense. Everyone was curious about Lord Brock's new wife."

"What a marriage it was," Kaya scoffed. "Because of him, now I've been left to rot in *here*." Her tone was unmistakable. She lacked any love for her former husband.

"Lady Brock—"

"No!" Kaya banged the steel door with her free hand. "I am Kaya *Gargan*! I know the laws of you Southerners. Cale and I didn't consummate the marriage," she pointed out with determination, "so I'm not a Brock anymore."

Thasus gave her a slight bow in respect to her wishes. "Fair enough. Again, I meant no offense. I only came to ask you about the other night."

Kaya made a noise with her mouth that was clearly a disrespectful gesture toward Thasus's comment. "If the great North King wants to send someone *else* to ask me about such things, then I have nothing to say."

Treating people with respect was a virtue amongst any man, or woman, of royalty. Unfortunately, Thasus had a knack for letting his emotions dictate the direction of a conversation. He was done with etiquette. "Just tell me what happened!" Noticing Kaya's eyes widen in shock, Thasus watched as she waved him off and turned around to walk away. "Wait! Please…" he pleaded. "I don't believe that you had anything to do with the assassination attempt. I *know* that you hated Cale."

The woman from Rikter's Hollow turned to look at Thasus once more, listening to the man's honest words. She made her way back to the door. "I *did* hate him. I despised him," she added. "It wasn't just because he was revolting – it was *his* idea to take on the Nortons in the first place. He put the idea into my father's head. If it weren't for him, my family would've stayed at Rikter's Hollow and never have been involved."

The East Prince was happy to confirm his thoughts about Kaya. He believed every word of what she said because *he* hated Cale as well, and her tone of voice sounded truthful in that regard. "Thank you, Kaya. Thank you for being so forthright. With Cale dead and the Brock army joining with the Nortons, I presume that your father will abandon any thoughts of taking the North." He may have been *too* optimistic.

Kaya's face twisted as she looked at the prince strangely. "Abandon? For all of your sakes, let's hope so."

Chapter 10

THE WAR ROOM

It was early in the morning. The sun had barely risen, but the Southern capital was already rife with commotion. Outside the castle, the overflowing crowds clamored for attention while they wondered about the rumors of an attack. South King Wilfred ordered Chancellor Lambin to address the people in an attempt to calm them, but the king's trusted advisor was no match for the commonfolk in times of distress. The man listening at the window could not help but shake his head.

Mika was quick to judge Gale Lambin the first time they met, solely on how the man cowered in the face of an impending attack. *This is war*, Mika had thought. *What does the chancellor expect?* With the knowledge that the Dukes had sided with King Kelbain, it was clear that they would try to conquer the Southern throne. The Orthanes of Summerhold needed to prepare…and Mika, though still recovering from his battle with the Lekuzza, would be there to help as much as he could.

In his bedchamber, the former soldier of Zenithor donned a new set of clothes. A change of scenery was always welcome, but Mika was not used to changing his attire. He had roamed throughout Areon in the same sort of clothes – usually a brown tunic with a black shirt underneath – for as long as he could remember. The red and gold colors of House Orthane were bright and extravagant. It was not in his nature to stand out and draw attention, but Princesses Mora and Saris had insisted that he bathe and switch into something else while they had his old clothes cleaned. Though, he had a strange feeling that he would not see those items again. He chuckled at the notion.

"Mika!" someone exclaimed at his open doorway.

He turned to see one of his previous travel companions. "Hello, Paxton."

The raven-haired knight edged into the room. "I was on my way to the war room. Are you coming?" Paxton asked, noticing that Mika was preparing to head out.

"I'm afraid not. I must see Prince Tomis. He and I have matters to discuss," Mika replied in a serious tone.

A concerned look crept onto Paxton's face. "Mika…the boy was only trying to help."

Mika formed a look of confusion. Of course, Paxton referred to the role that Tomis played in helping Mika heal from his wounds. The young prince had used his power as a Reader to dive into Mika's mind and attempt to help reconcile his past – in particular, the moments that caused Mika the most grief and agony. "I'm aware. Do not worry, my friend," he said casually as he continued to dress.

"Tomis is a Sage," Paxton remarked. "You're the Sage*slayer*. You could see why I'd be worried."

Mika stared at Paxton. The sound of his old moniker seemed to irritate him now. After everything that happened recently, from his battle with the Lekuzza to speaking with Aman, he felt he had left an old life behind. "No harm will come to him," Mika said of Tomis, "I swear it."

Paxton nodded, then laughed uncomfortably. "Well, since we're heading in the same direction," he said as he pointed down the corridor, "we could catch up. You can tell *me* about the beautiful Mystic that appeared out of an owl's corpse. I can tell *you* about the mad cult that tried to kill all of us. It'll be fun." The knight from Angelia was genuinely excited to talk about such things. Mika smirked, and the two of them departed the room, heading down the hall.

The story of Mika's encounter with Aman had already been told while they were all in the throne room two days earlier, but Mika indulged Paxton and spoke of the event once more. The same could be said about the battle at the Temple of Aman, though Mika was more curious about the details of the Patriarch, Oreus. "In all my years as a part of Kelbain's army, I never heard that he had a brother. Not once. I don't question the claim of this 'Oreus', but the news is still...intriguing," Mika said, looking deep in thought.

"The man is dead now," Paxton shrugged. "Nothing intriguing about it, if you ask me." The two of them continued to walk through the corridors of the castle. Paxton shifted nervously before broaching the next topic. "So, how long do you think it will take Rudi and Ashra to reach Woodhaven?"

Mika swallowed hard. The mere mention of Rudimere and Ashra just reminded him that he could not go with them. He wanted nothing more than to kill Draven Darkwood and finally avenge the death of his parents...but Jasian's life was at stake. Mika already felt immense guilt for bringing the young Bowlin with him when they first set out to kill Darkwood. After their failure, Draven captured Jasian and took Mika's axe – the one weapon that could harm the Evolutionary. *How could I have been so blind?* Mika thought with regret. After finding out the history of the Mystical Artifacts from Mora Orthane, Mika knew, without a doubt, that his axe was Harbinger, the axe that once belonged to the Mystic known as Rikter Brock. With such a weapon in Draven's hands, it was of the utmost importance that Rudimere and Ashra succeed in their quest. Still, Mika wished that he was well enough to accompany them. "If they don't run into any of Woodhaven's soldiers," Mika answered Paxton, "it shouldn't take them more than a few days."

Paxton nodded. "They're going to make it," he reassured Mika. "Darkwood will soon meet his end. Rudi and Ash will rescue Jasian." He turned to smile at the man beside him. "We'll all be celebrating when this is done."

"Your optimism is refreshing," Mika admitted. "Normally, I would feel the same…but I know what that man is capable of. Make no mistake: They are in terrible danger."

Paxton's smile faded. "That 'optimism' you spoke of? It's called faith, Mika."

"Faith? In the gods?" Mika was growing vexed. "Did Nira stay her hand when Draven put my village to the torch? Did Vemaris bother to breathe new life into my parents after their murder? Did the all-powerful Galdrafor lift a *finger* to aid me in my attempts to take Draven's life?" Mika stopped in the middle of the hall and rounded on Paxton. "Do not speak to me about the *gods* and their divine plans for us," Mika stated, shaking his head.

"You mistake me," Paxton said, clearly taken aback by Mika's sudden outburst. "I wasn't speaking of the gods. I care nothing for them." He noticed Mika's changed expression and continued. "When my parents were lost at sea, I blamed Tritus for allowing that to happen. I cursed him for *years*. 'The God of the Sea took my mother and father'. I would tell myself that every single night. Then, I was taken in by the Lord of Triton himself, Abacus Argon, for a time – I had no family left. That was where I met Ashra," Paxton said with a nostalgic smile. "We became friends and were almost inseparable until the day that I was sent to Angelia to learn how to become a knight. I started training with King Victor's grandson, Rudimere, and we became close friends as well."

"Forgive me, Paxton, but what meaning does this story hold?" Mika asked.

"Have faith in your *friends*," Paxton said simply. "I was lucky to have the hospitality of House Argon and House Palidor, and if I didn't have Ashra and Rudi by my side, then my life would've turned out much differently. I may pray to the gods at times, especially in respect of someone who has made their way to the realm of Volsi, but *they* are not responsible for my destiny."

Mika stared at Paxton for a moment, lingering on the man's words. "Hmph. I always thought that it was *my* destiny to kill Draven…but perhaps it is time I let go of what I cannot control." He sighed heavily, prompting Paxton to put a hand on his shoulder in support. He was almost surprised to see this side of the knight from Angelia. During their travels on the road, before the events at Squall's End, Mika had been unimpressed with Paxton's lack of restraint when it came to the subtleties of drinking. Since then, he only knew what he had heard from others: Paxton fought bravely as he helped fight the soldiers of Zenithor at Squall's End, and he personally confronted the Patriarch when it looked as if Rudi had perished at the Temple of Aman. Mika was busy fighting Draven within the tower of Squall's End, and he was not there for the fight against Oreus, so he was eager to see how Paxton fared in a fight. If the scouts were correct about Karthmere, then the city of Summerhold would play host to a battle one day soon.

"I *know* that Rudi and Ashra will find that bastard and kill him," Paxton stated, "but we need to prepare ourselves here. If it is our fate to help these people, then we should *not* ignore that."

Mika nodded. "You speak truly, Paxton. Thank you," he said sincerely. "Come, let us continue toward our respectful destinations while there are still hours in the day left." Paxton agreed, and the two of them began to walk down the hall again.

Reaching the fork in the castle corridor, Paxton turned and said, "I'm glad we were able to speak, Mika. I'll see you soon."

"Good luck with the battle plans," Mika remarked, referring to Paxton's upcoming meeting. With a slight bow of the head from both of them, they split up and made way to their next stop.

***

Searching throughout the castle and the grounds, Mika found his way to the same area he had viewed from his bedchamber window. Chancellor Lambin was still attempting to calm the townsfolk, with no success. Suddenly, Mika sighed with relief as he finally found Tomis, standing a few feet away from the chancellor.

The boy was having better luck with his portion of the crowd, it seemed, as the people were rarely speaking over him. This drew the attention of the rest, and they all listened to Tomis intently. He promised them that they would all have their answers as soon as the king and queen had something other than rumors to share. Apparently, hearing a similar message from a royal family member held more weight than the chancellor.

Afterward, the crowd dispersed, and Chancellor Lambin headed back to the throne room with haste. Tomis remained where he stood, staring at the golden city with a concerned look. Mika hated to interrupt, but the urge to clear things up with the young Orthane was too great.

Approaching the prince, Mika spoke without hesitation. "Hello, Tomis."

The boy jumped back, and his hair twisted wildly over his face. "By the gods! Mika, you startled me!" Realizing the possible reason for Mika's appearance, his voice quickly changed. "Please, I was only trying to help you."

"I am here to apologize," Mika stated to Tomis's surprise. "I should not have reacted the way that I did." Tomis simply stared at him, jaw dropped, and eyes widened. "Draven Darkwood sullied any childish interest that I ever had in Sages."

Tomis's expression changed once more. After peering into Mika's mind recently, he certainly sympathized with the man. "It must have been a terrible experience," he said, referring to the night that Mika's parents were murdered.

"It *was*," Mika replied, "but you and another friend helped me realize that there are some things that are out of our control. So, thank you for your assistance with…everything." He stopped for a moment and shook his head. "My past is not a pleasant one, but it was important to confront. What happened to my parents, my time as a soldier of Zenithor, my years of travel through Areon – it all shaped who I am today."

"I'm glad you see it that way," Tomis said with a smile. His mouth opened again, but no voice came out. He wondered if he should even bring up one of Mika's memories. "I am curious about something," he could not help but mention. "You were there when *both* of your parents were killed. But you told your friends a different story. You told them that you attempted to retrieve a sword from the stable racks to defend your mother and father. Why lie?"

Mika pursed his lips. "I have been telling that tale for a *long* time," he admitted. "Fighting back always sounded like the brave thing to do…much better than standing by and watching Draven murder my parents."

"I can help you again," Tomis offered. "If you allow me to enter your mind, I'll help you confront more of the memories that you don't want to."

"Thank you, Prince Tomis, but I will be fine. Strangely enough, however, I have been reflecting on my encounter with Aman."

"Oh!" Tomis exclaimed embarrassingly, clearly curious about the Mystic. "How so?"

Mika turned to look at the city and its golden features, mirroring Tomis's stance, so both were facing the same direction. "Sages have *always* been here. Well, not truly," he corrected himself. "Their powers have always been inside them. The Mystics just hastened the process." He turned his head and looked at the young Orthane again. "I used to think that all Sages were evil – a plague on all the land. But then I met Rudimere. After that, I met *your* family: you, your sisters, and your father." Mika put a hand on Tomis's shoulder. "You are all Sages, and you are all good people. I am proud to call you my friends." Tomis beamed. The two of them nodded to each other in mutual respect before Tomis left to rejoin his father in the throne room. Mika stood there a moment longer, then chuckled under his breath.

"*Sageslayer*," he said aloud to himself, "no more."

***

Paxton arrived at the war room, where he found Princess Saris engaged in a conversation with another woman. *By the gods, she's beautiful*, Paxton thought as he stared at Saris slightly open-mouthed. While Saris was dressed in more regal attire than Paxton was used to seeing, her form still commanded everyone's attention. The other woman was covered in golden armor, with the blue raven sigil of House Orthane on the chest plate. She also had red chainmail underneath and a sword attached to her belt. But it was when Paxton noticed the red cloak that he realized she was clearly a part of the Orthane's household guard.

Saris turned toward the doorway, and a smile formed across her face. "Ser Paxton, I'm glad you could join us."

"It is my honor," Paxton replied, returning the friendly facial expression. "I'm just glad that I could be of assistance."

"I'd like to introduce you to the Captain of the House Guard," Saris said, turning to face the other person in the room. "Valentyne St. Clare."

Paxton bowed his head. "A pleasure." Oddly enough, as he stood face-to-face with the woman in a brighter light, he noticed more details about her that he did not see when he first walked in. She had short, dark red hair, and her left eye was a shadow of blue. Her right eye was covered with a gold patch, held up by a leather strap wrapped around her head.

"Please, call me 'Val'. If we're to be discussing war strategies, it would do well to avoid such a long name," she chuckled. Suddenly, she caught sight of Paxton as he seemed to be focused on the decoration on her face. "Ah, *that* is a story for another time," Val said mildly.

"Apologies," Paxton said, his face full of embarrassment. "I meant no offense."

"No apology required," Val stated truthfully. "My Princess tells me that you fought well against the Patriarch and his followers," she said, attempting to change the subject. "I wish I could've joined you, but I was needed elsewhere." She snuck a glance at Saris, betraying her intent behind the remark.

"We discussed this, Val," Saris replied tiredly. "The House Guard was instructed to protect the king and queen. If I had failed, only the gods know what Oreus and Willard would have done…"

"Of course, my Princess. I live to serve House Orthane," Valentyne said with a bow. "I only meant that I would have fought by your side with honor."

Saris formed a half-smile and spoke softly. "I know, my friend. Your loyalty is *never* in question."

"What about the scouts?" Paxton inquired out of nowhere. "Their reports indicate that Lord Duke's army is massing outside of Karthmere's walls." He stopped to look around the room, making sure that the three of them were the only ones present. "Can they be trusted?" he asked, referring to the scouts. "Would any of them still be loyal to your brother?"

Saris looked deep in thought. After a moment, she said, "Willard answered to the Patriarch. They were about to move against my father." She shook her head. "No. Oreus would have wanted my brother to gather everyone involved in the coup. They were *all* there that night. Either *we* killed them, or they burned in the crumbling temple."

Paxton nodded, seemingly convinced. "Fair enough. We don't know when Karthmere will attack, however. We should plan as if they were going to be at the gates *tomorrow.*"

Saris and Val exchanged glances and then chuckled. "Forgive me, Paxton. As I told my father: We are on the top of Mount Gilder. We have the advantage," Saris stated with certainty. "No matter *when* they decide to attack, we will beat them back."

The last thing Paxton wanted was to disagree with a South Princess of Areon, but he was not convinced. "And if they have a *Sage* with them? If they have numerous Sages?" Paxton pointed out.

"We have Sages too, Ser Paxton," Saris reminded him.

"True. But how many of them were loyal to Willard? How many *soldiers* in Summerhold's army were killed in the Temple of Aman?" Seeing the look of realization on Saris's face, he pressed on. "Do we still have the numbers?"

Saris swallowed hard. She had not thought of the loss of the traitors as a loss to their own army. She quickly turned to Val. "Captain?"

Valentyne made a face as she attempted to figure out the numbers they now had in their army. "Willard commanded a large host," she admitted, "but not enough to affect our chances against Karthmere. Although…"

The Princess looked concerned. "What is it?"

Val sighed. "I've spoken to some of the men. Their morale has been shaken after the incident with the Convergence. A lot of them believed in your brother, even if they now curse his name for his dishonor. Losing a prince that way...it has dampened their spirits."

Saris lowered her eyes. "Because *I* killed him? That is what you mean to say?"

The Captain of the House Guard nodded. "Apologies, my Princess," she said nervously.

Saris put her hand up to stop Val from speaking further. "None required. Your honesty is always appreciated, Val. But you are right. I will address the men *myself* and make sure that they are prepared to defend our city," she stated. Sneaking a glance at Paxton, she noticed that the man's infectious smile was aimed in her direction. She formed the same expression at first but attempted to hide it to focus on the task at hand. "Gather them in the courtyard," Saris ordered Val. "I will tend to them shortly. Until then, Ser Paxton and I will continue the battle preparations."

Valentyne bowed to Saris. "My Princess." Before she left, she gave Paxton a sideways glance. "Thank you for your assistance, Ser Paxton."

"It was a pleasure to meet you, Captain St. Clare," Paxton responded with a courteous nod.

Once Valentyne had departed, Paxton turned to look at Saris, only to find her staring at the stone table in front of them. On the top, there was a detailed map of Summerhold. She had placed wooden markers behind the front gate and on two sets of battlements, specifically around the area of the city that met the mountain pass to the south.

"They'll try to come through here," Saris said, pointing to the front gate. "The road from the south leads straight there. With the Wilderness of Woe gone, Rayburn Duke won't hesitate to press his advantage. He'll knock right on our front door," she stated before she waved her hand over the wooden pieces that represented the army of Summerhold, "and we'll be waiting."

Paxton studied the map intently. *It's too simple*, he thought. Suddenly, Saris appeared next to him, looking directly into his eyes in an effort to grab his attention.

"Would you like to weigh in," she asked with a smirk, "or are you going to defeat the enemy by *staring* at them?"

Being that close to Saris, Paxton felt weak – almost completely vulnerable. He had loved Ashra Argon for the better half of his life, so he was familiar with the feeling. This was different. While his love for Ashra had not been reciprocated, Paxton could tell that Saris was fond of him. "I-I forgot what I was going to say," he admitted sheepishly.

"The map?" Saris asked coyly, her eyes widened. "Was *that* it?"

"Right, the map!" Paxton blurted out, surprising both of them. "That is, I meant the placement of your soldiers." He finally found his way back to his original intent.

"Oh?"

"Well, everyone knows where the mountain pass leads, especially Lord Duke. I think that it's all a bit too easy." Noticing the change in Saris's expression, he cleared his throat. "I meant no offense. I just think that we should anticipate other moves that he may have in mind."

"Hmph." Clearly, the moment between the two of them had passed, but Saris was determined to hear what the knight had to say. "Go on."

"We should call for aid," Paxton said simply.

Saris was taken aback. "Aid? You don't think that my people can hold the city?" Her face was beginning to turn a shade of red.

Paxton quickly shook his head. "On the contrary, my Lady, I believe that they *can*. I merely seek to divert the attention of the Dukes and throw them off-guard."

Saris listened intently. "How so?"

"If we call on Triton for assistance, then they can distract Karthmere's army at the bottom of the mountain. When *we* descend the pass to the south, we can use the high ground to flank the rear of their forces – trap them between Triton and us," Paxton explained.

"A good plan," Saris admitted, "but why would Triton help us?"

Paxton winced slightly. He had just revealed some of this tale to Mika in the corridor and did not care to relive his parents' fate. "It was my home once," he blurted out. Catching Saris's look of curiosity, Paxton ignored his desire to remain silent. "My parents died when I was seven – lost at sea, I was told. Lord Argon took me in for a short time, but he was already an older man with a child of his own. He told me that I would have a better life in Angelia, so he sent me to live with the Palidors." He laughed softly as he remembered the first time he met his adoptive family. "Luckily, Abacus Argon and Victor Palidor were *somewhat* close."

Saris laughed along with him. She clearly knew of the relationship between two of the Heroes of the Sorcerer's War, but it was exciting to hear Paxton's view of such renowned families from the East.

"I became King Victor's ward and, soon after that, Vandal Palidor's squire. That was where I met Rudi. Since I already knew Ashra from my time at Triton, the three of us became great friends." Paxton smiled half-heartedly. He silently wished for them to return safely and with haste.

"Your bond with the Argons of Triton runs deep," Saris stated. "Do you truly believe that Lord Argon will send reinforcements if you ask it of him?"

"I *know* it," Paxton replied confidently. "Even after he sent me to the capital, he and I spoke many times over the years. He still thinks of me as a son. He's a funny man," Paxton remarked with a short chuckle, "he always assumed that Ashra and I would marry one day." The thought of marrying Ashra *did* seem like a great idea to him for the longest time, but once he found out her true feelings for Jasian, he knew that his life was never going to be as he had dreamed. *Took a while to accept that pairing,* he reminded himself. Though he did not initially take the news of their tryst with grace, Paxton eventually accepted it and moved on. Looking at Saris at that moment, he was glad that he made the decision when he did.

"The Lord of Triton would have *arranged* for his daughter to be married?" Saris asked with sincerity. She presumed that someone as free-spirited and skilled as Ashra would not take well to such a ritual. The thought of her *own* father choosing her husband made Saris's blood boil. She felt lucky that arranged marriages were *not* a custom in Summerhold.

"Oh…well, no…Ashra and I have a complicated past," Paxton divulged without thinking. "I mean, it's not much of a past…Her father only thought…" he continued to ramble.

Saris tilted her head. "Do you love her?"

The knight from Angelia was shocked at the Princess's directness. He hesitated for a moment but finally collected himself. "I did once," he admitted. "She's one of my oldest and dearest friends. Nothing more."

"I see," Saris said with a slow nod. "Let us send word to Lord Argon," she abruptly changed topics. "Another force beside ours will be a welcome sight in the upcoming conflict."

Still recovering from the sudden switch in conversation, Paxton was surprised by Saris's decision. "I will begin writing to Lord Argon at once," he stated, clearly pleased that she welcomed his idea. While he waited for Saris to respond, she merely bowed her head slightly and walked out of the room, leaving Paxton to wonder what had just happened.

Chapter 11

A RESCUE UNDERWAY

The weather acted as an extension of the gods' wrath. It had been two days since the pair left Summerhold, and they seemed to encounter all sorts of changes in the air. First, there was the rain. For half a day, the heavy amount of water fell on them like daggers. To their misfortune, it had slowed their trek through the mountain, all the way until they reached the ruins of Coalfell. While they believed their journey to be easier from there, the sky decided differently. As they took the next day to travel the north side of Mount Gilder, carefully avoiding the road and sticking close to the rock formations, the winds began to push them back with an immense force. They surmised that they would have to contend with the gods' judgment until they found their way to The Great

Wood, as they were caught between the sea and the tall mountainside.

"Why do they hate us?" Rudimere asked his friend in a way that was half a jest and half-serious. "First, we find that the tunnel beneath the mountain is no longer clear, and now *this*."

Ashra sighed. "The tunnel was one thing, but for the last time, this *isn't* the work of the gods. Weather changes from time-to-time, Rudi – or had you not learned that simple lesson in your castle?" Her travel companion was clearly taken aback, leaving Ashra to feel a tremendous amount of guilt. "Apologies, Rudi. That was not right for me to say. I am just frustrated…"

"I understand," Rudi replied, forgiving his friend with ease. "This was all meant to be a simple task." Ashra's eyes grew large for a moment. Rudimere read her expression well enough. "You're right…*not* simple," he admitted. "I think '*simpler*' is a better word."

Ashra shook her head, annoyed. "Who's idea was this in the first place?" she pointed out.

"True. But we *both* want to rescue Jasian," Rudi countered.

The small mention of the man she loved had caught Ashra off-guard. Throughout the last couple of days, she and Rudi had been at odds with one another over minor troubles. She had not let herself think of the real reasoning for their mission. "You're right, Rudi. Maybe we should rest for now," she offered. "We could start up again in a short while." Taking out the small map that Mika had given them, Ashra surveyed the piece of parchment with determination. "Wait…we are almost there," she said suddenly. Racing forward, still clinging to the rocks, she arrived at a point where the mountain began to turn inward. Followed closely by Rudimere, she rounded the corner and stopped. The two of them raised their eyes high from where they stood, discovering trees that were larger than they had ever seen.

"The Great Wood," Rudi whispered.

Ashra inhaled sharply, which was then followed by a slow exhale. "Let's go," she told Rudi without hesitation. Leaving her friend behind once more, she charged into the thick forest with only Jasian on her mind.

Catching up to her, Rudi grabbed Ashra by the arm. "Wait," he said in a low voice. "We don't know who could be in here with us. Darkwood could have patrols throughout the entire forest," he reminded Ashra. "Now that we're here, we *should* rest as you suggested. We're very close to Woodhaven."

Not wanting to stop, Ashra thought of arguing, but she knew that Rudi was right. "Fine," she caved. *I'm coming, Jasian…I'm coming.*

After the two of them had set up a temporary camp, they decided it would be best to hunt for food. There were plenty of forests around Angelia and Stoneshield, so the two of them were no stranger to hunting woodland creatures, as they had been taught from a young age.

Ashra's father showed her how to wield a bow from the time that she could speak. Though their city of Triton was found on the coast, their frequent trips to the Eastern capital allowed them the opportunity to hunt big game in the nearby woods. As her father and Rudi's grandfather were close friends, it gave Ashra and Rudi plenty of time to grow in their own friendship. One thing that they had learned during all of those hunts was the joy of competition.

In The Great Wood, they hoped to keep that tradition alive. Their biggest target would be harts, a type of deer found in *all* forests of Areon. At first, they wondered if they would find one, but it did not take long to spot a handful of them along the way.

"Remember, Ash," Rudi said quietly. "It does not count unless they have at least 10 tines."

"We take what we can get," Ashra said, wanting to get to Woodhaven as soon as possible. "Let us hunt, eat, and get moving."

Slightly disappointed, Rudi frowned. There was a part of him that held onto the memories of childhood — and how he enjoyed those times with Ashra, Paxton, and Jasian — but it was sometimes hard for him to let go of those things and focus on the present.

"Right," he said. "Eat and leave."

After a few more minutes of sneaking up on the harts in the distance, Rudi and Ashra took their positions, ready to take their shots. Ashra held her bow as an archer would, yet Rudi's style was a bit more sloppy. He admitted to Ash that he had not practiced with his bow in a long while, prompting her to chuckle for the first time since they had departed for Woodhaven. At last, the moment of truth arrived, and the pair had fired their arrows. Ashra's arrowhead pierced the animal with precision, but Rudi had missed. The commotion sent the beasts running in a haze of confusion and fear. Rudi cursed under his breath, pulled back on his bow again, and fired. The second arrow found its mark, and the hart fell to the ground.

Rudi looked at Ashra, who had already been staring in his direction with a dumbfounded look. "I know, I know..." he said. He and Ashra approached their quarries, intent on making sure that they were fit to be cooked. While Rudi examined the animal, Ashra made a small triumphant noise.

"Hmm. Hart of ten," she stated with a smirk.

"What?" Rudi's voice grew shrill for a second. Ashra had fooled him into thinking that they were *not* competing. "You're full of tricks," he pointed to his friend and laughed.

"Count them," Ashra demanded.

By her request, Rudi counted the points on the hart's antlers. He threw his head back and groaned. "Hart of eight," he said with dismay. After Ashra laughed at him, the two of them made way back to their camp, where they prepared their meal.

Sitting around the fire, after stuffing themselves, Rudi and Ashra took the time to talk before heading out. They discussed their plan for rescuing Jasian and retrieving Harbinger from Draven Darkwood. While neither of them knew Woodhaven's layout, they would make the best of it when they arrived, but the purpose was still the same.

"Do you really think that you can kill him?" Ashra asked Rudi in a serious tone. "Darkwood has been an Evolutionary for years – even while Mika was a child."

"I will certainly try," Rudimere said with honesty. "If we can get the axe away from him, I'll have a better chance."

"Why do you say that?"

"I never told you, but there was a moment when I was fighting the Patriarch," Rudi explained. "He told me of a weakness to Evolutionaries. Well…he *showed* me." Ashra looked perturbed. "Physical contact. He *hit* me."

Ashra leaned back in shock. *"That's* it?"

"Yes. While we may become immune to *objects* and *substances*, skin-to-skin contact is where we are vulnerable."

"Rudi…this makes things a bit more complicated," Ashra said with worry. "If anyone gets their hands on you—"

She had warned him of something similar while they infiltrated the Convergence, Rudi remembered. "They can hit me," Rudi interrupted her, "they can tie me up. No matter what, my life is in danger, Ashra. Being an Evolutionary makes me better-suited for a battle – like the one we're about to face."

"It makes you more of a *target*," Ashra countered. Her friend merely shook his head and waved her off. "Look, Rudi…I know why you're doing this. Why you want to save Jasian, I mean."

"He's my cousin," he replied in an obvious manner. "What more reason do I need?"

"I heard you speaking to Mora before we left Summerhold," she revealed to him. "You feel responsible for his capture. You also feel responsible for Merroc's death." Her words caused Rudi to lower his head with guilt. "It is *not* your fault, Rudi. None of it. You can't protect *everyone*."

"Maybe," he said, "but it was still my duty. You all followed me when we left Angelia. My cousins followed me from Stoneshield. Look what happened to the Dragoons at Squall's End…"

"They all knew the risks, Rudi. They were soldiers of Angelia. Merroc and Jasian knew it too. *All* of us tried to fight our way out of that tower. We wouldn't be here if Merroc hadn't killed Dirce," Ashra reminded Rudi, hatred for the Illusionist on the tip of her tongue.

Rudimere shrugged. "Perhaps one day I'll see things the way that you do, Ash."

The sudden sound of a snapped branch alerted them, causing Rudi and Ashra to douse their fire and draw their swords. As they did so, they hid behind a couple of nearby trees, awaiting the origin of the noise. Two men in green armor came into view, both of them walking slowly toward the location of the camp.

"Quiet!" one of the soldiers said in a hushed shout to the other. "You scared them off!" As they approached the makeshift camp's center, one of the men bent down to touch the spot where the fire had been. "It's fresh. I told you."

Rudi, still feeling upset about the topic that he and Ashra had discussed, grew impatient. Choosing to face the soldiers head-on, he left the cover of the tree and walked into plain sight. "Hello," he said casually.

"What are you doing?!" Ashra whispered.

"I don't suppose you know anything about a prisoner at Woodhaven? Black hair? Loves his swords?" Rudi attempted to goad the two soldiers into a fight – and it worked. As they unsheathed their blades, Rudimere walked toward them with his hands outstretched. Without pause, one of the men from Woodhaven swung his sword at Rudi's chest. The East Prince watched the look of surprise form on the man's face when the steel shattered. While the second man ignored the feat and charged at Rudi, an arrow found its way into his neck. As Rudi turned around to see Ashra wielding her bow, the wounded man fell dead to the floor.

"Please!" the remaining soldier begged as he fell to his knees. "I won't tell anyone! I don't even know who you are!"

"Where is the prisoner?" Rudimere asked calmly. The nervous man shook his head wildly. "Where are the rest of your men? There were only two of you on patrol." This time, the Woodhaven native hesitated to respond. "What is Lord Darkwood planning?!" Rudi shouted, his suspicions rising at the lack of forces in The Great Wood.

"M-Most have gathered for the t-trial," the man quivered with fear. "There was a m-man brought to Woodhaven. He will be p-put on trial for his crimes."

Rudi looked to Ashra with concern, and she mirrored his expression. Sighing, he lifted Vulcan from its scabbard.

"No, wait!!"

In an instant, Rudi cut down the pleading man, silencing him forever. He wiped the blood from Vulcan before sheathing it once more. "We couldn't let him go, Ash," Rudi said out of nowhere. "He would've told them we were out here."

"I know," Ashra replied gravely. "There was no other choice." Grabbing Rudi's shoulder gently, she added, "Don't do that again, Rudi. Walking out like that with no weapon…"

"I'm immune to steel, Ashra. I have Oreus to thank for that one. I was in no danger."

Ashra shook her head. "You don't listen," she said softly. "Too many things can happen to you, Evolutionary or not. Don't let your Sage power make you arrogant," she cautioned him. "You're better than that."

The East Prince took heed of his friend's advice and nodded. "I will do well to remember, Ashra. But now," he said, turning toward Woodhaven, "we must hurry. Our rescue attempt just became a lot more difficult." Thinking about the possibility of facing hundreds of Woodhaven soldiers – all who were probably in attendance for Jasian's trial – Rudi grew internally worried.

"The gods will protect us," Ashra stated confidently.

"Let us hope that you're right," Rudi replied as the two companions continued onward to Woodhaven.

Chapter 12

PANDORIM

The old tower stood tall, looming over what remained of a forgotten area in the West. Skeletal in appearance and bony in structure, it had wasted away since the days of the Demon Sorcerer. Few knew its name, but even less knew its purpose, for the tower of Pandorim was also known as the Temple of Magor.

A large host, all clad in black armor, marched toward the ancient temple. Led by a single man on a dark horse, the army's standard-bearers held the sigil of Zenithor proudly, waving the dark red shark fin high for all to see. As they closed in on Pandorim, the man atop the horse held up his hand, signaling for his followers to halt.

"Hmph. He is late," he muttered under his breath.

Just as the slender Zenithorian had remarked, a cracking sound was heard from the sky above. While he and his army raised their heads with curiosity, they witnessed a figure hovering just under the clouds as it descended to meet them. Uncertainty turned to realization as the army of Zenithor gazed upon their king – and the son of Magor – Kelbain.

As his feet touched the ground, the West King focused solely on the man before him, a look of annoyance spread across his face. "I don't care for flying," Kelbain said.

"I was surprised, to be honest," the other man replied. "Normally, you don't dabble in your Wind Elemental ability."

"My horse was slowing down as we crossed the Deadlands. I left it behind and flew the rest of the way," Kelbain said with an icy tone. He cared nothing for the animal that he left in the barren stretch of land. His only concern was that he could not use any other element for a time, or he would be rendered weak from the strain of his powers. "Now tell me, General Soros: Are the men ready?"

The general cocked an eyebrow. "We wouldn't be having this conversation if they were *not*. We are ready to attack Woodhaven at your command."

"Glad to hear it," the West King said, ignoring the insolence. "We shall take back what is mine. As for Draven Darkwood," he started to say as he turned to look at The Great Wood in the distance, "well, he will soon learn what it means to cross *me*."

"Of course, Your Grace. But I wonder," Soros added, "what do you think has happened to Rhobu?"

The man that Soros spoke of was another of Kelbain's generals. After Kelbain had taken Woodhaven from the Prastors, he appointed Rhobu as its steward. To his regret, he had not left many troops to support General Rhobu. The oversight led to Woodhaven's fall into the hands of Draven Darkwood.

"He's probably dead," Kelbain said callously. "If he had lived, I would've had him executed for his failure." Noting the small jerk in Soros's neck, Kelbain continued in an intimidating manner. "How fares Zenithor, General?"

"Perfectly well," Soros replied, feigning a casual voice. "We have anxiously awaited your return."

"Spare me the groveling," Kelbain shot back. "You and your brother are like sharks in the Crimson Sea. I left *both* of you as co-stewards of Zenithor because neither of you could be trusted to take care of my father's fortress single-handedly."

"Malos and I would never betray you, my King," Soros stated, choosing his words carefully. "If either of us have offended you—"

"You have not," Kelbain admitted. "Let us hope it stays that way. Remember who gifted you – *all* of you – with longevity. Do not make me regret that decision."

Long life, Soros reminded himself. The man knew better than to allow Kelbain to question his loyalty. If he and the other generals had wanted to disobey the son of Magor, they would not have accepted his offer of longevity after helping him all those years ago. "Your will, Your Grace," General Soros pledged.

Internally, Kelbain accepted, though he offered Soros no response. Turning his head toward his father's temple, he started to walk with haste. "I must pay my respects before we leave."

After ascending the endless amount of steps outside, Kelbain made his way into Pandorim. While he had been there many times, this was the first since he had killed Fulton Prastor and started the war with the people of Areon. His breathing was uneven, and his long black hair began to sweat – this caused Kelbain to chuckle under his breath. Many believed Pandorim to be the entryway to Mistif. Furthermore, those same people thought they would meet Saurius, the God of Death and Lord of Mistif himself, if they ventured into Pandorim. *Fools*, Kelbain mused. In his eyes, they continued to prove why they were lesser than him, but their ignorance protected his father's temple. Almost no one dared to enter, save for a few greedy adventurers who met their demise within.

Kelbain walked through the desolate halls, passing by the bones of the fallen, avoiding all of the traps that he had created years ago. Wind rushed through the corridors, whistling in the hollow structure. Anyone else would have experienced a sense of dread, but to Kelbain, the place was sacred. Walking up another set of stairs, he finally reached his destination: a large, square-shaped room that contained a stone sarcophagus. It was Magor's tomb.

Thinking about the letter that he had received at Karthmere, Kelbain started to breathe heavier. His chest pounded with anticipation. Stepping in front of his father's resting place, his foot triggered one of the traps that he knew well. Streams of fire launched at the West King from all directions. Any normal person would have been scorched alive for their curiosity, but Kelbain was a Sage. Using his abilities, Kelbain stopped the fire in mid-air and redirected it at the stone walls, putting out the flames instantly. Suddenly, he winced in pain and almost collapsed to the ground. His usage of different elements was too close together in time, and he began to pay the price. Just as he had let the pain in to have its moment, Kelbain watched as the sarcophagus in front of him opened up, revealing the mummified remains of Magor. Even in agony, Kelbain smiled darkly at the thought of irony as he glanced at all of the bones that surrounded the room. Anyone who had stepped on the same trap in the past would have seen the body of Magor…but only for a moment before they were burned alive.

Reaching the stone edge of his father's resting place, Kelbain held himself up and stared inside with wide eyes. "I'm here, Father. I'm here." Shifting his eyes from the wrapped skull, he glanced at his father's hands. They sat crossed on Magor's chest, covering a dusty weapon. Kelbain made a slow movement to lift his father's hands from the item, making sure to take great care not to damage anything. Within a brief moment, Kelbain retrieved the small weapon from Magor's tomb and examined it deeply. "I am ready,

Father," he whispered. "Ready to fulfill my destiny. I'll show them all just how wrong they were." As he departed the tomb, his father's sarcophagus closed, sealing itself once more.

Outside of Pandorim, the West King strode toward his army with pride and purpose. They continued to wait for him in relative silence. Stopping in front of Soros, Kelbain said, "Give the order, General." Soros stood at the ready, awaiting his king's command. "We march through The Great Wood," Kelbain announced. "Let us pay a visit to the new Lord of Woodhaven."

Chapter 13

EVERMOUNT

The world was changing. While word reached the East of the emergence of pirates on the seas, rumors spread of chaos in the Southern cities. Andemar had spent the night in Stoneshield, and so he had made it a point to visit the local tavern. The patrons there whispered of another coup at Karthmere, but none could speak of the outcome. They also mentioned Summerhold and the destruction of a temple. *Something about a false religious group,* Andemar thought the next morning, unable to recall what had been said. He was more interested in his next destination.

After Andemar said his goodbyes to his Aunt Hana, he left Stoneshield and set out for Evermount. His next step was to speak to Lord Varian and gain access to the Shadow Sanctum, then retrieve the Mystical Artifact. It was a simple enough plan, but things always had a way of deviating from the original intention, Andemar considered.

On his way to his destination, he chose to set up camp and rest for a night. While the act of falling asleep had been simple enough, it was his dream that plagued him the next morning.

"Will...of...Ragnarok."

Victor's last words took form in Andemar's mind more than usual on the trip, though the prince did not know why. He began to think that the meaning would make itself known sooner rather than later. He welcomed the truth. It had been too long since the riddle was presented to him – even Horus failed to decipher it. *Either that or he would not tell me at the time*, Andemar considered. Pushing the thought to the side once more, he concentrated on his next task.

The prince and his horse rode hard. A long stretch of land stood between Stoneshield and Evermount, though as one approached the latter, they would immediately realize the difference in the soil. Evermount was known for having some of the most fertile lands in all of Areon, as evidenced by the numerous farms surrounding the large city. It also helped that the metropolis was so close to a massive lake. There, the people would venture out and fish for more food, assisting in the sustainability of Evermount.

Once the great city came into view, Andemar began to think of the history that was forever tied to it. His father had once told him of the legendary battle in which Vulcan Palidor freed the people of Evermount from the grip of a tyrant. It was the event that led to Vulcan's ascension as the very first East King and the dawning of Angelia. Not much else was known, as the tale of Vulcan Palidor took place centuries ago, even before the Mystics arrived in Areon, and before the sudden rise of Sages. It was a time that Andemar wished he were alive to see.

Approaching closer to the city, the prince took note of the structures at the center – the infamous Citadel. They were so large that they could be seen from far outside the walls. The Citadel was comprised of the main building, which he assumed was the lord's hall, and three towers that stood behind it. The hall, while enormous in its own right, displayed a statue of a large, golden phoenix on its roof. Evermount was known to worship the Goddess of Life, Vemaris, who was represented by a phoenix – The animal also stood as the sigil of House Varian. Connecting to the main hall, the center tower stood the tallest, as it almost reached the sky. It was aptly named: the Sky Tower. The other two towers stood the same height as one another and were evenly spaced behind the Sky Tower.

Andemar reached the gates and was let through without incident, as the guards immediately recognized the Prince of Angelia by his attire. The blue cloak with the white horse is what gave him away, Andemar figured. He continued to ride onto the street ahead of him. Evermount was entirely circular in shape, with rings of streets surrounding the Citadel, so Andemar was tasked with riding from the outer ring around to the center of the city. Passing by all of the homes of the city's inhabitants, he took note of their appearance. Each home seemed to be almost identical in height and overall size, except for unique writing that adorned each door. It was a curious thing, as Andemar could not read what was written on them.

Finally, he circled the city enough times and arrived at the Citadel. Looking up into the sky, he was not prepared for what he saw next. A handful of people were *flying* from tower to tower.

"By the gods!" he exclaimed.

"Wind Elementals," a voice sounded from up ahead.

Andemar brought his eyes down from above and saw a guard standing in front of the doors to the main building. The man wore shiny, blue armor with a gold phoenix on his breastplate. The sigil was surrounded by golden flames, just as their house banners were.

"Something you see every day?" Andemar asked the guard.

"Sure," the man replied with a light chuckle. "This place is full of Sages."

That made Andemar uncomfortable, to say the least. The last thing he needed was a Reader to dive into his mind and uncover secrets that he did not want to divulge, or for a Watcher to have seen his arrival months ago.

"My name is Andemar Palidor, Prince of the East," he declared. "I come to speak with your lord, Drudorn Varian."

The guard acted quickly, having only realized who he was speaking to so casually. "Right away, my Prince. Lady Lucille attends court in the Sky Hall."

"Sky Hall?" Andemar inquired.

"We call it that sometimes," the guard explained. "Entry to the Sky Tower is found directly at the back of the great hall, hence the nickname."

Andemar nodded as the guard allowed him to pass. "Thank you," he said. Passing through the double doors, he inhaled sharply as he glanced around the hall. In his eyes, it seemed to be a cross between the splendor of Angelia and the humble setting of Stoneshield. The stone walls were tinted in a yellowish hue, mostly due to the torches that surrounded the room, and the ceiling was lavishly decorated with the same unknown writing that Andemar had seen on the homes throughout the city.

Further ahead, he noticed a woman sitting on a robust chair, her long, yellow dress flowing to the floor. She was young and beautiful, her smooth-looking skin radiating in the light, and her lengthy, blonde hair appeared to be perfectly suited to her in the way that it sat atop her shoulders. She was surrounded by noble-looking individuals, presumably some of the more wealthy citizens of Evermount. At her side, there stood a scrawny man dressed in gray robes. His dark hair was slicked back and allowed his abnormally large forehead to protrude for all to see.

"Lady Varian," a voice sounded from behind Andemar. "I present to you: Prince Andemar Palidor, of Angelia."

The prince had only just realized that the guard from outside followed him into the hall to make the announcement. Murmurs started up amongst the nobles in the room – and Andemar observed as the skinny man next to the shocked Lady Varian began to whisper in her ear. *Must be the chancellor*, he assumed.

"Prince Andemar," Lady Varian addressed him courteously. "Welcome to Evermount. It is an honor to finally meet a member of the royal family."

Andemar could not help but take offense to the comment. Normally, if a lord had a wedding, then the king, queen, and their family should be invited. Lord Drudorn wed Lucille without so much as a feast but chose to have a rather small ceremony. Andemar assumed that it was because Drudorn did not want to make a fuss over his *second* wedding. It was understandable, yet it still went against tradition.

"The honor is mine, Lady Lucille," Andemar responded in kind.

"Allow me to introduce you to Theodore Graves, Chancellor of Evermount," she said as she motioned toward the man standing next to her.

The hollow-eyed man stared at Andemar without changing his expression. For some reason, the prince immediately felt a sense of unease around the chancellor. He could not explain it but decided to stay on his guard all the same. With respect, Andemar addressed Graves with a nod.

"How can I help you, Andemar?" Lucille asked.

"I was hoping to speak to Lord Drudorn, my Lady." Andemar made his request without hesitation. He was eager to learn everything he could from the man.

Lucille chuckled nervously. "I'm afraid that is not possible. My husband is in poor health and cannot receive visitors."

"Apologies, Lady Varian," Andemar began to say carefully, "but that wasn't exactly a *request*."

Lucille glared at Andemar with an annoyed look on her face. Before she could say anything, Chancellor Graves leaned down and started to whisper in her ear again. After a moment, she sighed and finally replied to the prince.

"Forgive me. You are our East Prince. If it is an audience with Lord Drudorn that you command," she said with sincerity, "then we will oblige." With a wave to two of her guards, she told them, "Please escort Prince Andemar to Lord Varian's chambers."

"Thank you, my Lady," Andemar said. As the guards bowed to their lady, they led Andemar out of the Sky Hall and into the next corridor, heading in the direction of the Sky Tower.

In time, after climbing numerous amounts of stairs, they had reached a floor with another passageway. They walked a few feet and turned again, where they reached a wooden door on the right.

One of the guards knocked – seemingly out of courtesy – before entering right away, leading Andemar into the bedchamber.

"Lord Varian," the guard spoke up. "This is Prince Andemar Palidor, of Angelia. He wishes to speak with you."

Andemar moved into sight and got a good look at the Lord of Evermount. The man was lying in his bed, sickly and frail, but appeared to be no older than his own father, King Vandal – he even had a similar amount of gray hair that reflected the validity of his age. A rush of memories flooded into Andemar's mind as he started to think of his grandfather, Victor. He was weary of seeing people in such a fragile state.

"A Palidor? *Here?*" Even with a weakened voice, Lord Varian expressed surprise at the unexpected visit. "Apologies, my Prince. I'm afraid that I cannot greet you properly. This malady…has taken its toll on me," he said wearily. A look of defeat crept onto his face. "What can I do for you, Prince Andemar?" His tone of voice changed to one of slight disinterest.

Andemar had waited for the guards to leave the immediate area before he started talking with Lord Drudorn, as secrecy was of the utmost importance. But before he prodded the man for information regarding his mission, he inquired about more personal matters.

"If I may ask, Lord Varian, how did this happen?" He was referring, of course, to Drudorn's sickness.

"Yes…well, I suddenly woke up one morning feeling ill," Drudorn explained, "and proceeded to get worse as the day went on. Two days later, I collapsed to the floor of the Sky Hall. I don't remember much after that, but I awoke right here." He let out a sigh before continuing. "I'm told that our healers have done everything they can to find a cure. Sadly, they have found nothing."

After a moment, Andemar pulled a chair from the corner of the room and brought it to Drudorn's bedside. Sitting next to the Lord of Evermount, he said, "I am truly sorry this has happened to you. I wish the gods would aid you in—"

"Oh come now, Prince Andemar," Drudorn interrupted. "You didn't come all this way to hear my sad tale. I have two sons who will do that when they return home." He chuckled lightly under his breath, thinking fondly of seeing his sons again. The two young men had been gone for quite some time. Lord Varian did not worry much about his youngest son, Dorian, but was forever protective of his oldest, Randar. While his eldest son proved himself to be a capable warrior, he suffered from an unknown illness – one that Drudorn had tried to help his son conquer all of his life.

"You're right," Andemar replied, catching the Lord of Evermount's attention once more. "I seek passage to the Shadow Sanctum." He decided to speak bluntly rather than hide his intentions.

Lord Varian had that look of detachment again. "Oh?" he responded casually. "What's *that*?"

"Your cousin, Hana, mentioned it," Andemar divulged only a portion of the truth. If Drudorn had no knowledge of the Shadow Sanctum, then perhaps it was not the *real* Drudorn. *What if this is a Changer?* Andemar pondered many possibilities, but he did not let paranoia rule his thoughts for long. "She said that I could find…something valuable there," he said cautiously, waiting for Lord Varian's next response.

Drudorn's eyes narrowed. "If she told you *that*," he countered, "then that's not all she would have said." The Lord of Evermount gathered what strength he had and sat up in his bed. "Tell me," he said simply.

Andemar nodded, believing that the feeble man before him was truly Lord Varian. He finally spoke the words.

"A storm rises from the shadows."

Drudorn formed a look of shock before he closed his eyes and let out a shuddering breath. Opening his eyes again, he asked, "Why did Hana tell you that? What reason did she have to reveal our family's most guarded secret?"

Andemar then shared his entire story about his visits with the Foreseer, Horus, and what he had learned of his own destiny. After he had taken a few minutes to explain, Andemar concluded by saying, "Aunt Hana confirmed the existence of the Sanctum and told me the words, so that I may come to see you and learn more. Retrieving the Mystical Artifact is vital to our survival."

"Shhh!!" Drudorn shook his hands at Andemar like a madman. "Quiet, my Prince," he said in a hushed voice. "The phrase that my cousin shared with you may be enchanted, but speaking openly about the Artifact is *not*."

"Enchanted?" Andemar asked, confused.

"Yes. It's a better one of ours, if I may say so. It wards off any Readers," he said proudly. "They could search your mind for days and never discover what those words meant."

Andemar, out of sheer curiosity, wanted to hear more about the enchantments but chose to stay on the topic of his mission. "Lord Varian, this weapon will help us all win the war against Kelbain. I must find it before it falls into the wrong hands." He was sure to speak more softly when mentioning the Artifact so as not to attract any unwanted attention from anyone outside their walls.

Drudorn, out of necessity, went on to explain the dangers of the Shadow Sanctum. "Many in the past had ventured there but never came back," he warned. "Some say that a thing of evil dwells deep within. My father found the weapon during the Sorcerer's War, long after Garis had abandoned the temple."

"Garis?" Andemar asked with bewilderment.

"The Mystic of the East, yes," Drudorn affirmed. "The Sanctum was once the Temple of Garis." He then continued to share his information with Andemar. "We sealed the weapon and the entranceway using the same enchantment that I mentioned earlier. Old magic," he revealed, noticing the look of interest on the prince's face, "from a time before the Mystics came to Areon. The weapon was far too dangerous for any man to wield – but, no longer." Smiling, he added, "I believe you are worthy, Prince Andemar, as is your cause. Though, getting there will not be easy," Drudorn admitted.

Andemar had let everything sink in. In another example of Vandal's overprotective ways, Andemar and his brothers never knew any bit of what Lord Varian had just told him. Luckily, he was growing accustomed to learning more about Areon's hidden history.

"You'll have to get by the Tempest," Drudorn cautioned.

Andemar blinked. *What is that?* Andemar thought to himself as he shook his head in disbelief.

Chapter 14

THE TRIAL BEGINS

The roar of the crowd was deafening. Their cheers for blood sounded throughout the arena but also echoed in the corridors that surrounded it. As all of the accused sat there in wait, staring at the umber wooden doors that led to the grassy battlefield, they contemplated many things. One, in particular, could only think of how he would kill the Lord of Woodhaven, Draven Darkwood, and get away in one piece. While the former was already quite improbable, the latter seemed to be impossible.

Three days, Jasian thought to himself. Everything centered around that number. He had trained for his first day of the trial for the past three days – as Darkwood had permitted – and if he were to survive against his first three opponents, the next portion of the trial would be held in another three days. A part of him thought that Draven had been playing a strange joke on him, but that was how the rules of their trials played out.

Jasian raised his chin. The thunderous sound of the crowd rang throughout the corridor once more. He could slightly hear the voice of someone else between the shouts of the people. *Darkwood*, he correctly surmised. No doubt, the Lord of Woodhaven was preparing his people for a spectacle. The thought sickened Jasian to his core. Darkwood already knew that he was guilty of killing soldiers from Woodhaven – the 'trial' was just about giving the honor of Jasian's death to one of their own. Draven had admitted as much when he first told Jasian about the trial. *Just survive*, he told himself. *Survive long enough to kill him…*

Throughout the last few days, the only thing that Jasian found comfort in was his memories. He thought a lot about his time back home, where he would train night and day under the instruction of Ornell Balgon – a surly old man without sympathy. Balgon was the commander of Stoneshield's forces but also played the part of master-at-arms to Lord Bowlin's sons. Jasian was very fond of those moments because he would occasionally be in Ashra and Rudi's company during his training. Chuckling to himself, Jasian remembered when his cousin commented about Commander Balgon in earshot of the man.

"He's old enough to be my grandfather," Young Rudimere had remarked back then. "I'm surprised that he can still hold a sword." Much to his dismay, Jasian and Ashra did not laugh, but their faces formed the same expression of fear. Once Rudi realized that Commander Balgon was behind him, his face turned sour.

"I could put this sword right through your eyes without breaking a sweat," Balgon threatened young Rudimere. "But your family would be quite upset, I think." He held his broad sword at Rudi's bright blue eyes, the tip of it sitting on the boy's nose. "Or *would* they?"

Afterward, Jasian and Ashra laughed at Rudi's expense, but the three of them learned that Commander Balgon was a force to be reckoned with. Living within the same city walls, Jasian grew to respect the old man over time and would come to appreciate the man's insightful training. Even when Jasian wanted to fight with two swords like his older cousin, Andemar, his father tried to discourage the idea – but Balgon nurtured the thought…to an extent.

"If you're going to wield two blades," Ornell said in his usual gruff voice, "be sure that *you're* the one in armor. If the man you are fighting has armor on, then you'd be a fool to use two swords at the same time." Jasian had questioned him back then but was met with an immediate retort. "If you're trying to find the weakness in a plate of armor, you need *both* hands on your sword, boy! The only real time that you should use two swords is when you're both without armor – and when would *that* happen?"

Jasian let a smile creep onto his face as he remembered the lesson. No one would be wearing armor in the upcoming fights in the trial. *That's all I needed to know*, he thought. Darkwood had informed him of the details before he was allowed to train – and once he found out, he began to use two swords to prepare for his first day of battle. Though he never took issue with dual-wielding in the past, he presumed that he would have no problems during the trial if his opponents wore no armor of any kind.

"You look deep in thought," a voice called out to him.

Pulled from his ill-timed nostalgia, Jasian turned to his left and found another shirtless prisoner sitting in the hall just a few feet away from him. The man's brown hair met his shoulders, and his beard fell beneath his chin in a tangled mess. "Hope you're concentrating on what you need to do in there."

Jasian narrowed his eyes. "What does it matter to you?"

"It *doesn't*," the man responded rudely. "But we are both here in the dirt, *eagerly* awaiting our moment to fight for our lives. No one else to talk to before our time here is over, is there?"

Before Jasian could reply, the wooden doors parted, allowing the sounds of the crowd to spill into the corridor with intensity. A single guard approached Jasian and forcibly lifted him to his feet.

"Well, that was short-lived," the prisoner said disappointingly. "I'll see you in Volsi, friend."

Jasian ignored the rambling man in the corridor and entered the arena to the jeers of the people. Looking around, he could not help but notice that the crowd was much smaller than he imagined. He almost forgot that Kelbain slaughtered most of the people of Woodhaven. To his disbelief, he felt sorry for them – regardless of his feelings toward their current lord.

Before he reached the center of the circle, he was instructed to choose his weapons from the sword rack that stood outside the grass. Having prepared for this, Jasian chose two short swords that would be perfectly light and manageable for the upcoming fights. After walking away with his choice of weapons, he stood in the middle of the arena and waited. He immediately looked to the balcony when he saw a figure begin to stand up. While the man hushed the crowd, Jasian's eyes became slits as he realized who was about to speak.

"People of Woodhaven," Lord Darkwood announced in a loud, projected voice, "you are here to bear witness to today's trials. The guilty men that will fight before us have all committed heinous acts against our glorious city." The words drew the ire of all in attendance. They were keenly aware of the sort of 'acts' that Draven spoke of. "Our first man to defend himself today," Draven said, pointing to Jasian, "is responsible for the deaths of multiple soldiers from Woodhaven. This *monster* from the East cut down our honorable and brave men, and today he will experience justice!" Lord Darkwood's impassioned speech, exaggerated as it may have been, was met with the roar of his people.

The Young Bear stood unmoved, glaring at Draven with hate in his eyes. He thought that he caught a glimpse of a smirk on the Lord of Woodhaven's face. His fists suddenly clenched around the sword handles tightly.

"I give you: Jasian Bowlin, of Stoneshield!" Draven shouted. After the crowd reacted in the way that Lord Darkwood expected, he introduced the first opponent for Jasian. "Representing Woodhaven, a soldier that I have personally led into battle: Fane Treeleaf!"

Woodhaven's denizens cheered for their warrior as the man raised his arms in acceptance of the praise. Jasian watched the man, studying him as he approached. Treeleaf was slim, muscular, held a sword in one hand, and a shield in the other. It was all that Jasian needed to know. His opponent would most likely be fast – and if he was wielding a shield, he probably learned how to use it. *Get it out of his hands*, Jasian told himself. *Do it quickly.*

Once Treeleaf had reached the circle, Draven held a hand up to silence the crowd before he spoke again. "Fane Treeleaf, why do you fight today?"

"To honor the fallen and bring justice to their murderer!" Treeleaf replied with the traditional words.

Lord Darkwood nodded, and his warrior turned to face Jasian. When Fane moved into a fighting stance, the Young Bear followed. Holding his hand up once more, Draven made a fist, signaling the start of the battle. "Begin!" he cried.

Jasian jumped back as Treeleaf charged toward him right at the start. The soldier from Woodhaven swung his sword without restraint, attempting to dispatch Jasian swiftly. The useless attacks were avoided, though the man also used his shield as a weapon, thrusting it forward with deadly purpose. Jasian continued to dodge the sword attacks but used his two blades to counter the shield when he could. Fane slashed at Jasian's gut, missing entirely – but as the Young Bear leaned toward his opponent at the same time, Treeleaf used his shield to bash Jasian's mouth, sending him tumbling to the ground. Jasian recovered quickly, even with blood pouring from between his teeth.

"I draw first blood," Fane mocked Jasian. Then, turning to the crowd, Treeleaf raised his arms in early celebration, much to the joy of the people.

A bloody mouth he could handle, but Jasian became vexed when he witnessed Fane's gloating. Grasping his swords again, he stood up and awaited his opponent. "Are you finished!?" Jasian shouted. He watched as Treeleaf turned around to stare at him with widened eyes. Twirling the steel in his hands, he stood defensively, ready for the next attack. "Come then!"

In a move that was expected, Fane charged at Jasian again, but this time the Young Bear left his defensive stance and attacked the man head-on. The barrage interrupted Treeleaf's offensive strikes and caught him off-guard. Forced to defend, Fane began to lose his footing as he backed up. Jasian took advantage and used both swords to knock Fane's shield out of his hand. Before he let the feeling of surprise truly set in, Jasian impaled Fane with one sword...then the second. The soldier of Woodhaven fell to his knees, shock spread across his face – and as the man's eyes shut, Jasian retrieved his swords from Treeleaf's chest before the fighter dropped to the grass.

Noting the jeers from the crowd in the arena, Jasian sighed with relief – even after he looked up to the balcony and saw Draven smiling and clapping. Suddenly remembering the rules that Darkwood had explained, Jasian tried to calm himself for the five minutes he had until his next opponent appeared. *One down, two to go*, he told himself.

Time flew by, but Jasian was ready. His next match was against a large man that called himself 'The Marked One'. His name originated from the vast number of tattoos covering his body, including atop his bald head. The oversized giant wielded a one-sided axe, in which the blade was as big as Jasian's torso.

Shortly after the introductions were made, the fight began. Jasian was much faster than The Marked One, having no trouble avoiding the beast's attacks. *Tire him out*, Jasian thought, *Get him to keep swinging*. He did just that, as he forced the man to grunt and swing his axe over and over again. Within moments, Jasian ducked under the man's legs and sliced both shins with his swords. The behemoth growled and fell to his knees, just as Fane Treeleaf did. Jasian plunged his sword into the gut of The Marked One, causing the man to spit up dark red blood. To Jasian's surprise, the man quickly grabbed him by the throat and pulled him close. Before the Young Bear could react, his head had involuntarily connected with the tattooed skull of The Marked One. Jasian flew backward into the grass, disoriented and unable to see – his opponent, still on his knees, laughed. While one of his swords remained in his opponent's belly, Jasian recovered and used his other sword to slice the throat of The Marked One, spraying a red mist into the air.

Once again, the people of Woodhaven showed their disappointment with the outcome, but Lord Darkwood nodded and clapped. "Well done!" he shouted down to Jasian. Hearing the angry cries of the crowd, he attempted to assuage their complaints. "Not to worry, dear friends! There is still one more fight for today!"

Breathing hard through the pain and retrieving his sword from the fallen, tattooed man, Jasian braced himself for the next encounter. He was happy to have made it past the giant, but that head-butt had almost knocked him out. *Have to protect myself better.* A part of him was starting to worry about his next opponent. He had faced a soldier and a monstrous warrior already. Jasian wondered what could be next. Not having to wait long, Jasian watched as Lord Darkwood stood to announce the final participant in the trial's first day.

"The accused has fought with honor today. Has he not?" Draven's words were countered by the crowd's disdain. "Yes, truly, he has fought well. But now, he must face his greatest challenge. His next opponent is a knight of Woodhaven – given the title by the *great* Fabien Prastor," he proclaimed, clearly meaning to insult their most recent lord, *Fulton* Prastor. While Draven had served Fabien honorably, he had later tried to take the seat from his son, Fulton, which resulted in Draven's banishment from Woodhaven. A smile crept across Darkwood's face as he thought of how far he had come since that day.

The doors opposite Jasian had opened to reveal a simple-looking man. He held a pole with a banner attached at the top – the black cloth displayed a silver eagle. Jasian had noted the crowd's unrestrained screams at the sight of the man's sigil, and he became quite curious as to the reasoning.

"I give you: Ser Hardegin Highwind!" Draven shouted, prompting the people to shout all over again.

*Highwind…*Jasian thought as he let out a sigh. He was not too knowledgeable about the West, though he knew the surname. While other names like Prastor, Darkwood, Redwood, and so forth were given at birth, 'Highwind' was given to those who served the Lord of Woodhaven with prestige. The Highwinds were renowned for their bravery and loyalty, having made a name for themselves during the years of civil war between Woodhaven and Zenithor. Suddenly, Jasian's brows furrowed. *How many survived Kelbain's slaughter?* he wondered.

The knight approached the grass circle and turned toward Draven, who silenced the crowd before speaking. "Ser Hardegin Highwind, why do you fight today?"

"To honor the fallen and bring justice to their murderer," Hardegin replied calmly.

After the traditions were upheld once more, Jasian stood tall with his swords at the ready. The knight that walked toward him also held two blades and moved into a similar fighting stance.

"Begin!" Draven yelled, wasting no time.

Jasian and Hardegin circled each other, determining who would strike first. As the Young Bear looked into the eyes of the battle-weary knight in front of him, he saw a man who was fighting for more than the whims of his lord – he saw a man that was tired of losing the ones that he loved. It was the same set of eyes that Jasian displayed after Merroc died.

"I don't want to fight you," Jasian said abruptly. "But I must survive this."

Ser Hardegin looked taken aback at first but then nodded respectfully. "Good to know that you are not a coward," he said in a low voice. "Fight with honor, Young Bear. One of us will travel to Volsi tonight." Swinging his swords, Hardegin clashed with Jasian, and the two men stood frozen, locked in battle.

"I fear it is so," Jasian replied, struggling to gain the upper hand against the veteran knight. A fleeting thought found its way into his mind – one of Ashra, her eyes shining in the sun, smiling and welcoming him home to her arms. He pushed the distracting thought out of his head. *Focus! Need to focus,* he reminded himself. Using his swords to push Hardegin back, Jasian went on the offensive, striving to quickly end the fight. The two of them were evenly matched as they continued to attack and parry each other's blows.

"You are not without skill," Highwind commented. "I've fought better, but you show great promise. Shame…" The knight countered Jasian's next flurry of strikes, then swiftly dislodged one of the blades from Jasian's hands.

As the sword clattered to the ground, Jasian fixed his eyes on Highwind and held his remaining sword tightly with both hands. Winded and growing tired, Jasian mustered the strength for one final assault. Catching his opponent off-guard, Jasian used his sword to block both of Hardegin's in succession. The speed that he exhibited caused the man to falter in his defensive style, which Jasian exploited – he noticed that Hardegin seemed to block more heavily with his right hand. Clashing his single weapon against both of Hardegin's swords one more time, Jasian sliced down on his opponent's right wrist, severing his hand. The Highwind of Woodhaven yelped in pain, but before he could retaliate, the Young Bear knocked his other sword to the ground. With his opponent standing before him, unarmed and maimed, Jasian pulled his sword back in preparation to strike. He hesitated for a moment, if only to give the doomed man a chance for final words. Hardegin seemed to take the hint.

"Well done," Highwind offered praise to the young Bowlin. "You saw that I favored my right hand. Well done, indeed." Suddenly, he began to look around the arena with a joyful expression as a single tear ran down his cheek. "I've given my life to this place. But I look forward to meeting my brothers again in Volsi." Lowering his eyes again and locking his gaze with Jasian, he said, "I wish you good fortune during the rest of your trial, Young Bear."

Nodding to the respectful knight, Jasian quickly ran him through then watched as Hardegin crumbled into the grass below. Realizing that the day was done, Jasian dropped his sword and exhaled in relief.

Lord Darkwood stood up on his balcony and quieted the shouting jeers of the crowd. Speaking loudly for all to hear, Draven said, "That was well-fought, Bowlin. Your fighting prowess has surpassed my expectations. That concludes the first day of your trial. In three days, we shall see if you are up to the task when you face your next opponents." Leaning on the edge of the balcony, Draven attempted to gain Jasian's full attention. "The next time you enter this arena may well be your *last*," he cautioned.

Jasian scowled at Draven. Internally, he swore – once again – to kill his brother's murderer and make sure that the reign of Lord Darkwood was a short one.

Chapter 15

A ROYAL WEDDING

It was a glorious day for the North. Only days ago, two of the houses in the region were in open rebellion against the king. While it was still unknown if the civil war would continue, the people in the capital of Whitecrest celebrated as their king married for a second time.

North King Cyrus stood tall – as much as he could, anyway – while he held hands with his soon-to-be bride, Amasha Gargan. His hair shone with a bright hue as the sun poured in through the large windows in the throne room. The giant block of ice that composed the entirety of the back wall was a fitting decoration for a royal union in the North. King Cyrus wore a fancier version of his normal attire but added a cleaner fur coat to drape over his shoulders for the occasion. Amasha, in her slender form, was dressed in a light blue gown that seemed to be too tight, though she did not appear to mind. She, too, wore a cloak of fur to protect her from the cold winds in the castle. She also displayed a coy smile throughout the ceremony, as she gazed upon the king with an almost ravenous look.

The prince from the East, who had been looking on from the front row, knew exactly what sort of woman Amasha was. After the engagement was solidified, he had only spoken to Cyrus about her once while they were all traveling back to Whitecrest. The king mentioned that she seemed to be overly enthusiastic about romantic entanglements. Thasus presumed that to mean she was happy to lay with *anyone*. The night of the feast confirmed their thoughts on the matter, as she was quick to cling to Cyrus's side. They had barely known one another for a day. While Thasus took no issue with that kind of arrangement, he had a feeling that Cyrus may not have much experience with such boldness. But as they stood before him, ready to bind themselves to each other, Thasus admitted that he did not know people as well as he thought.

While the pair were about to exchange their pledges of eternal love and loyalty, Thasus surveyed the rest of the attendees in the room. The king's mother, Celia, stood behind Cyrus with a look of pure discontent. It was almost as if she disapproved of the match and had no qualms about letting everyone know. To his left, Thasus found Cyrus's son, Prince Saul, standing at the end of the row. The boy was smiling weakly, but there was something hidden behind his blue eyes – something that made Thasus very curious, yet almost worried.

The sound of heavy footsteps broke his concentration. Vyncent Reign, dressed in his new, shining, sapphire armor, was tasked with bringing the king his ceremonial armband. As Thasus understood it, the band had been given to Cyrus when he became of age and would only then be given to his bride on their wedding day. Earlier that day, Vyncent was made the commander of the new Royal Guard. But the king wanted to ensure Vyncent's happiness in his new position – he also granted him the title of 'thane', making him 'Vyncent Reign, Thane of Whitecrest'. It was a title that did not exist in any other region, but Thasus knew it to be purely celebratory and not based on merit.

Suddenly, out of the corner of his eye, Thasus spotted another individual as they were dragged into the throne room from one of the side entrances. Two of the guards had brought in Kaya Gargan, chained from her wrists to her feet and barely able to walk. In this light, Thasus was able to see the extent of her treatment in the dungeons. Her clothes were dirty, as was her hair, and her arms were scraped – most likely due to the lack of vision in her cell, Thasus imagined. She was a curvy woman, though if she were anything but a prisoner, it would have been more noticeable. *Hard to tell through the rags,* Thasus thought contemptuously, as he became more and more disappointed with King Cyrus. Realization dawned on him – the only reason Cyrus let her out was to see her sister get married. *He may never let Kaya out of her cell again.* Knowing what he knew, after speaking with Kaya himself, he could not accept her imprisonment any longer. He would speak with the king after the ceremony.

As the wedding proceeded, the crowd was silent while King Cyrus and Amasha exchanged their solemn vows. The king then took the armband he had been holding and placed it around Amasha's left arm. Following that moment, Amasha placed a new, golden armband – one that was made recently for the king's wedding – and gently coiled it around Cyrus's left arm as well.

After that, Amasha took off the flowered circlet that she had worn for the occasion – Northern tradition called for the man's *father* to be involved in the next step, but, in place of Cyrus's father, Celia was required to place the queen's golden crown atop Amasha's head. Celia acted the part when the time came, though her smile was anything but genuine. Amasha failed to notice, as she was too enamored with her new accessory. The new queen looked into Cyrus's eyes, smiling from ear-to-ear. From there, the ceremony soon reached its conclusion, and the priest announced the two of them as 'King Cyrus Norton and Queen Amasha Norton, rulers of the North'. The crowd clapped and shouted with excitement.

At the same time, Thasus glanced over at Kaya to ascertain her reaction – she had already been staring in his direction. The look on her face was one of pity, or so Thasus thought. He flinched, believing that her gaze was focused on his scars. He imagined that her curious observation could have been for a different reason, but not one that he could immediately figure out.

Later, the guests poured into another hall for the reception. The king wanted to make sure that the festivities did not stop. If the reception had taken place in the throne room like the ceremony, there would have been a long delay in between. During the gathering, Thasus made his way through the sea of guests, journeying toward the ale. He happened to notice Kaya's abrupt departure – though it was more of an *escort* – from the reception. She had been in an embrace with her sister, the newly crowned North Queen, but then quickly taken back to the dungeons by the guards. Thasus cursed the king's indecision regarding Oswall Gargan while taking note of Kaya's devastated facial expression. *The woman doesn't deserve to sit in a cell*, he thought. *I must find Cyrus at once.* Along the way, he overheard many unwanted opinions about the king and queen's wedding.

"Did the king retrieve a sword?"

"Oh my! Did you see the queen's dress? By the gods..."

"Where was the sword exchange?"

Thasus found the complaints about the swords to be interesting. He, too, had been expecting certain Northern traditions to be upheld but understood why they were not. Usually, the groom was supposed to retrieve a sword from an ancestor's tomb to present it to the bride at the wedding ceremony – this was to ensure the sword's safekeeping until a son was born from the marriage. The people failed to realize that Cyrus had already liberated a sword, many years prior, at his first wedding. From what Thasus could figure out, Cyrus had retrieved his father's sword and given it to his first wife, Cassie. After she died giving birth to Prince Saul, Cyrus had the sword entombed with his first love. Understandably, that was why he would not attempt to take the weapon for his second wedding.

The sword exchange, which the guests spoke of, referred to a part that Amasha should have played. If Cyrus had given her a sword, she would have presented him a sword from her ancestral line, symbolizing her father's protection being passed on to the husband. But considering that the betrothal was decided upon at the recent meeting at the crossroads of the Fool's March, Amasha could not have obtained a sword for her new husband.

"Lord Gargan did not attend his daughter's wedding?" Thasus heard from another attendee, just as he was about to approach the king.

Cyrus was seated at the head of the table, feasting on a small plate of meat, while his wife drank wine from a glass, seemingly new to the concept. Amasha stared at the glass after she downed the liquid in one breath.

"This is incredible, Cyrus!" she exclaimed. "A very sweet ale, this is."

"That is wine, my dear," Cyrus corrected her, smiling as he did so. "You reside in Whitecrest now. You have your choice of *all* kinds of pleasures."

Thasus wondered if it was the best time to speak with the king, as the man appeared to be a little drunk. Then, he considered the idea again. *Perhaps it's a* better *time.* People tended to be more accommodating while the drink took hold of their senses, he thought. Locating an empty seat, Thasus brought it over to the king's side and sat down.

"Thasus!" Cyrus shouted as he embraced the East Prince from his chair. "Mighty Thasus! Come, drink with me!"

"King Cyrus," Thasus addressed the inebriated man. He turned to the new North Queen next. "Queen Amasha," he said, courteously lowering his head. The woman seemed to be as befuddled as Cyrus.

"Thasus, of Angelia," she remarked with a sly grin. "*You're* the one that killed the Fenrok. My sisters hate you. Did you know that?" The queen proceeded to ogle the Prince with a lustful expression.

"Ohh no!" the king said loudly. He was trading gazes between his wife and Thasus, his eyes blinking rapidly as he spoke. Finally, he stopped to look at Thasus while holding a finger up. "You have had many women, my friend, but this is my wife," Cyrus slurred as he spoke. "The only one who will be having her tonight is *me*." The king and queen smiled at each other and then found themselves locking lips in a messy display of affection.

After a few moments, Amasha excused herself from the table to go and greet other guests. Thasus was glad to be rid of any distractions, as he needed to speak with Cyrus alone. "Your Grace, it looks like you are having a good time. I'm happy for you."

Cyrus turned to face Thasus, still grinning foolishly. "Thank you, Thasus. You are a true friend. Just between you and I," he said as he leaned closer, "it is still strange to be married again." The king looked down at the table and closed his eyes, clearly becoming emotional. "I miss her...my Cassie. She left this world too soon," he lamented. "Alas, Amasha is my wife now, and I will honor her."

Thasus nodded in an attempt to understand the king's loss. But losing a wife during childbirth was something that he could never understand. He often wondered what it would be like to have a wife and children. After spending so many years avoiding a serious partnership, he was starting to realize that he wanted something more than a single night with a woman. Shaking his head, Thasus tried to think of a way to broach the topic of Kaya's imprisonment with Cyrus.

"So...I take it that you weren't expecting Lord Gargan to show up tonight." It was the best he could start with.

"Of course not," Cyrus replied with a short laugh. "Word has it that Oswall hates his daughters – well, a few of them, anyway – and Amasha told me herself that her father would not come to the wedding, especially on such short notice. Besides, there was barely enough time for him to make the journey here." The ale was still affecting the king's words, but he seemed to master his senses for a little while as he spoke with Thasus.

"I'm sure Grenna and Jorga have already informed him of the treaty. Do you think that he has heard about Cale's execution?" Thasus asked.

"Hard to say," Cyrus shrugged. "But we hold his daughter in the dungeon. Even if he *has* found out about Brock, he'll think twice before attacking us."

The king's words were clear, though there seemed to be some fear or doubt behind them. Thasus could wait no longer. "Your Grace," he began carefully, "I have spoken with the Gargan woman."

Cyrus's browed dropped. "You have?"

"Yes. At length. She told me that her father had *no* intention of rebelling until Cale introduced the idea," Thasus explained. "Cale even extorted a marriage to Kaya because he knew he'd be able to solidify the help of the Gargans with the match." He stopped for a moment, noticing Cyrus hanging on every word. "I do not think that Oswall will attack you, Your Grace. Now that Lord Brock is dead, and you have taken in the rest of his army, Lord Gargan will abandon any thought of attack." Thasus reminded himself of what Kaya had said the last time they spoke. She was slightly hesitant regarding the idea of her father giving up on the rebellion. The East

Prince did not think much of her demeanor at the time, but it was still puzzling.

"You spoke to Kaya?" Cyrus focused on anything but the points that Thasus brought up. "I *told* you that we would get the information out of her. You just decided to do it yourself?" The king was starting to get angry, and Thasus looked defensive.

"She doesn't need to be in that cell," Thasus said bluntly. "Why is she still there? You gain *nothing* from her imprisonment."

"She could be *lying* to you, Thasus. Did you ever think of that? Did that not occur to you while you skulked into her cell to get the information that you desired?" Cyrus was quickly sobering up. "You don't know Oswall as I do," he pointed out. "Holding his daughter captive *will* keep him at bay." Cyrus truly believed in what he was doing, though it *did* begin as a ploy to cover up his involvement in Marc Bowlin's death. Cyrus did not know what to do after the incident, so his mother came up with everything – the lie about Cale's assassin, putting Kaya in the cell to keep Oswall in line, all of it. *Thasus may be right*, the king thought, *but it's too late now.*

Biting his tongue, Thasus was forced to accept the king's command. "As you wish."

At some point, Thasus decided to leave the hall while the celebration continued – he had enough for one night. Still, he could not get the Gargan woman out of his mind. *No reason for her to be there. No reason at all.* Though he could not convince King Norton of Kaya's innocence, the East Prince struggled with the prisoner's situation. Stopping in a windy corridor, he closed his eyes. *Do not go down there again.* Sighing, he made the familiar turn toward the dungeon and walked with haste. He even stopped once more to Pathfind his way to Kaya's cell, ensuring that the way was clear of any guards. He assumed that they were all back at the reception – even the guards that took Kaya back to her cell earlier.

Arriving in the cold, dark of the Northern dungeon, Thasus made his presence known. "Kaya?" he called out.

"I was w-wondering when you would c-come back," the woman said, shuddering in the blackness of the cell.

"Are you alright?" Thasus asked, concerned about the frigidness of the room. As he approached the door made of iron, Kaya stood up and walked toward him. She had no fur skins covering her, and she barely had on a full amount of clothes. "Kaya…"

She waved him off. "Pay this n-no mind, East Prince. I grew up in Rikter's H-Hollow. I've been in colder weather."

"Not without proper clothes," Thasus remarked as he removed his own cloak of fur. Holding the heavy apparel, he pushed it in between the bars, offering it to Kaya. "You *need* it."

Kaya was hesitant at first but then nodded and took the cloak – it was large enough to cover her whole body. Wrapping it around her shoulders, she used both of her shivering hands to pull it tightly across her midsection. Immediately, she breathed easier as she felt the comfort of some warmth again. "Thank you, Thasus."

"Who took your cloak from you?" the man asked, edging on anger. "Was it the guards?"

Kaya let out a harsh, derisive laugh. "They thought it'd be fun to see me beg. I gave them no such satisfaction." She caught Thasus's smile after her comment, and she smiled back. "So I used the torches for warmth – what little they have, anyway." Suddenly, she scoffed. "My father would *not* have approved."

Thasus cocked an eyebrow. "Why?"

"He can be very…rigid. He preferred that we all had as much exposure to the cold as possible. My sisters and I, we'd take turns climbing in and out of the crater – sometimes from breakfast to supper – so Father could make us wake in the morning and do it again." Her face became sad.

Thasus had never been to Rikter's Hollow, though he was fully aware that the village of the Gargans was at the bottom of a crater – the same one that was caused by the Mystics' arrival to Areon, or so the legend said. Seeing the look on Kaya's face, he said bluntly, "Why would he do such a thing to his own daughters?"

"To make us strong," she replied, shaking her head. "Turns out that Grenna and Jorga were the only two that benefited from that sort of parenting." Noticing the expression on Thasus's face, she added, "My father and I don't see eye-to-eye. While he can have a more brutal outlook on things, I try to see the beauty of it all."

"Beauty?" Thasus asked, not sure where she was heading with that statement.

Kaya laughed at him. "I'm no savage, *Prince* Thasus. I *do* see the world in a different light than some of the other Northerners."

"Your sisters painted a very different picture when they tried to have me killed," the man retorted sarcastically.

"I am sorry about that. They are more like my father than I care to admit…"

"It was nothing I couldn't handle," Thasus said confidently.

Kaya looked closely at the man's face for a moment, wondering about the truth behind the tale. "What was it like?" she asked. The East Prince expressed a look of confusion. "You fought and killed the Fenrok. Tell me about it."

He observed Kaya's eyes when she asked about the battle. *She wants to know about the scars.* A part of him wanted to leave the past in the past but could not help but *want* to share it with her. He turned around to find a wooden stool placed against the wall. Pulling it next to the iron bars, he sat down and told Kaya the entire story.

Afterward, Kaya expressed her thoughts on the man's account of his legendary fight. "That must've been frightening. It *really* stood up on its hind legs?"

"*That's* not something to forget," Thasus recalled. "It was a massive beast." The two of them sat for a moment before Thasus spoke again. "You spoke earlier of the beauty that you see. Now, it's your turn to tell *me* a tale," he said with a smirk. It was unlike him to show much interest in anything, let alone a conversation with a woman. He was used to one-night trysts, where *"It's time for you to go"* were the only words spoken. Perhaps it was because he did not need to pay her gold for her services – that, and Kaya seemed to be interested in what he had to say.

"Have you ever seen the Ironforge?" she asked.

For a moment, Thasus had forgotten where the renowned forge was located. Deep in the heart of the crater, the forge was supposedly built within its wall. The Gargans of Rikter's Hollow had access to it for as long as anyone could remember. The only way that others could see the forge and use it was to pay the Lord of Rikter's Hollow a hefty fee. Thasus remembered when he and his brothers had argued whether their swords were created at the Ironforge. Andemar and Rudimere believed it to be so, while Thasus was harder to convince. Sure, their father and grandfather had the means to pay Lord Gargan, but none of them knew for sure where they were made. All the same, Thasus knew that the Ironforge was famous for producing great weaponry but had always assumed that the best blacksmiths were responsible for that claim. "I have not," he replied.

Kaya inhaled sharply. "It's the most wondrous thing I have *ever* seen. It is difficult to explain." Her eyes blinked rapidly as she tried to find the words. "Imagine a place so serene – so calm – that you feel at home there. You could even forget your worst experiences, if only for a time." The East Prince looked at her skeptically but remained curious. "I have had my share of terrible memories," she said with a look of fear, "but being in the Ironforge made me feel…at peace."

Thasus chuckled. "I've never been to a forge as miraculous as that."

Kaya frowned. "You're mocking me."

Clearing his throat, Thasus shook his head. "My apologies. I have heard many things about this Ironforge, but half of the stories don't make sense."

"*Must* they make sense? Sometimes things are beyond our understanding."

"Not for *me*," Thasus retorted. "All of these wild tales of the Mystics. The Ironforge. Sages. If I wasn't a Pathfinder, I'd never believe any of—" His eyes widened. Kaya's eyes were identical to his. "Shit," he cursed into the darkness.

Kaya let the shock run its course, then she spoke plainly. "Why are you afraid?"

"Afraid?"

"Yes. You felt the need to keep your power a secret. Why is that?"

He had never really thought about it before but was forced to now. Realizing the truth, he told her, "I'm afraid of what others would think. I've always been the one that jumps into a fight – the one to lead the charge – but many distrust Sages. What if those who count on me to be heroic look at me differently when they find out that I'm a Sage?"

Peering into the man's eyes, Kaya reached out with her hand and placed it on Thasus's face. "*I* wouldn't look at you differently." She noticed that the man flinched at her touch. "Does this bother you?"

"I thought that *you* were bothered," he placed his hand on hers, "by my scars. I saw you staring at me in the throne room."

"You thought that I was looking at your scars?" Kaya asked gently. After Thasus nodded, she said, "I was looking to you because you are the *only* one that has cared enough to come and visit me. The only one who has taken the time to question me about the Lord of Stoneshield. *You* haven't left me here to rot," she said sorrowfully.

Thasus felt emotions running through him that he thought to be impossible. He wanted more than anything to set her free. He wanted to pry open the door with his bare hands and kiss her. Then, sanity flooded his mind once more. If he freed Kaya, he would have to combat the majority of the North – all of them under King Cyrus's command. Weighing Kaya's freedom against the alliance with King Cyrus was one of the most difficult choices he ever had to make.

"No, I have not," Thasus replied. "But…I have spoken to the king. He still thinks that your father may attack. He will not release you…" Thasus had trouble saying the words. He knew it was wrong for her to be locked up, but there was no getting around it. The stakes were too high.

Kaya removed her hand from Thasus's face and looked to the ground with disappointment. "I see. That's…unfortunate."

Thasus shifted where he stood. "I am sorry," he muttered before abruptly turning to walk away.

"Thasus, wait." Kaya sought to gain his attention once more. She watched as he stopped to turn around and look at her. "Will you please visit again? I enjoy your company." She was able to form a half-smile, given the circumstances.

The East Prince smiled back at her. "You have my word."

Before he left the room completely, Kaya called out to him again. "You told me that you've never been to the Ironforge."

He looked at her, befuddled. "I *haven't*."

"Ah," she said curiously. "Well, I could spot an Ironforge sword anywhere. *Yours* is one of the largest that I've seen. Someone must've paid quite the amount of gold for *that* one." She observed the man's stunned expression as he gazed at her open-mouthed. "Goodnight," she said with a grin before heading to the back of the cell.

Chapter 16

IN THE CAULDRON

"You lied to me," The East King continued to accuse his wife. It had been three days since the incident with their grandson, Anden, yet the king could not help but dwell on the topic. Vandal sat on his throne while the queen stood before him, defending herself with every breath.

"I tried to protect him, Vandal – in my own way. We both know how our children felt about *your* method of protection," Serena pointed out.

Vandal winced at the insinuation. Long ago, after he had visited with Horus – the Foreseer in the city – he had sworn to keep his sons away from anything to do with Sages or the Mystics. He even went so far as to keep them from battle, though he *did* allow them to train. It was not until Kelbain started this new war that Vandal changed his mind and became more understanding of such things. *But she lied*, he kept repeating to himself.

"Serena…you *lied* to me. We do not keep things from one another," he said matter-of-factly. "You should have told me that Anden was an Elemental. By the gods, he's practically a *Sorcerer*."

"We don't know that," Serena denied. "He *has* the ability of multiple elements, but he has not shown me anything else."

"That's bad enough," Vandal retorted. "You *know* what people are going to say. They'll think that he's Magor reborn." He shook his head before broaching the next issue. "This business with the curse…Why didn't you tell me the truth about Andemar?" He was referring to their son's journey and the reason for it. Sure, he knew that Andemar was in search of the Mystical Artifact that supposedly resided in the Shadow Sanctum, but Vandal was not aware of his son's intention to end the curse on their bloodline. By doing so, Andemar would not have had the wish to return home with the weapon – he would most likely attempt to go further west, toward the war.

"He knew that you would not fully understand," Serena explained.

Vandal shot back, "Meddling in the affairs of the Mystics never did a goblet of good. My own father put us in this situation." His voice trembled as he spoke, almost embarrassed to speak ill of the great Victor Palidor. "It's the reason why we're *cursed*…"

The queen approached her husband and gently placed a hand on his shoulder. "If it were not for your father – if he had not been there with his companions 60 years ago – Magor would still live." Vandal looked up and into Serena's eyes with a look of sadness but also acceptance. "Besides, my love," Serena continued, "we both know why you're upset about Andemar's true intentions."

King Vandal nodded. "They are all gone," his lips quivered. Thasus, Andemar, and Rudimere had all left the city with the purpose of saving Areon in one way or another. Still, Vandal wished that they were by his side at that moment. "I miss them," he confided in his wife. "Is that not allowed?"

Serena chuckled. "Of course it is," she said with a smile as she embraced Vandal. "They *will* be back. I know it in my heart."

Just as the two of them had reached a point of joy in their conversation, the doors to the great hall opened to reveal a member of the household guard, striding toward them with haste.

"My King. My Queen," the man bowed as he addressed Vandal and Serena. "A message from the North. Sealed by the sigil of House Norton."

As the guard handed him the letter, King Vandal felt something in his gut – something was wrong. "King Cyrus's seal," he pointed out to Serena. She nodded between him and the letter, motioning Vandal to open it. "Thank you, that will be all," he said to the guard. While the man left the room, Vandal had already opened the seal and began to read. His eyes darted back and forth, from the top of the parchment to the bottom, until he had finished. Closing his eyes, his hand slowly met his forehead as he agonized over the contents of the letter.

"What is it, Vandal? What news?" Serena asked as she took the letter and started reading the news for herself. Halfway through, she let out an audible gasp, which was soon met by a shuddering cry, as she put a hand over her mouth. Her brother, Marc, was dead – murdered by Lord Cale Brock, of the Frostford, according to King Cyrus.

"I am deeply sorry, my love," Vandal said as he glanced up at his grieving wife.

"What of Thasus?" Serena blurted out. "He could be in danger. The letter doesn't mention him at all." The sound of her voice was full of worry.

"That is a good thing," Vandal stated carefully. "With any luck, Thasus will be on his way home now. King Cyrus says that Brock was hung and that the army from the Frostford has joined with him. We have allies now."

Serena shook her head, tears still flowing down her cheeks. "But Cyrus also said that he was almost assassinated. If Cale Brock was allied with Oswall Gargan, it might not be over yet." Suddenly, her head sunk as she uttered, "Marc...you fool..." After a moment, Serena handed the letter back to her husband as she attempted to stand taller. Taking a deep breath, she said, "He saved the North King. For that, I am proud of him." Smiling through the pain, she resolved to push on and honor her brother's memory.

Vandal nodded, agreeing with his wife's words, but began to slowly run his fingers through his facial hair, down to the point at the bottom of his beard. Contemplating everything that had happened recently, from Marc and Merroc's deaths to the battle at the strange temple in Summerhold – where Rudi and his friends were almost killed – Vandal thought long and hard about his next move. Then it hit him. All of this tragedy, all of this turmoil between the houses in the North, and even the threat of King Kelbain, could have been stopped by one person. One man, alone, could have *seen* it all happen and prevented it from taking place. *Enough*, Vandal thought to himself.

The East King crumpled up the parchment in his hands and let it drop to the floor. Rising from his chair, he told Serena, "I have to go."

Dumbfounded, the queen watched as her husband walked hastily toward the doors at the entrance of the hall. "Where are you going?"

"To get answers," Vandal replied shortly.

Walking through the halls, Vandal carried a new sense of determination with him. He would find out everything this time and leave no stone unturned. *None of this should have happened. If only I had—*

"I'm sorry," a small voice said as he bumped into the king around the corner of the corridor.

Vandal flinched, then looked down and locked eyes with his grandson, Anden. The boy formed a sad expression, most likely believing Vandal's recoil to be about him, though it was just a reaction of surprise. *No time to explain.*

"Go and see your grandmother, Anden. She could use the company right now. I shall return soon." With that exchange, Vandal was off to make a visit that he should have made years ago.

***

Watching the bubbling liquid in front of him, the old man smiled broadly through his thick gray beard. He had put in much effort to see his spell come to fruition.

"Almost time," he spoke to himself. "Yes…the time draws near." Hovering from one cauldron to the next, Horus studied each item with a keen eye, observing the water's complexity as they changed colors. Sighing with relief, he made his way to a large shelf in the corner of the room. As he opened the satchel that he carried, the Foreseer began to shove things from the shelf and into the pouch. He made it a point to treat a few items more delicately than others – a small bronze statue, a black dagger with gold edges, and a misshapen rock were all handled with care.

CRASH

The front door of the shop had been busted open with a thunderous force. A group of soldiers, armored in white from head to toe, made their way inside and lined themselves around the edges of the main room. Following close on their heels was the East King himself, Vandal Palidor.

"Ah! Greetings, Your Grace. I *knew* you'd be back again someday," Horus said with a smirk.

"We must speak, you and I," Vandal stated as he pointed to the hunched-over old man. "I'm going to ask you some questions, and you're going to *answer* them."

"I will help in any way that I can, King Vandal," the Foreseer said, obviously feigning an astonished reaction. "Though, I must say that this is quite the show of force. Surely, *you* do not need such protection."

Vandal's eyes became slits. The Foreseer knew of the King's power, of course – and making that kind of remark made Vandal trust Horus even less. Ignoring the comment, Vandal asked his first question.

"I'm going to be as plain as I can, Horus. You have had many meetings with my son, Andemar. Why is it that you never mentioned the tragedy that would befall our family?"

Horus looked confused. "You're going to have to be more specific," he said.

"My nephew, Merroc." The King took a step closer toward the Foreseer in an attempt to invoke some level of intimidation. "The

Lord of Stoneshield – my brother, by law, Marc Bowlin." Vandal's expression became a mix of anger and sadness as he spoke. "They are now gone from this world."

Horus nodded gravely. "Prince Andemar mentioned Merroc. I am truly sorry, Your Grace." The Foreseer made a strange face as if he were squeezing his eyes together. "The future is always moving. It flows steadily like the most serene river. Sometimes it rages like the Crimson Sea." Opening his eyes again, he said, "I may be a Foreseer, but I cannot see all. Your son knew this, as well."

King Vandal's face jerked at the mere mention of Andemar. "He left the city at *your* insistence," Vandal accused the Foreseer. "Why were you so eager to convince him to leave?"

Horus let out an unexpectedly loud chuckle. "Ho, ho! I believe your wife also had something to do with that! Did she not?"

"*Also*, by your instructions," Vandal said in a resentful tone.

"Your son needed the push," Horus shrugged as he spoke casually. "As did *you*, many years ago. But you ran out of my shop before I could reveal your true destiny."

Vandal took another step toward Horus, which caused the soldiers in the room to put their hands on their hilts. They remained still, ready to obey the King's command if need be.

"*My* destiny is my own, Foreseer. I knew it then, and I know it now. But you've sent my son on a fool's errand – and for that, you must tell me why." Vandal fixed himself to the ground so as not to act prematurely. He wanted to hit the old man. He wanted to take out all of his frustration on *someone* and had even considered the possibility that Horus was not the one to bear the extent of his vexations. But his suspicions about the man stood at the forefront of his mind.

"A *fool's errand?*" Horus repeated back to the king. "To save all of Areon? To bring peace to all four of the kingdoms? You call your son a 'fool' for wanting to fulfill his role in our salvation?" The Foreseer was in genuine shock as he stared at the king. Shaking his head, he continued. "You never understood what was at stake. *That* was why you ran that day – and you never wanted to admit the greatness of your family. You only wanted to tuck away your children, hiding them in your great, big castle." The disappointment in the Foreseer's voice was palpable.

Enough. The King held out his left hand in front of Horus's face, pointing at the man and igniting from the fingertip down to the wrist. His entire hand was ablaze for all in the room to see – Vandal was oblivious to the fact that his soldiers knew nothing of his secret before that moment.

"Do not speak of what you do not know," the King threatened.

"Oh, but I *do*," Horus retorted, unfazed. "I have seen more than you can imagine."

Extinguishing the flame, Vandal turned and walked toward the entrance of the shop. "Seize him," he commanded his men. "The Foreseer will divulge everything from a dungeon."

Sensing the King's impatience, Horus backed away from the soldiers and stood behind his black cauldrons, which were bubbling with more intensity than they had been earlier.

"Did you notice these?" he said, bringing the men's attention to the objects in front of him. Vandal had turned to look at the Foreseer once more. "Ho! I've been working on something special for a long time." Raising his head, he locked eyes with the king. "I *saw* this visit. Long before I ever wrote down a single note about the contents of these cauldrons. You see, there was plenty of time to prepare."

"Guards," Vandal said calmly to his men, shooting glances to both sides of the room where soldiers were slowly circling Horus.

"Andemar will still need guidance before his task is done." Before anyone could make a move, Horus dropped an unknown item into the center cauldron and then ducked behind it.

"Guards!" the King shouted.

It was too late. The cauldron exploded with white light, setting off the other two cauldrons nearby. Sound seemed to disappear as the men in the room opened their mouths to yell, yet nothing was heard. They also appeared blinded by the light that engulfed the room. Moments later, King Vandal and his guards found their troubles to be temporary – they stood up to find that the Foreseer had vanished.

Vandal seethed with fury. "Find him!"

Chapter 17

A KNIGHT AND HIS LADY

Summerhold had been in a constant state of disarray as of late. Though promises of safety had calmed the townsfolk, King Wilfred and all those who surrounded him were endlessly preparing for a war that would soon be on their doorstep – but they still did not know *how* soon.

Paxton tried to keep up with any news from the scouts to find out where the army of Karthmere was, but he grew impatient with their lack of new information. Seeking out Mika, the knight from Angelia hoped to learn something that would aid their cause. It was all he could do to keep his mind off of Saris, as he had not spoken with the South Princess at length for a couple of days. Confusion began to take over his thoughts. *Have I read the signs wrong?* he wondered. From the moment he and Saris first had words with one another, he felt a connection that could not be ignored. However, after their conversation in the war room, things seemed to change, though Paxton did not know why.

Making his way toward the training yard behind the castle, he pushed all distracting thoughts from his head and focused on greater issues. As he rounded the nearest corner, he spotted Mika amongst a few Summerhold soldiers in the circular training area. The former Zenithorian looked to be instructing the men and women in *his* methods of swordplay. While Paxton wished to speak to Mika, he did not want to interrupt the lesson. Leaning against a nearby pillar, Paxton observed his friend's obvious skill with a weapon but was surprised to find out that Mika was also an exceptional teacher.

"Try not to stand still," Mika informed the attending soldiers, circling one in particular. "An opponent that is always on the move can avoid being hit. But more importantly, it gives you the ability to spot openings," he said as he brought his practice sword to the trainee's underarm, finding a small weakness beneath the golden armor, "that may have eluded your sight otherwise." The young soldier's shocked expression turned to one of realization after Mika removed his wooden weapon. "Once you discover your enemy's weakness, the fight could be over in moments. But learn to guard these same openings. You have shields. *Use* them." Out of the corner of his eye, he spotted Paxton standing nearby. He had matters to discuss with the man, so he ended his lesson abruptly. "That will be all for today," Mika announced to the soldiers. "Take heed of what I have said."

As the men and women of Summerhold continued to train, Mika and Paxton met with each other and spoke about the city's defense. Paxton informed Mika that they were no closer to finding out the whereabouts of Rayburn Duke's army. Mika, however, was concerned about other issues.

"These soldiers," Mika said, pointing to the group in the yard, "they are good people. But they have not seen much in the ways of war. I fear for them."

Paxton considered Mika's words but reminded him, "They've trained for this. You must trust that they will be ready when the time comes."

Mika shook his head. "If that army has any Sages…if they have a *Reader*, they could end the battle before it begins."

"Ah. The King has something in mind for that scenario," Paxton revealed. Before Mika could ask what he meant, Paxton went on. "I worry about our reinforcements. We have not heard back from Triton, even after I wrote to Lord Argon about my plan."

Mika looked curious. "What plan?"

"Well, if Lord Argon's forces marched from Triton to the bottom of Mount Gilder, they may not get here in time. I suggested another path. If they were to *sail* from Triton to Seaside Harbor, they could disembark and then march to the bottom of the mountain in less than a day. The whole trip would be cut in half."

Mika's eyes widened. Suddenly, a smirk crept along the edges of his mouth. "*That* is an astounding plan, Paxton. You continue to surprise me."

"Hey, don't act *too* surprised," Paxton remarked. "I have good ideas from time-to-time." The two men laughed and began walking toward the castle. "I just hope that Lord Argon received my letter with enough chance to prepare."

"Patience, my friend," Mika assured Paxton. "We will probably hear from them within the next few days."

The knight from Angelia nodded. While he knew that Lord Argon would not fail to respond, he only wished the answer to come soon. Unexpectedly, Paxton found himself staring at the sword that was sheathed on Mika's belt. He thought of the revelation that Mika's former weapon – now in the hands of Draven Darkwood – was a Mystical Artifact known as Harbinger. A part of him still could not believe that they had all been in the presence of such a weapon as they fought beside each other at Squall's End. "How are you faring?" Paxton asked randomly. "Using a sword? Is it troublesome?"

Mika looked down and noticed that his hand was already sitting atop the pommel of his sword. "I used a sword for *years* before I took the axe from Baldric Brock," Mika replied, attempting to preserve his dignity. He sighed as his face turned sour. "Still…I do miss it terribly. Harbinger felt like an extension of my arm. Losing it has been difficult."

"The weapon doesn't make the man," Paxton stated. "For years, I wanted a sword from the Ironforge. Often, I dreamt about it as a child. But then I was knighted by *Victor Palidor*," he spoke fondly of the moment, "one of the Heroes of the Sorcerer's War. He charged me with defending the people of Angelia, upholding the honor and values of the Eastern kingdom…and he presented me with a sword." Paxton reached down and touched the hilt of his blade. "*This* sword. It represents one of the proudest moments of my life – and to me, it will always hold more value than anything I could have made at the Ironforge."

Mika smiled again and shook his head. "When we first met, I thought you were a drunken fool. But I've come to know you as an honorable man. You certainly showed that quality at Squall's End and the Temple of Aman." He placed a hand on Paxton's shoulder. "Your great deeds far outweigh the actions of a lovesick man."

"Thanks…" Paxton said hesitantly.

"Thank *you*," Mika said, oblivious to the awkwardness of his previous statement. "From what I hear," Mika continued, "you've moved on to another lucky woman."

Paxton displayed a half-smile at the mention of his affections toward Princess Saris. He wanted to confirm his friend's assumption, though he was unsure if Saris felt the same way. *Perhaps it is time to find out*, Paxton thought to himself.

***

"You need to find out," Mora tried to convince her sister.

Saris sighed, not wanting to have this conversation. "Please, Mora. Not right now."

"If the two of you feel this way for each other, then you should not delay."

"What about *you*?" Saris shot back, annoyed at Mora's insistence. "You have your own issues to tend to, do you not?"

Mora lowered her head sullenly. "Rudimere and I…we long for each other, that much is clear. I know that it has all happened quickly, but you know the feeling, Saris," she pointed out. "Ser Paxton has stolen your heart, yet you do nothing."

"He's in love with someone else," Saris blurted out.

Mora looked at her sister, unconvinced. "You do not know that. Have you asked?"

"I feel it in my heart," Saris said before sitting down next to the war room table. Mora approached her slowly and sat next to her.

"You *must* find out, Sister. War is about to begin. He is within these walls – you do not have to wait as *I* do."

Saris turned to her sister, noticing the sadness upon her face. Throwing her arm around Mora and pulling her close, she said, "Apologies, Sister. I know not what you must be going through right now. If anyone can return from such danger, it is Rudimere and Ashra," she admitted. Though Ashra was at the center of Saris's insecurity regarding Paxton's affections, she held the woman no ill-will. Saris longed to leave the Southern capital and travel the world – as most already knew – so, in truth, she admired Ashra's ability to roam Areon freely. When it came to Rudimere, Saris believed the man to be a worthy suitor for Mora, even *if* she thought he was impulsive at times.

"I know," Mora replied. "I believe that he will return. I just miss him."

Suddenly, the door to the war room opened with a loud noise that rang throughout the quiet area. Ser Paxton walked in, clad in simple clothes, devoid of his shining white armor that he usually wore around the castle. He spotted Saris almost immediately.

"My Lady," he said with a courteous tone as he bowed to the Princess. Catching sight of Mora, who he had not seen sitting right beside Saris, Paxton bowed again in order to remain respectful. "My Lady," he repeated.

"Ser Paxton," Mora addressed the knight as she stood. "Forgive me, but I must see my father about urgent matters."

"Oh?" Saris asked suspiciously.

Mora turned and stared at her sister, her eyes large. "*Yes.*" Walking toward the door with haste, she spoke to Paxton one more time. "Thank you for all that you have been doing to help. It means the world to our family," she said with genuine appreciation.

"It is my honor," Paxton said before Mora took her leave. Turning toward Saris, he noticed that she was already staring in his direction. He could not take his eyes off of her. Though he wanted to discuss more personal matters, he began by asking, "Have you heard from Triton yet?"

Mildly disappointed, she answered, "Nothing. No letters have come. But Father expects a reply soon." She did not mean to be short with him, but the thought of discussing his relationship with Ashra irked her. Rather than speak of such things right away, she elected to start with something less complicated. "You know, I haven't had the chance to say it, but you were a superb fighter at the temple."

Taken by surprise, Paxton returned the compliment. "As were you, my Lady. A beautiful princess who could fight like that – well, any man would be lucky to be in your presence. Not that your looks would have anything to do with your skill in battle," he stumbled to say. "I only meant...I think that..." Paxton sighed before finally speaking from the heart. "You are everything that a man could ever want."

"Is that so?" Saris asked, tilting her head. "I wondered if a woman like *this* would be more to your liking." Using her ability as a Changer, Saris shifted her body until her skin had lightened. Her brown hair became blonde, but her curls remained. As her brown eyes turned blue, she gazed upon Paxton until his mouth opened slightly. Saris had grown weary of avoiding the question, so she thought the image of Ashra might force Paxton to divulge his true feelings.

"What are you doing?" Paxton inquired with a mix of concern and shock.

Saris approached the knight and put her hand on his chest in a flirtatious manner. "What is it that you truly want? Do you even know?"

"I do not want *this*," Paxton quickly replied. "Please, stop."

"What do you want, Paxton?"

"I want *you*, Saris. Now, stop!"

The South Princess reverted to her original form, stunned by his answer. She chuckled slightly, a wave of relief washing over her, and placed her hand on his cheek.

Paxton lowered his eyes to meet with hers. "I do not like games," he said firmly.

"Then, let us stop playing one."

The two of them embraced in a fiery kiss – one that was long overdue. Soon enough, they let their passion speak as they removed each other's clothes and found themselves atop the war room table in an act of pure love. Even amidst the threat of an impending attack, Paxton and Saris had never been happier.

Chapter 18

FEARFUL CONFESSIONS

It was eerily quiet throughout the castle. For most Northerners, it was hard to believe that there had recently been an execution right in the courtyard. Not only that, but the people in the capital also bore witness to a royal wedding, as Cyrus Norton, king of all the North, married Amasha Gargan. Since then, tensions have risen in Whitecrest.

The king laid in his bed, thinking of the events from the last few days. He still felt tremendous guilt for killing Marc, and his argument with Thasus plagued his mind as well. Their war of words revolved around the imprisonment of Kaya, Amasha's older sister, though the king could not help but think about the repercussions of murdering the Lord of Stoneshield and what the

Prince of Angelia would do if he found out the truth. Interfering with his thoughts, Cyrus's new queen stirred beside him, attempting to begin a romantic entanglement that had not yet occurred.

"My King," she started, "are you not ready yet?"

"Apologies, Amasha. I am just distracted."

"We haven't consummated the marriage yet…" Amasha remarked.

The king was well aware that he had not yet bedded his new wife. It was insulting, he thought, that she had even brought it up. "I realize that."

"Do you not want an heir?" she asked.

Ignoring her blunt question, Cyrus sat up. "As I said, I have a lot on my mind."

"Is it my father?" she inquired in a sincere tone. The king merely sighed as she put a hand on his shoulder in a comforting manner. "You've married one of his daughters, widowed and imprisoned another. You have nothing to fear. He will *not* attack," she assured her husband.

King Cyrus considered her for a moment. Perhaps she was right, he thought. Cyrus had been focused on any threat to his power for long enough. The voice inside of his head – the one that usually sounded just like his mother – kept telling him that he should always be prepared for the possibility of rebellion. A part of him agreed with his mother, but there were times when he believed her to be a bit too paranoid.

"On the subject," Amasha continued, "when *will* you be releasing Kaya?"

There it was: another request for the woman's freedom. *I have to stick to the story*, he convinced himself. "As long as your sister remains in her cell, Oswall will remain at Rikter's Hollow."

Amasha scoffed. "You may put too much faith in that decision. When she married Cale, she was no longer our father's problem. But that's why you have *me*." Her attempt at levity did not seem to change the king's expression. "So if you could release her—"

"I cannot!" Cyrus was done explaining himself. Thasus had already angered him when the man asked the same question, and now his wife had done the same. Kaya's imprisonment may have started as part of the lie that Cyrus's mother created, but the king had no choice but to go along with it. He had already committed to it for an extensive amount of time. If that meant that Amasha's sister had to stay in a dungeon, then it was fated to be so. "You would do well not to ask me again," he said with finality.

The queen rose from the feather bed in a huff. "I'm finding another place to sleep tonight," she said with frustration. As she gathered her necessities before storming out of the room, she turned to her husband and said, "Unless you change your ways and let my sister go, you won't be consummating *this* marriage. Then

SHARDS OF THE SUN

you'll truly be the laughingstock of the entire North. What is a man if he has no heir?" The tone of her voice was rising quickly with contempt.

"I *have* a son," the king responded darkly. His wife's eyes widened in shock, and then she was gone. Truly, tensions *were* growing in Whitecrest.

The next morning, Cyrus sat on his throne, lonely and speechless. The lie that he and his mother had started was causing everything to crumble. There were times when his mind would go back to the fateful night of Marc's death. He would reassure himself that the Lord of Stoneshield deserved to die for laying a hand on Celia. But then he also felt incredibly sorrowful – he murdered a man who was only grieving the loss of his son. From there, the Lord of the Frostford, Cale Brock, was executed, an innocent woman was thrown into a dungeon, the Prince of Angelia and the North King were at odds, and the new queen was already unhappy in her marriage. Cyrus was feeling truly lost.

With a thunderous crash, the doors to the throne room opened, and two figures began to approach the king. A rare smile crept along Cyrus's face as he noticed his son was walking beside his mother. The boy's lessons were probably done for the day, so the king was more than happy to greet him. "Saul," Cyrus said happily, "it does me good to see you. How was your day?" Suddenly, as the king reached out to his son, gesturing for an embrace, Saul flinched and walked away. After his son hastily left the room, Cyrus grew concerned. "What happened?" he asked Celia.

The king's mother waved off the question. "Your son didn't like being told what to do," Celia replied, absent sympathy.

"Ah. Children will be children," Cyrus said with a shrug. Though it was common for children to give their teachers grief when it came to their daily lessons, the king was still hurt that his son refused to embrace him. He could have used some comfort at that moment.

Sensing her son's internal struggle, Celia asked, "What is troubling you, my son?"

Cyrus thought he masked his emotions well, but apparently, he did not. His mother tended to see right through him. "It's nothing," he lied.

Celia gave the king a look of disbelief. "Cyrus, you have made the same face since you were a boy. I *know* when you are lying. Tell me," she said in almost a demanding voice.

The king sighed. "It's Amasha," he admitted. "She and I had an argument."

Cyrus's mother laughed under her breath. "You two haven't been married for a *week*. What was the nature of this argument?"

"It seems that she disagrees with her sister's imprisonment. Before you say anything – I defended our actions for keeping Kaya in her cell. Unfortunately, my wife doesn't share the same reasoning." Cyrus could not help but divulge all of the details to his mother. He was used to it, as he confided in her about everything throughout his life. "In all honesty, she claims that her father will stay his hand because I already have *her* for a wife. I won't lie to you, Mother…perhaps we should set Kaya Gargan free. I worry that Amasha's frustrations will lead to her eventual betrayal." Catching himself before speaking any further, Cyrus scoffed. "What am I saying? I'm probably just overthinking it."

Celia stared at the king, expressionless. After a moment, she blinked slowly and then inhaled sharply. "I don't believe that would ever happen," she said calmly. "You shouldn't worry so much, Cyrus."

"And the Gargan prisoner?" he asked, going back to his idea of freeing Kaya.

"We spoke about this," Celia reminded him. "As long as Oswall lives, your rule over the North will never be solidified – especially not after finding out about Cale and Oswall's little rebellion."

Cyrus thought about when he had dragged Thasus into the castle after the man's battle with the Fenrok. The East Prince had revealed what he knew about the coup attempt, effectively saving everyone in Whitecrest. Cyrus would always be thankful for that. Shaking off the distracting thought, Cyrus told his mother, "I married Amasha so there'd be *peace* in the North."

"Peace?" Celia ridiculed her son. "Have you ever known those barbarians in Rikter's Hollow to be *peaceful*? We don't know what they're planning, but I promise you: It will not be pleasant. But as far as the Brocks go, we were very fortuitous."

Cyrus's eyebrows dropped. "How so?" he asked.

"Cale Brock would have been a dangerous enemy to have, Cyrus. Lucky for us, Marc Bowlin's anger got the better of him. In the end, he helped us. Without his death, we would not have been able to take out Lord Brock so easily. Absorbing the rest of Cale's army was just an added benefit."

The king had a stunned look on his face. *She speaks as if these terrible events were in our favor.* "Mother," Cyrus spoke carefully, "if Marc had lived, and if *Cale* had lived, peace in the North might have been an actuality."

"You don't know that," Celia retorted.

"Neither do you!" Cyrus exclaimed in defiance. "You weren't at the crossroads, Mother. When Thasus defeated the warrior from the Frostford, Cale honored his agreement and made peace with us."

"Then Lord Gargan would have still marched on us," Celia stated matter-of-factly.

The King threw his hands into the air. "Against *all* of us? I don't think so, Mother."

Celia was taken aback by her son's newfound courage. She felt the need to remind him of her status. "That's right, Cyrus. I *am* your mother – and you will do as I say. Kaya Gargan will remain in her cell. We will prepare for war against the Gargans...and we will not speak of this again." As her son showed signs of countering her, she slammed her hands on the arm of his chair. "*Not. Again.*"

Cyrus recoiled into his kingly throne. He wanted to argue his point, but there was no winning when it came to his mother. "Of course not..." Cyrus reluctantly agreed.

The next morning, Cyrus was back in his bed, but his wife was nowhere to be found. He lamented that she had not slept at his side overnight, and he also regretted the argument that they had about Amasha's sister. His mind took a turn and found its way back to the last conversation that he had with his mother. It was difficult to defy her, though a part of him knew that he should do so someday. Whenever Cyrus argued with his mother – no matter how small the quarrel – he always remembered that she handed over the throne to him when he came of age. She taught him how to rule after Cyrus's father fell from the tower. Shaking his head, he thought, *What am I supposed to do now?*

Suddenly, Cyrus's door burst open. He was startled at first, but then he saw his wife run in with excitement.

"Cyrus! Oh, my dear husband, I missed you!" the woman from Rikter's Hollow shouted. She nearly jumped into the feather bed and proceeded to shower her king with kiss after kiss. "Apologies for the other night," she said more softly. Amasha grabbed Cyrus and pulled him in closer, touching her lips to his with more force. "I was a fool. Let us not fight again."

Cyrus did not know what was happening or why, but he did not object to the unusual display of affection, especially after their recent disagreement had been so hostile. As the queen climbed atop him, he looked at Amasha with a longing in his eyes. For once, his former love was *not* at the forefront of his thoughts – and he was able to move forward with Amasha as he should have days ago. It was a bright moment that eclipsed the dark days of late.

Sometime later, Cyrus found himself smiling as he walked casually down the icy corridor of his castle. Passing by all of the portraits of the previous kings, he felt a sense of pride, knowing that he may soon become a father to another son. At the same time, his mood soured. He had not seen Saul since their last encounter in the throne room. A feeling of guilt overwhelmed him, and he decided to turn around and head to his son's room.

Arriving outside Saul's door, the king walked through the open threshold and discovered a disturbing scene. He found Saul seated on the bed, rocking back and forth and staring at the wall. The boy was muttering under his breath and did not seem to change his blank expression.

"Saul…" Cyrus spoke softly to his son. "What is wrong?" Saul responded by shaking his head, never taking his eyes off of the wall. "Saul," Cyrus repeated, "talk to me." He placed a hand on his son's golden head and rubbed gently. "Son…what's troubling you?"

Without so much as a look in his father's direction, Saul whispered, "Please...I can't." He began shaking his head again. "I can't, Father...I can't."

Instinctively, Cyrus lifted the back of his son's shirt in an attempt to check him for any marks, bruises, or any other injuries that his son may have incurred. He found nothing. Where they would have come from, even if he *had* found something, Cyrus did not know. But something was hurting his boy, that much was certain. The king sat next to Saul and simply held him. Feeling helpless, tears filled his eyes and fell down his cheeks.

In a moment of clarity, Cyrus's eyes widened. Contemplating recent events, he remembered how strange it was that Saul would act differently after his daily lessons. He then thought of the night that Marc died. The Lord of Stoneshield made many claims about Celia's past, including her supposed hand in Marcel's death. Marc had also said that Celia tried to kill their twin sons. Cyrus did not believe any of it at the time, but he knew that Marc tried to reveal more before his death. The king suddenly felt sick. He had never questioned his mother's character before, but if Saul was burdened in any way, then he needed to find out the truth.

Before he could confront his mother, Cyrus wanted to make another stop. Along with everything that was affecting his son, he thought of his wife's abrupt change of heart regarding their argument about Kaya's imprisonment. He wanted to think that they *could* grow to love one another, but he had to be sure that she was sincere with her affections.

Reaching his destination, Cyrus opened the door to his room at the top of the tower, only to find his wife in an unsettling state. She was staring out the window, a blank look on her face, just as it had been with Saul. In this instance, Amasha turned toward the doorway when she heard Cyrus, and she immediately perked up.

"Cyrus!" she exclaimed, her smile as false as her eagerness.

The North King took a few steps in her direction and wasted no time. "Have you seen my mother?" The queen's demeanor changed as she formed a confused expression. "Recently?" he added.

Amasha's eyes seemed to grow larger than her head. "W-Why?" she asked nervously. Quickly, she tried to change the tone of her voice to sound more convincing. "I mean, why would I have seen her?"

"Speak," Cyrus demanded. His face was a mix of desperation and anger.

Amasha turned her eyes downward. "I can't..." she said fearfully, avoiding Cyrus's gaze.

She sounds as scared as Saul. The king grabbed Amasha by the arms and pulled her in close. "You must," he pleaded. "What happened to Saul? What happened to my *son?* To *you?*" At the mere mention of Saul's name, Amasha shook her head vigorously, prompting Cyrus to push her further. "You tell me *now*. Why are you so afraid?!"

"She'll kill me!" Amasha screamed with the entirety of her voice. Terrified, she finally broke down into tears but soon began to divulge things that she knew she was not supposed to tell her husband. "It was after our argument. I wandered the castle to clear my mind, and I came upon a room that I had not seen before. I was curious…so I went inside." The queen shuddered as Cyrus released her. He was intent on hearing the rest of her tale. "Your mother…she was in the r-room with Saul. She was *hitting* him." Her face twisted in disgust, and as she looked to her husband, noticing the look of bewilderment that he displayed, she explained further. "She was hitting him with the edge of a sword." After a moment, she started to speak defensively. "I-I thought that it was some form of punishment! So I apologized to her for the intrusion…but she *ran* at me and then threw me against the wall. She told me…" Amasha began to sob.

Cyrus sat his wife down on the bed and joined her, attempting to lessen her anguish. Calmly, he told her, "Go on."

Nodding, Amasha said, "She told me that if I breathed a word of what I s-saw, she'd strap me down and *cut* me in more ways than I could imagine. She said this while she had the sword to my throat. Then she told me…" Amasha hesitated for a moment. "Your mother told me that if we did not have a child, I would not *live* to see our first wedding anniversary."

Realization dawned on Cyrus. "That was why you forced yourself on me."

"At first, yes," she admitted, "but I'm happy that we did." The queen searched her husband's eyes, hoping to find forgiveness. "Please, Cyrus," Amasha said in between frightened sobs, "don't tell her that I said anything. I want to be *yours*. I don't want to die..."

The North King tried to digest everything that he had heard. While he had difficulty believing that his mother was capable of the things that Amasha claimed, he knew one thing: Amasha was not lying. She was too petrified, Cyrus thought. As they sat next to each other, he turned to his queen and placed a gentle hand on her cheek, wiping the tears away. "*Nothing* will happen to you," he stated. The words prompted Amasha's eyes to widen and fill to the brim with wet tears of relief. Suddenly, as though he were hit with a bolt of lightning, Cyrus had a moment of clarity. "Amasha...you said that my mother used a *blade* on my son?"

She nodded. "Yes. Why?"

Cyrus's eyes darted around the room while his mind raced. *There were no marks on him. None.* Worry filled the king's heart. Although he was concerned about his son, he was also growing agitated about his mother's secrets. *What are you hiding, Mother?*

Chapter 19

THE SIEGE OF SUMMERHOLD

They gazed into each other's eyes, lost in the utter bliss of the moment. With the window open, they could hear the birds singing songs and the distant commotion within the city. Having made their way from the war room to Saris's luxurious bedchamber, Paxton and the South Princess laid next to one another, caught in a state of serenity and happiness.

"What are you thinking?" Saris asked the knight.

Paxton sighed. "I think I don't want to leave."

"Oh?" Saris beamed and kissed Paxton vigorously. Once their lips had parted, Saris sunk back and let out a sigh of her own. "We've barely shown our faces in the last two days. We should probably report to my father."

Paxton nodded. "Agreed. I still cannot believe that we haven't heard anything from Triton," he lamented.

Worry revealed itself as Saris lowered her eyes. Suddenly, a loud noise could be heard over the tranquil sounds that the pair had been listening to all morning. Paxton and Saris jerked their heads toward the window, looks of realization spread across their faces.

RING. RING. RING.

Bells rang throughout the Southern capital, followed quickly by the cries of panicking denizens in the city. The knight of Angelia and the South Princess immediately put their clothes back on, intent on finding out what had happened.

A series of booming knocks echoed off of Saris's door, startling her before she allowed the person entry. The Captain of the House Guard, Valentyne St. Clare, made her way inside.

"My Princess!" she exclaimed fearfully. "They are coming! The army of Karthmere is marching as we speak!"

"Slow down, Val. Tell me how you came to know of this," Saris said in a calm voice.

Taking a moment to breathe, Val explained further. "Two of our scouts. They were attempting to find out more about Lord Duke's movements. Arrows were fired in their direction, meant to silence them. One made it back…one did not."

Saris inhaled sharply and looked back at Paxton. "This is it."

"Let's head to the throne room," Paxton insisted.

The three of them proceeded to run down the corridor, passing by numerous members of the House Guard. Valentyne gave her orders without stopping, commanding them to head to the throne room as well. There, the Guard would take their place by King Wilfred's side until they were instructed otherwise.

Minutes later, Ser Paxton, Captain St. Clare, and Princess Saris stood in the throne room of Summerhold. In their company, Princess Mora, Prince Tomis, and Mika Gainhart also attended the king and queen. The House Guard was all accounted for, as they stood in formation around the royal family. The only other person who stood in the room was Chancellor Lambin — and he was more terrified than ever.

"My K-King…the Viper Legion w-will be with the regular army," he mumbled. "They will have Sages, Y-Your Grace. We must be prepared."

"I am *more* than aware of this, Gale," King Wilfred dismissed the chancellor. "They will never get close enough to the city to become a threat, and they can only get here by way of the southern mountain pass. We shall focus our defense there, of course." Without standing, the rounded man turned to Saris, granting her permission to speak on the matter further.

They had all gone over the plan for a while by that point. Though Saris was fully prepared to issue battle commands, she still retained a bit of nervousness that any soldier would feel before battle. "We all know our stations," she said, demanding everyone's attention. "We have two walls at the main gate. Our infantry will remain between the inner and outer walls in the event that Lord Duke's forces break through. Our archers will take position atop the battlements of both walls and rain a volley of death upon them before that even happens," Saris stated with determination. Waving her hand toward the raven-haired knight beside her, she said, "Ser Paxton and I will lead the infantry." The princess addressed the former Sageslayer next. "Mika, as you still suffer from injuries, we'd like you to join the archers on the lower battlements."

In his mind, Mika was ready to fight, but his battle with the Lekuzza had left him physically unfit for a position on the front lines. "I will assist you in any way that I can," Mika replied sincerely, though he was still disappointed.

"King Wilfred will command from the upper battlements," Saris continued. At that point, she caught sight of her mother's expression – it was one of absolute fear. She knew that the queen must have argued against the king's involvement in the battle, but the army's morale depended on his presence.

"Father," a young voice had called out from the side of the room. Everyone present had stopped to look at Prince Tomis as he stepped forward. "I can fight. Allow me to join you all."

Even before he could utter a word, Wilfred received a sideways glance from Queen Kayla. Her eyes spoke a thousand words. Wilfred did not need to be a Reader to understand what she wanted to say aloud. "No, Tomis," the King started, "you and

Mora must stay behind. I need you both to help the people in the city and get them to safety." He hesitated for a moment before voicing his next concern. "If Summerhold falls, lead the people through the northern pass toward the ruins of Coalfell." Though his son seemed to accept his command, he knew that Tomis disagreed. "Now, if no one else has—"

"I'd like to speak," Queen Kayla said abruptly. Her husband looked at her with surprise but bowed his head slightly, giving her a moment to address the others. "It has been a while since this was pointed out, but we are preparing to defend our city from my brother. *My brother*, who marches here as we speak, aims to take the South for himself. Make no mistake," she stressed, "Rayburn will not show mercy, and he will not take prisoners. We all know what he did to take Karthmere in the first place..." The queen's voice trembled as she spoke of a memory that haunted her for many years. Her brother had been a decent man once, but it was hard for her to remember when that was. When she heard about Rayburn's coup against Samus Weyland all those years ago, she severed any ties to him and the Duke name for good. Though her husband was required to remain cordial with Rayburn for the benefit of the Southern region, relations were never the same. "Do not hesitate. If any of you have the opportunity...kill him," Kayla announced with ice behind her words.

There was a mix of surprise and acceptance around the room. Everyone knew what had to be done, but they were still shocked to hear it out of the mouth of Queen Kayla. From there, the gathering came to an end. All who were present began to separate and head to their posts.

As Paxton left the throne room, he overheard a small portion of a conversation between Mika and Tomis.

"Do not worry. You will get the chance to prove yourself one day," Mika had told the young man.

Paxton noted Tomis's disappointment. He knew all too well what it was like to be told such things at that age. Strangely enough, he was the same age as Tomis when he saved Vandal Palidor's life and received his knighthood. *One day, indeed*, Paxton thought to himself with a smile, knowing that Tomis would do well in the future.

Paxton and Saris were back in the princess's room within a matter of minutes, donning their respective armor for the upcoming battle. Paxton assisted Saris with her bright, golden armor, and then Saris helped the knight put on his newly-polished white armor.

"Have you had the chance to speak to the soldiers yet?" Paxton asked Saris. "To ease their minds?"

"I *have*," she responded with a proud nod. "I'm confident that they are ready."

Soon enough, the two of them were fully prepared to take their positions at the head of the Orthane army. Before they left the room, they turned to each other and embraced in a long, emotional kiss. The second their lips parted, Saris spoke, hoping that it would not be the final time. "Don't die out there," she said breathlessly.

"I wouldn't dare, my Lady," Paxton assured her. "There are too many places outside Summerhold that I must show you." Knowing her wish to travel throughout Areon, Paxton was happy to see that his words were the cause of Saris's wide smile.

***

Midday had arrived, and all were in their positions. King Wilfred surveyed the approaching army, who had taken the southern pass up the mountain, as he had predicted. One of his scouts suddenly appeared next to him, out of breath.

"Report," the king commanded.

"No banners are being held, Your Grace," the scout said. "No sigils in sight."

Wilfred's eyes narrowed. "Odd," he commented. Waving off the strange tactic of Lord Duke, the king stated, "No matter. Today, we show Karthmere why Summerhold rules the South." Turning to the members of his House Guard, he raised his chin, signaling them to return to the throne room. While their duty was, in most cases, to protect the king, Wilfred instructed them all to head back and stay with Queen Kayla and Chancellor Lambin in the great hall. "Captain St. Clare," he called out to the woman, stopping her in her tracks. "You will stay here."

The Captain of the House Guard was dumbfounded. "Your Grace?"

"The others can see to the queen," Wilfred told her. "I need you by my side."

Valentyne fought back tears. After her mother died, she had searched endlessly for a way to pay tribute to the former head of the House Guard. Finally, the moment fell into her lap. "It would be my honor, Your Grace," she said, ready to prove herself worthy of her mother's old title.

With Captain St. Clare to his left, King Wilfred stepped forward until he reached the edge of the battlements. From the soldiers that surrounded him to the ones on the lower ramparts – and even further to the ground below – all stood in anticipation of the king's next move. Though he had managed to squeeze into a suit of armor, King Wilfred was not much of a warrior. But his abilities as a Sage gave him an equal footing in his own right. Closing his eyes, Wilfred stretched his powers as a Reader beyond normal means. He was able to peer into the minds of every single one of his city's defenders, though he did so with their permission. His reasoning was not to search their thoughts but to guard them all against any enemy Readers. It was a feat that would take all of his concentration during the siege.

At the same time, the army of Karthmere advanced on the front gate with haste. The men and women in black armor rushed forth, shouting their battle cries as if the Readers within their ranks were now aware that their powers would be useless in the upcoming fight.

Mika stood on the lower battlements, the warm breeze blowing through his hair, waiting for the king's orders. Suddenly, he faintly heard Wilfred shouting to his men up above.

"Archers!" the king commanded. "Loose!"

The arrows' scattered noise that left the upper battlements found their way to the attacking army on the ground below. Mika continued to await his orders.

"Gainhart," the king spoke in Mika's mind out of nowhere. *"A volley from your archers, please."*

Mika turned to the archers beside him on the lower battlements and immediately relayed King Wilfred's command. "Archers!" He watched as the men and women locked their bows into place, ready to fire. "Loose!" Mika shouted. The rain of arrows dropped down hard onto the Karthmere soldiers. *This siege will not last long,* Mika thought, wondering how Lord Duke could think that this was a good plan.

Meanwhile, on the ground below, Saris and Paxton stood at the ready between the front gates. They watched patiently as the gate was pounded endlessly by the enemy's battering ram. The wooden door shook violently but held strong.

"Daughter," King Wilfred spoke to Saris, *"stand firm. Our archers are making quick work of them."*

"They continue to batter the door, Father," Saris responded aloud, prompting Paxton to face her with a confused expression. "But, we are ready."

***

Elsewhere in the city, the great number of people who could not fight were being led to safety. Princess Mora and Prince Tomis guided their townsfolk toward the northern entrance, intent on leading them to the ruins of Coalfell if the battle turned for the worse.

In the midst of calming the people, Tomis stopped abruptly and became nervous. His demeanor changed again, and he started to tremble.

As the group of people they traveled with continued forward, Mora shot her brother a look of concern. "Tomis, what is wrong?"

He swallowed hard. "A feeling," he replied quietly. "Thoughts. Coming from nearby." Tomis closed his eyes and began to rub his forehead gently. "Deceit…cockiness…distant, but not far." His eyes shot open, and a new look of terror engulfed his face. "Mora, we must head to the western side of the city – to the cliff edge."

The Princess shook her head, confused. "Why?"

"They are coming," Tomis said gravely.

Leaving their people safe at the northern gate, Mora and Tomis rushed to the city's western edge, hoping that Tomis's Reader ability had failed him. Tomis attempted to reach out to his father using their joined power, but he was still much too far to do so.

Once they finally arrived at the cliff edge, their worst fears were realized. Creeping over the top of the mountainside and into the city itself was a giant formation of ice. Slowly, the siblings peered over the cliff, only to be met by an incoming barrage of fire. Jumping back, Mora yelled to her younger brother, instinctively trying to get him away from the danger. Once the fire stopped, Mora looked over the edge again and quickly counted more than a dozen soldiers – they were climbing the ice as if it were a ladder. The one who led them to the top seemed to be creating steps as he went.

"A Water Elemental," Mora said to Tomis as she backed away from the cliff. "You must reach Father. I'll try and hold them back."

"How?!"

"Did you forget, little brother?" Mora asked as she approached the top of the mountainside once more. Using her own ability as a Sage, she summoned a large gust of wind and aimed it down at the invaders, knocking at least four soldiers from the ice-ladder. "I'm an Elemental as well." Repeating the feat, Mora whisked two more from the slippery structure, but the rest remained. The Fire

Elementals who had attacked a minute earlier sent balls of flames in Mora's direction from the ground, protecting their fellow soldiers' ascent. Mora jumped back into cover. "Go!" she shouted to Tomis.

Tomis nodded and began to run toward his father's location, attempting to use his Reader ability to contact the king before physically reaching him. After a moment, he felt his father's presence within his mind.

"Tomis! I lost contact with you and Mora. What has happened?"

"We were too far," Tomis replied hastily. *"Father, we must pull back to the keep. They're here! Mora is trying to stop them, but they are still climbing!"*

After his son calmed himself enough to explain further, Tomis told his father everything he knew, which caused the king to turn a sheet of white. Without hesitation, he spoke to his commanders that led his forces down below.

"Saris, gather the infantry, fall back and defend the keep!"

The princess turned around and looked up high toward the upper battlements. *"Father, what's wrong?"*

"They've climbed the western cliff!" he replied. *"Your mother and Gale are in danger!"*

It was all she needed to hear. "Fall back to the keep!" Saris shouted to her fellow soldiers. "King's orders!"

"What's happened?" Paxton asked as he kept his eyes fixed on the gate in front of him.

"I'll explain on the way," Saris said. She noticed that Paxton was still worried about the front gate. "If they break through, they'll still have one more gate to tear down. Quickly, now!" Reluctantly, Paxton followed Saris through the inner gate, and they made their way back up through the city.

"Mika," King Wilfred addressed the former soldier from Zenithor, *"continue the barrage. I've pulled the infantry back. Duke's army is in the city."*

"How is that possible?" Mika inquired as his eyes narrowed. Suddenly, raising his chin, he realized the truth. "Sages," he said aloud.

"The Viper Legion, most likely," the king added. *"Remain on the battlements. Saris and Ser Paxton will attempt to intercept the invaders."*

"We cannot hold them forever. They will *break down the gate."*

"Hold them as long as you can. If they break through the first gate, have the water at the ready. They may still try and burn down the second."

"As you wish, Your Grace," Mika responded with a hint of regret. He knew that he should stay at his post, but he grew concerned about Paxton and the Orthanes. Cursing under his breath, he turned to one of the archers nearby. "I must leave."

"Now?" the archer asked in shock.

"I must assist your people up above. King Wilfred has commanded that you continue the volleys, even if they break through the first gate. If they use fire on the second, use *that* to douse the flames," he said as he pointed to the buckets of water nearby.

"You heard him," the archer said to his companions. As the group readied their next round of arrows, the man shouted, "For Summerhold!" and they all fired at will.

Leaving the lower battlements, Mika made his way to the throne room alone.

***

Paxton and Saris, out of breath from running through the city, arrived in the courtyard outside the great hall, ahead of the infantrymen that had accompanied them. Scanning the area rapidly, they saw no one.

"Check the western cliffside," Saris said to Paxton. "I will head into the throne room."

"Be safe," Pax warned the princess before they separated.

Making his way a short distance to the cliff, Paxton began to hear a loud commotion – familiar sounds that he knew all too well. *A battle*, he surmised. After turning the next corner, his eyes widened in awe. The army of Karthmere had made their way to the top of the cliff and into the city. But they were all attempting to fight something at once – a Wind Elemental in the sky.

Mora Orthane was flying from side-to-side, using her powers to throw groups of soldiers over the edge of the mountain. The black-armored invaders attempted to use what weapons they had to bring Mora to the ground, but she fought back with purpose. She was almost sure that she had disposed of any Sages that remained, but she was then blindsided by a ball of flames that raced by her face. Jerking her head toward the attacker, she prepared herself for the next projectile. As expected, another attempt was made to burn her from the sky. But Mora used a great squall to return the fire to the Sage, burning the man to death in the process.

Paxton continued to watch from the ground until a hand found its way to his shoulder. Instinctively, Paxton rounded on the person behind him, only to come across a frightened young man that had just emerged from the shadows. "Tomis!"

"Ser Paxton, thank the gods you are here!" Pointing to his sister above them, Tomis said, "She has been fighting them all by herself, but she's getting tired. I searched her mind. She *cannot* last much longer. And…" Tomis's face twisted. "I lost him…"

"Who?" Paxton asked the prince.

"The Water Elemental. The one who made the ladder of ice that brought the Viper Legion into the city. I read his mind, Paxton…but he purposely thought things – random things – that hindered my ability. I do not know where he went."

Out of the corner of his eye, Paxton saw a group of golden-armored soldiers charge toward the Viper Legion. The infantry had arrived. He sighed with relief, as Mora would be able to rest after her heroic efforts.

"Need some assistance, my friend?"

Paxton turned to find a friendly face staring back at him. "Mika! What are you doing here?"

"When I heard about the Dukes' treachery, I had to do something. Besides, I am not much of an archer," Mika stated as he drew his sword confidently, despite the fact that he was still healing from his previous injuries. "Come, Paxton. Let us fight side-by-side, at last."

The knight from Angelia smirked. Unsheathing his sword, Paxton joined Mika in the battle against Karthmere's forces.

***

The South Princess approached the door to the great hall. Saris was fully aware that her mother – as well as their chancellor, Gale Lambin – were stashed away in the throne room, safe from any harm. Seeing as she had not found a trace of any threats outside, Saris felt at ease while opening the door. As the wood's creaking sounded throughout the hall, Saris's relief and optimism faded away in an instant. Bodies of the House Guard were scattered about, some of their limbs covered in ice. Chancellor Lambin hung on the wall, impaled by multiple spears made of the same ice found on the Guard members. "Oh, Gale…you poor fool," Saris lamented. Suddenly, her eyes grew large as she gazed at the throne at the end of the great hall. There lay her mother, the

Lady of Summerhold and Queen of the South, on the floor and in a thick, crimson puddle. Her hand moved to her mouth in horror. "Mother? MOTHER!" she cried out, tears rushing down her cheeks. She darted to the queen's side, trembling as she stared at her mother's empty visage. Saris wanted to take her mother into her arms and rock her, just as the queen had done with *her* when she was a child – but the echoing sound of slow footsteps distracted her and forced her to look to the side of the room.

"Welcome, Princess," the unknown voice said. "You're a bit late, I'm afraid. I tried to introduce myself to these fine people, but," the man made a disapproving noise with the tongue in his mouth, "your mother's courtesy left much to be desired."

Saris leaped at the murderer in her family's hall, roaring with anger. Swinging her sword wildly, she narrowly missed the man's head.

"Dear girl," he said condescendingly as his right hand began to trickle with water, "what do you hope to accomplish against *me?*" The droplets hardened in mid-air and turned sharp. The Water Elemental launched the pointed drops of ice at the princess, but she quickly rolled herself out of the way and behind a stone pillar. "You cannot hide, Princess. Why not come out? Face your destiny."

The man continued to goad Saris into fighting, though she knew that she needed to get him outside and into the open courtyard. Battling an Elemental in such a confined space was madness, she thought. Making her way from pillar to pillar, avoiding the iced projectiles of her mother's murderer, Saris finally reached the door. She noted the man's frustrated grunt as she slipped outside. Taking a moment to catch her breath, she pushed away all thoughts of sadness and despair. *No time for any of that,* she told herself, determined to fight and win the day. Before she could gather her strength, the door behind her began to change into nothing but a block of ice. A second later, the cold object shattered, and the Elemental walked outside with a vexed appearance.

"I tire of this, my Lady."

Saris sighed and faced the man with her sword in her hands. "Finish it, then."

The older man – with blonde hair now visible in the daylight outside – chuckled with amusement. "Truly? So be it." The water and ice around his hands evaporated, and he drew his sword.

As the two of them engaged in their own fight, sword-to-sword, the remnants of the battle on the western side of the city began to spill toward the courtyard. Mika and Paxton fought bravely, taking on vast amounts of soldiers alongside the forces of Summerhold. Mora was back in the air, wind-rushing the enemy and forcibly removing them from the field of battle. Tomis – who had originally hidden from the enemy due to his lack of training – found his father and brought him to the fight in the courtyard.

King Wilfred was not a great swordsman but could hold his own. His loyal Guard member, Valentyne St. Clare, never left his side.

"Stay back, Your Grace!" Val yelled to the King while she parried an attack.

"Oh no, I won't have you outshining *me*," King Wilfred replied competitively. The king was blocking each attack that came his way when out of nowhere, he thrust his sword into the gut of his opponent. Shocked at what he had done, he noticed the dead man's silver medallion gleaming in the sun. "Look, Val! I killed a Legionnaire!" He smiled broadly. "Kayla will be so proud," he said softly to himself.

Valentyne saw the look on her king's face, and she smiled as well. It vanished within a moment when she saw the steel tip of a spear rip through Wilfred's shoulder. "King Wilfred!!"

Not far from the shouts of her friend, Saris turned from her fight with her mother's murderer and watched as her father fell to his knees. Almost immediately, he was run through by numerous swords from the surrounding Legion members. The sound that left Saris's mouth was deafening yet indiscernible. Overtaken with grief, Saris dropped her guard and was then met with a blade at her throat.

"Enough!" her captor shouted to the two armies that were locked in battle.

The forces of Karthmere had ceased their attack at the command of the mysterious Water Elemental. Summerhold's remaining soldiers grieved for their fallen ruler. Mora and Val knelt at Wilfred's side, while Tomis stood with a supportive hand on Mora's shoulder. Mika and Paxton finally noticed where Saris was as she stood a captive with a sword held to her neck.

Paxton began to race toward her. "Saris!"

"Not one more step," the blonde-haired man warned. "You don't want *another* Orthane to die by my hand, do you?"

Paxton's eyes became slits. "Who are you?"

The man smiled. Rather than address the young knight personally, he spoke loudly to the entire crowd. "My name is Harlan Wallis. I am the Lord of Karthmere." His proclamation was met with surprise, which was to be expected. "Rayburn Duke is dead. Dalton Duke is *dead*. In the name of King Kelbain, you will all surrender to me." He watched as the people of Summerhold looked to one another in confusion. Pulling the blade back further, he stressed his demand once more. "King Wilfred is gone. I've killed his wife," he stated as he spotted the King's other children, who were stricken with grief. "Surrender now, or the princess dies."

"No," Paxton said, looking Harlan dead in the eyes. "This city will not fall today." He took a step toward the Lord of Karthmere.

"Stop. I'll kill her right in front of you, boy." Lord Wallis warned again.

Halting mid-stride, the knight from Angelia continued to lock his gaze with Harlan. "You're not my equal, and you're no man at all."

Lord Wallis's eyes widened. He surveyed the courtyard and found the members of the Viper Legion. All of them, including their new captain, Loreena Stenwulf, stared at him and awaited his decision. They knew the customs of Single Combat as well as he did…and the price of refusing the challenge. He would not lose Karthmere, or the title that he held, but refusing to fight meant the loss of respect of all who followed him. As a ruler, that was something that he was not willing to part with. "I'm as much a man as you," Harlan replied in a venomous tone.

Sometime later, with the Single Combat made official, the battle had come to a halt. The outcome of the contest would determine the fate of the entire South. Under normal circumstances, each participant in the duel would be given a customary amount of time to prepare – but with both armies still winded from the battle, and the loss of both King Wilfred and Queen Kayla still too near, Harlan Wallis and Paxton Korba agreed to hasten the process.

As both men stood on opposite sides of the courtyard, backs to each other, they chose their respective Witnesses for the duel. Lord Wallis chose Captain Stenwulf.

"You have done well, Loreena. Leading the Viper Legion is no easy task. I am confident that this boy will die my hands quickly," he remarked as he unsheathed his sword, "but should I lose, I want you to take the reigns at Karthmere." His proclamation caused Loreena to blink rapidly.

"My Lord?"

"The Stenwulfs have long been a proud family of Karthmere," Harlan stated. "They would prosper under your rule."

Captain Stenwulf bowed to Harlan. "I will not disappoint you, my Lord."

Harlan chuckled under his breath. "Do not jump into my seat so quickly, Loreena. First, let us see who stands triumphant after Single Combat."

"You are a man of honor, Lord Wallis. You shall emerge the true victor."

Harlan smirked after Loreena's generous statement. He turned to face his opponent, who was still preparing for their duel.

On the other side of the yard, Paxton said his final words to those who had fought beside him in the unfortunate event that he should lose against Wallis. While he struggled to speak at times, knowing that this could be his final living day, he found himself staring at Mora and Tomis. The pair were holding each other, grieving for their parents. Paxton wanted to tell Mora that Rudi would come back to her, but in his heart, he knew that nothing would ease the pain of her loss at that moment. He also knew, for Tomis – as young as he was – the day had taken a toll. There was nothing that he could say. No words at all. But he came to know the Orthanes during his time at Summerhold. Fighting for them was *his* choice. Fighting Lord Wallis was also his choice, but it also meant that he could honor the king and queen and save their city.

Tomis lifted his head and stared at Paxton. As if he had read the knight's mind, he nodded respectfully in the man's direction.

Paxton returned the gesture and moved along to Mika, stopping right in front of the former soldier. "If you'll accept, I'd like to select you as my Witness," Paxton said.

Mika nodded soberly. "Of course, my friend."

"If I should fall," Paxton continued, "bring my remains to Triton. It is where I was born. It's where I belong." He reached his hand out to Mika and grasped his friend's arm. They held on for a moment as Paxton asked Mika for another favor. "When Rudi and Ashra get back…tell them I'll meet them at the tavern in Volsi." With a half-smile spread across his face, Mika agreed. Paxton smiled back before he turned to face Wallis. As he took out his sword, his smile faded, and he focused on the man across from him.

"You don't need to do this!"

Paxton shifted his gaze to the sidelines. Saris was still a prisoner of the Karthmere army, held back by a pair of soldiers. His mind raced, thinking of all the places he wanted to show her. The Silk Isles. The top of Squall's End. The view from Lord Argon's balcony at Triton.

"It is done," Paxton replied sadly. Turning back toward Lord Wallis, he began to take a step while he announced, "As the challenger, I declare that there will be *no* Sage powers during this duel!" He said it loud enough so that all in attendance would hear.

Harlan agreed. "Yes, yes, of course." He had anticipated that request, but he also had one of his own. "And as the challenged, I invoke the rule of Second Combat." The declaration was met by murmurs throughout the crowd. He presumed that *his* demand was *not* expected.

In Second Combat, once a participant was killed, their Witness could challenge the winner if they chose to. It was the only form of retribution or revenge that was allowed within the confines of Single Combat rules. The Witness would then have the opportunity to change the outcome of the entire proceeding and win back what the original participant lost.

While the people surrounding them continued to whisper about the stipulations, Harlan and Paxton scowled at each other. With their swords in hand, they advanced and began their confrontation. The audience grew silent as they watched the fight in awe.

Lord Wallis, the more seasoned veteran, was surprisingly aggressive in his choice of fighting style. Using both hands, the Lord of Karthmere swung his sword swiftly and ferociously, narrowly missing Paxton's body with each attempt.

The knight from Angelia blocked as much as he could before backing up into a heavier defensive stance. Staying light on his feet, he continued to move to try and circle Harlan, but Lord Wallis anticipated many of Paxton's tactics. Keeping his eyes fixed on his opponent, Paxton parried the next blow and swung his weapon with precision, landing a slice on Harlan's arm. The wound sent Wallis tumbling backward, and the crowd behind Paxton cheered.

Harlan growled in frustration as he wondered how the raven-haired knight could get the better of him. Suddenly, he remembered the story that Kelbain told him before the king departed Karthmere. Kelbain had battled his own son, Zane, in Single Combat – and while the rules they fought under were similar, Kelbain ignored them and used his power as an Elemental against his son…killing him in the process. The part of the story that stuck with Harlan was that Kelbain faced no dishonor for betraying the rules. No one questioned his tactics because they feared him.

Looking to his opponent once more, Harlan started to believe that he could keep his people in line the same way Kelbain had done in Zenithor. With a quick wave of his empty hand, water turned to sharp and deadly ice daggers around his fingertips. Many gasps sounded in the courtyard, but before anyone could say a word, Harlan flung the daggers in Paxton's direction. At least one of them contacted the knight, as Harlan saw the man's head jerk backward.

Paxton was shocked. His hand moved up to his face instinctively, and as he brought it back down, he noticed the blood trickling from his fingers. Lord Wallis had thrown many daggers of ice, but luckily only one had cut his face open. Out of the corner of his eye, Paxton saw Mora and Tomis step out of the sidelines with concerned looks upon their faces.

"Stay back!" Paxton warned, not wanting either of them to fall victim to Harlan's powers.

"He betrays the rules!" Mora shouted.

The fact could not be denied. Paxton turned back to glare at Harlan. "Your treachery runs deep, Lord Wallis," he stated.

"You've no idea who I am or what I'm capable of," Harlan countered. "My hand has dealt more crippling blows to the lords of Areon than anyone. It was *I* who took the life of Samus Weyland," he revealed. "*I* killed Dalton Duke and ended their line. Queen Kayla would have lived had she just surrendered the city to me." His words drew the reactions of many in attendance. "My name will live throughout history," he said with finality.

Paxton narrowed his eyes. Battling a Water Elemental was not something that he had desired, but it was the scenario in which he faced. He charged at the Lord of Karthmere, despite his disadvantage. Harlan attempted to use his power again, but Paxton grasped his wrist before any water could be conjured. The maneuver angered Lord Wallis, and the man tried to use his sword-hand to catch Paxton off-guard. The knight was prepared for that and used his own sword to knock Harlan's weapon to the ground. As he kicked the sword away, he was met with a strike from Harlan's fist – the force behind the man's punch was great enough to knock Paxton to the grass.

Seizing the advantage, Harlan spun around and spoke to his Witness. "Sword!" he commanded. To his surprise, Loreena Stenwulf stood motionless, her face contorted into a look of disgust. "Give me your sword, Captain!" When the woman remained fixed, the Lord of Karthmere turned to the rest of his Viper Legion for support. "I *demand* that you give me a sword!" But none of them budged. It slowly became clear that his choice to break the rules had not worked in his favor. Yelling in anger, Harlan turned again to find his opponent on the ground. "No matter," he said, ignoring the disloyalty of his soldiers. Using his power once more, he summoned a great deal of ice and formed it into a new sword. "It is time to end this." Approaching the fallen knight, he waited until the man saw him coming. Without hesitation, Lord Wallis plunged his sword of ice into Paxton's heart. As he stared into the man's hazel eyes, watching them grow larger as the blade went deeper, he heard the cries of the distraught crowd that surrounded them. Pulling the cold, frozen sword from his victim, Harlan stood triumphantly and sighed. "It is over," he said, out of breath. Shifting his attention to the remaining Orthanes, the Lord of Karthmere spoke loud enough for all to hear.

"You have lost. Abdicate Summerhold to me *now* or watch everyone di—" In an instant, Harlan choked on his words while the blood from his mouth spilled quickly. Confusion spread across his face as he slowly looked down at his gut. He could feel the sensation of something there but did not see a thing. Bringing his hands down, he started to feel a sharp item protruding from his belly – and at the same time, a sword materialized before his eyes. At the other end of it stood Ser Paxton, who was alive and well. His gaze darted to the ground, where he witnessed the body of the knight that he killed fade away into nothingness. "W-What...is...happening?"

The knight from Angelia removed his blade from the Lord of Karthmere and watched as the man fell to his knees. With a sideways glance, Paxton turned and nodded to the young man standing a few feet away.

Lord Wallis looked in the same direction and found Prince Tomis, a strange look of concentration on his face. "*You!*" Harlan shouted, blood gurgling from his lips. "You insufferable cheat! Creating illusions?!" Violent coughs followed the complaints.

"You broke the sacred rules, Lord Wallis," Tomis replied defiantly. "I just made it an even match."

Harlan had nothing left. He was going to die, but he was not going to give up easily. Turning to face his soldiers again, he issued one last command. "Avenge me...Kill them all."

The Captain of the Viper Legion was the first to respond, though it was in silence. Loreena stepped forward and dropped her sword. The other Legionnaires followed in turn and did the same. With the clattering of their swords ringing throughout the quiet courtyard, Harlan Wallis had truly lost.

"You...traitorous lot." The Lord of Karthmere dropped to the floor and groaned, dead and dishonored.

As the crowd stood unmoving, both sides looked to each other, anxious about what would happen next. While Tomis reeled from the amount of power that he exerted from conjuring such a vast illusion in Harlan's mind, Mora held her brother up in support. Paxton never took his eyes off of the soldiers of Karthmere. He lifted his sword again, ready to do battle if Captain Stenwulf chose to fight in Second Combat.

The woman from Karthmere stepped into the middle of the dueling circle, still unarmed, and spoke with conviction. "Harlan Wallis dishonored us *all*. There will be no Second Combat, Ser Paxton. Karthmere yields."

The words sparked celebration amongst the people of Summerhold. Regardless of their losses – tragic as they were – relief swelled within the masses. None were as relieved as Princess Saris, who was no longer a prisoner. She ran into the arms of her knight, embracing him tightly and kissed him until the necessity of air eventually broke them apart.

"I told you I would not dare to leave this world," Paxton told Saris with a smirk on his face.

Saris smiled broadly and kissed Paxton again while the crowd cheered for their savior: a man from the East that saved the South.

Chapter 20

DESCENSION TO DESTINY

Luck was on his side. The son of King Vandal reached his destination in less than a day from the time that he left Evermount. Fully expecting the entirety of his journey to be difficult, he was happy that he had not encountered any trouble on the way to The Tempest – and since the location hung over a cliff that overlooked the sea, Andemar was looking forward to a change of scenery.

Thinking back to his short time at Evermount, he thought of the fact that he had stayed in the city for a couple of days at the behest of Lord and Lady Varian. At times, he found that Chancellor Graves would ask him many questions about his journey – more questions than the prince was comfortable with. Andemar was not exactly used to confronting suspicious individuals regularly – not like his brother, Thasus – but ended up conjuring a story for the chancellor.

"I'm here to secure the support of Evermount. We're at war," Andemar had told Graves. All of that was true, though Andemar refused to share any information regarding his quest to the Shadow Sanctum.

"I would be most astounded if Evermount lent their support," Theodore Graves had replied with doubt, "but I suppose anything could happen."

Believing the response to be a strange one, Andemar reminded the chancellor, "Evermount is within the Eastern region. You are to answer King Vandal when called upon. I'm sure *Lady Varian* knows of her husband's oaths to the king."

Chancellor Graves scoffed, then walked away with an annoyed expression.

Later, just before Andemar had departed the city, he spoke with Lord Varian once more. Drudorn had reminded him to speak the secret words in front of the entrance to the Sanctum but added the important detail of waiting until nightfall to do so. Still in a bit of disbelief about the old magic that Drudorn spoke of, Andemar asked, "Will this truly work, my Lord? I've seen Sages before, but the magic of the—"

"The Magians, yes," Drudorn confirmed.

"Right. What if it isn't real?"

Lord Varian sat up in his bed and stared into the eyes of his prince. "Believe it, Prince Andemar. The Magians existed centuries ago. Not all of their magic is known to us – most of it is long forgotten, as I told you – but what we *do* know is that Evermount was once home to a school that taught such things," Drudorn remarked matter-of-factly. "The place was a ruin even before Hana and I were born. Eventually, it was restored into a library, where the citizens of Evermount could read and learn about the history of Areon."

"Have you ever been there?" Andemar asked.

"When I was a child, yes," Lord Varian said as he laid back down. "My father took me there and showed me an area of books, magically protected and hidden from those who did not know the secrets of our family. There, I learned the mysteries of the Magians – the wielders of rune magic. That was also when my father told me of the Mystical Artifact's location within the Sanctum."

With a perturbed look, Prince Andemar inquired further. "When we first met, you said that Garis abandoned his weapon *and* the temple…Why would he do that? Where were he and the other Mystics during the Sorcerer's War?"

"With respect, my Prince, I am almost sure that *no one* knows," Lord Varian said honestly.

After digesting all of the information that Drudorn had to offer, Andemar stood up to leave. "Thank you for everything, my Lord."

"I wish you good fortune, Prince Andemar. May Vemaris protect you," he said, speaking of the phoenix – the Goddess of Life. "I hope we meet again someday."

A shudder ran through Andemar's body. Lord Drudorn seemed to speak those words as if he thought he would not live through his sickness. He wondered if Drudorn was more ill than the healers would admit. Not wanting to reveal his thoughts, Andemar feigned a happy reply. "So do I, Lord Drudorn. It was a pleasure speaking with you."

Afterward, the prince made his way back to the great hall and thanked the Lady of Evermount for her hospitality.

"The East Prince is always welcome in Evermount," Lucille responded kindly. "And I assure you, now that my husband has given you the support of our troops in the war, Evermount will see it done."

Andemar nodded, accepting her pledge, though he saw something strange occur. As the words left Lucille's lips, she looked to the chancellor with a stern expression. Andemar assumed that she found out about the chancellor's initial dismissal of his request. "Glad to hear it," he replied, thinking that the situation was better without Graves's odd interference.

"Safe journey home," Lucille remarked before Andemar left the hall.

He would have been thankful if he did not feel a small amount of guilt for lying to Lady Lucille. It was Drudorn's wish that

Andemar not tell anyone else of his true purpose – of his quest to the Shadow Sanctum. The prince stayed true to his word and headed to his destination.

Shaking off the memories of the previous day, Andemar inhaled slowly as he looked over the cliff and out to the ocean. He had arrived at The Tempest. Strong gusts of wind, as well as a mist of water, covered him from head-to-toe, inviting him over the edge. It took every ounce of strength to stay rooted to the ground as the winds bombarded him. Viewing the moon in the distance, he was happy to see that its light cast over the cliff rather than leave him in complete darkness for his descent. Suddenly, he stopped. *How do I get down?* As he slowly approached the edge, he peered downward and watched as the waves at the bottom crashed forcefully against the rocks. To his surprise, he discovered an old rope ladder to his right, but his face turned sour. The rope was worn and had not been used in quite some time. He knew it would be a dangerous climb down to the Sanctum, but it was necessary. *Need to get that weapon*, he reminded himself. *Areon depends on it.*

Placing his feet on the shoddy ladder, he began his descent. The wind continued to be unforgiving as he made his way down, nearly blowing him off the rope on countless occasions. Having his entire suit of armor on made things more difficult. It was not as heavy as his soldiers' armor, but it added enough weight to affect his trek down the ladder. Andemar's swords, Phanes and Thanatos, clanged against the stone cliffside with each step down the rungs –

the noise was loud enough to travel from his location to the bottom.

Andemar suddenly felt a tugging sensation and grew curious. Shifting his gaze to one of his feet, he saw that he had become entangled in a loose portion of the rope. Trying not to panic, he attempted to release himself but was unsuccessful. The winds started to pick up. *And now I'm caught in a rope ladder on the side of a cliff.* If he fell, the drop would have surely killed him from that height. Carefully, he unsheathed Phanes and cut the loose piece of rope that held him in place. As the ladder began to shake, now that it was less stable, Andemar's grip wavered. Reaching the nearest rung with both hands, he was forced to drop Phanes, and he watched as it fell into the sea. He cursed, then started his descent once more, holding on to what was left of the ladder. Andemar finally caught sight of the landing that was only a short distance away.

Out of nowhere, the rope ladder gave out, and the prince gasped loudly as he fell. Landing hard on the ground that barely protruded from the cliff, Andemar groaned in pain. He took a moment to gather himself – even turning to peek over the edge that he had almost tumbled off of – before standing up.

Walking a short way inward toward the entrance of the Sanctum, he was shocked to find a mere cave entrance that seemed to be closed. It was not the sealed entrance that confused him, as he knew that he would find it that way, but he had expected the former Temple of Garis to be more grandiose. Sighing, Andemar was glad that it was already night – he would not have to wait long to open the Sanctum.

Wasting no time, Andemar spoke the words. "A storm rises from the shadows."

Nothing happened. He tried again, only to encounter the same result. *It doesn't work.* Sitting on the ground, frustrated and befuddled, Andemar started to think that his journey was pointless. He doubted his destiny, wondering if Horus had made a mistake in telling him that *he* was the one who should save Areon...

Looking behind him at the spot where the remains of the broken ladder fell, he soon realized that there was nowhere else to go. Glimpsing the moon as it hung over the ocean, Andemar was reminded of Lord Varian's advice about waiting until nightfall. He narrowed his eyes as his mind began to race. He jerked his head back toward the cave entrance and discovered something that had not been there a moment before: The moonlight touched the edge of the entrance, revealing strange symbols...ones that Andemar had seen before. *Those markings on the houses in Evermount,* he realized. *Runes...The Runes of the Magians! It is true!*

Unsheathing his remaining sword, Thanatos, the prince raised the blade high in an attempt to reflect the moonlight onto the entranceway of the Sanctum. He was only able to manipulate it slightly, but it was enough. More symbols began to appear, the more that Andemar slowly moved his sword. Revealing each mark as he went along, he felt a sense of nervousness and excitement in the pit of his stomach. *This is it.* Once he reached the end of the entrance, and no more symbols appeared, Andemar lowered Thanatos and spoke the magical phrase again.

"A storm rises from the shadows."

The cave rumbled thunderously. The stone began to lift from the bottom of the entrance, revealing a bright, wondrous light. Standing in awe, Andemar turned for a moment and saw that the moon shone its glow into the heart of the Shadow Sanctum. As he walked in, he breathed a sigh of relief. While he had expected darkness, he was glad to see nothing but a blinding view of his destiny.

Chapter 21

THE APPRENTICE OF FIRE

"Still no sign of the Foreseer," the guard in white armor revealed.

The East King nodded and sunk back into his chair. He had much to ponder as of late. Marc Bowlin was dead. Horus escaped. His sons were all still out in the world, rather than safe at home. *Could I have done something more to prevent such a catastrophe?* Suddenly, Vandal found himself shaking his head – he had given his blessing to all of his young men before sending them on their quests. It was something that he continued to remind himself of, as he was not used to the idea of putting his sons in danger.

"That will be all," Vandal said to the guard. "Report back if you receive any word of his capture." He was not done with Horus yet. The Foreseer may have claimed to be helping Andemar, but Vandal did not trust him.

Out of nowhere, a loud noise echoed off the walls. From across the room, Vandal saw the large doors of the great hall open to reveal two figures, both heading in his direction. He watched as his wife and grandson made their way into the throne room. Earlier, the king had requested Anden's presence, hoping that Maryn would not object – ever since his son's wife found out all of the family's secrets, she had refused to speak to both the king and queen.

Anden could not help but keep his head down, much to Vandal's disappointment. The last time he and his grandson spoke, it had been slightly unpleasant. But he sought to make amends with Anden if only to make the boy realize that he had nothing to fear from his own kin.

"Thank you, Serena," Vandal addressed his wife. "I'd like to speak to Anden alone."

The queen smiled at her husband first and then looked to Anden with the same expression. "It will be alright, child. He just wants to talk." Anden looked into her eyes and nodded. Before she left the room through one of the doors behind the throne, Serena stopped and leaned toward the king. "He thinks you're afraid of him," she whispered sullenly. Placing a hand on Vandal's shoulder as she moved to walk away, her gesture was returned when her husband gently grasped her hand, signifying that he understood her concern.

After the queen had taken her leave, King Vandal motioned to his grandson. "Come, Anden. Sit."

The young Palidor took a deep breath and took a seat where his grandfather had guided him – the chair of the second heir. Anden always loved the fact that the Eastern kingdom had three seats in its throne room – one for the king and two for the next heirs in line for the throne. If one was sitting on the King's throne, the chair to the right was occupied by the first in line, while the chair to the King's left was for the second heir – in this case, Anden's father, Andemar. While he sat in the place where his father should have been, Anden became increasingly sad. He missed his father more than anything and truly wanted to speak with him about his troubles.

"I miss him too," Vandal said with a half-smile. Anden nodded, unable to hide his feelings. "I must apologize, Anden. The way that I reacted when I found out about your powers..." His voice trailed off as he shook his head. "I am sorry, my boy. To be honest, I think that I was angrier at your grandmother for hiding your secret. You can understand that, right?"

Anden nodded. He understood, but he still felt as if he had done something terrible. "Grandfather...I want to apologize too."

"For what?" Vandal asked with genuine curiosity.

"I'm sorry that I have these powers," Anden said, his face beginning to contort into one that would soon produce tears. "I wish that I could make them go away."

The king leaned in closer to his grandson. "No," he said. "They are a part of you now. You must learn to accept that and everything that goes along with being an Elemental." Vandal surprised himself a bit, as the words he spoke made him feel proud to be a Sage. It was a feeling he was not familiar with.

"What about the curse?"

The candidness of his grandson's question caught Vandal off-guard. "The curse?" he asked, his head cocked to its side.

"I overheard my mother talking about it with Grandmother – something about a 'blood curse', I think."

Vandal sighed. *The boy is almost 11. He can handle the truth.* The king surmised that it was time to be completely open about their family history. He began to tell Anden everything. From the moment Victor Palidor was stabbed with Magor's dagger – a dagger that carried Magor's own blood on it – to the role that Horus played in telling their family of their affliction. He also went into great detail about Andemar's quest to the Shadow Sanctum, telling the boy of his father's bravery.

After a few minutes, Anden sat in silence. It was a great amount of information, and he needed to let it all sink in. Finally, the boy spoke. "So…am I *dangerous?*" he asked with a fearful gaze.

Laying a hand on Anden's shoulder, Vandal addressed his grandson's unease. "Of course not. The truth is, only Magor has been known to have controlled all of the elements – perhaps his son, Kelbain, could as well. We don't know for sure. It's likely that you're able to do such things because of the curse that we bear, but that does *not* mean that you are dangerous," Vandal stated with conviction. "You're a Palidor. We forge our own destiny."

Anden smiled briefly, but the expression faded fast. All of a sudden, he felt lonely. "But I'm the only Sage in the family," he said.

The king looked into his grandson's eyes knowingly. Removing his hand from the boy's shoulder, Vandal held an open palm in front of him and conjured a small flame. The brilliant light flickered and crackled, causing a sound that filled the hall, as there was nothing else but silence.

Anden's face turned into one of astonishment while his jaw dropped. He was sure that he had been dreaming the day that his powers grew out of control. He remembered seeing his grandfather get rid of the fire somehow; only he had no idea how it was possible. Now that he knew the truth, he was starting to feel better about his Sage abilities. He was *not* alone.

"You should continue your lessons with your grandmother," Vandal said as he manipulated the flame in his hand, "but she'll be sticking to books from now on. *I* will teach you how to control the flame," he decreed as he closed his hand into a fist, extinguishing the bright element. "Then, perhaps, you may learn to master the *other* elements as well."

Anden's full smile came rushing back, along with newfound confidence.

Chapter 22

THE TRIAL CONTINUES

The sounds of the crowd drowned out any other noise within the corridor. Three days away from the arena, and he already longed for the silence. Well-rested from the grueling fights with some of Woodhaven's finest, Jasian sat and waited for the start of the second day in the trial.

Out of the corner of his eye, he saw a man a short way down the hall – the same man who had tried to spark a conversation with Jasian three days prior. The prisoner was in the midst of bathing himself, from what Jasian could discern, as the man poured a bucket of water over his head and ran his hands through his hair, pulling the wet strands back. The man's head jerked, turning toward Jasian in surprise.

"See anything you like?" the man jested.

Jasian shook his head. "I was only curious," he replied, "why would you even bother removing the dirt? We're going to fight out there again anyway."

"Keeps me sane," the prisoner responded in a serious tone. "Besides, I had little sleep last night. Today is the final day of my trial as well."

"You fought on the same day that *I* did?" Jasian asked, thinking back to when he first met the prisoner.

"I *did*. But I have been fighting for much longer than *you* have, I'm afraid," the man revealed as he walked toward Jasian. "One opponent a day for weeks now."

Jasian's eyes grew large. "Weeks? How can that be?"

The man tilted his head with a small hint of modesty. "I've been killing soldiers of Woodhaven for quite some time, young one. I'm just paying for all of that *now*. Lord Darkwood felt it was best to break my spirit day-by-day." He let out a light chuckle. "But I keep proving him wrong," he said with a smirk.

"That's impressive," Jasian admitted. "I thought Draven wanted *me* dead."

"Oh, he *does*," the man confirmed. "Making you fight three opponents within minutes of each other? The odds of survival were completely against you. But you shoved your victories in his face, didn't you?"

"You saw?" Jasian wondered.

"Of course. I had just finished my latest battle before you were brought into the arena, and I was curious. Defeating that Highwind was no small accomplishment," the prisoner commended Jasian on his last match.

The Young Bear shrugged. "I just want to live," he stated. "Though I'm no fool...Even if I win my next three fights, I do not believe that Darkwood will be true to his word and grant me my freedom."

"You're wise to think like that," the man said. "I gave up any thoughts of freedom days ago – at least by way of winning in the arena." He was met by a puzzled look on the face of the young Bowlin. Leaning closer, he spoke softly. "If it's freedom you desire, I think you and I should work together."

Jasian could not hide his interest but scoffed with doubt. "Darkwood will try anything to keep us here. You must realize that."

"Yes, he will," the man agreed. "That is why we must go along with the trial as planned. When we win," he said confidently, "we will kill Darkwood and escape during the chaos. They will not know what to do without him."

The thought of killing Draven Darkwood had been at the forefront of Jasian's mind ever since Merroc's death. He wanted nothing more than to see the man's head parted from his neck, but he had lost in a fight against the Evolutionary twice already. *Perhaps with some help*, Jasian considered. "If we do this," Jasian began to offer, "there is something that you should know about Darkwood."

"By the Mystics, I know the bastard is an Evolutionary," he replied defensively. "His *head* is the only thing that stands between us and freedom." Holding his arm out to Jasian, he sought to confirm their alliance. The young Bowlin smiled and returned the gesture. Nodding, the man said, "Be ready, then. I'll see you after." He stood up and walked away casually, not wanting to arouse suspicion of his and Jasian's length of time in conversation.

Sometime later, as Jasian continued to wait for his time in the arena, he was paid a surprise visit by the Lord of Woodhaven himself. Draven strolled toward him with a sense of regal authority that Jasian could not stand.

"Hello, Jasian," Darkwood said, bowing his head courteously.

"What are you doing here?" Jasian asked rudely. "I thought that I wouldn't see your face until I was done winning the fights in this trial."

Lord Darkwood's grave expression betrayed another reason for his appearance. "News from the North," he replied, ignoring Jasian's comment. "Your father has been murdered."

The bluntness of Draven's words caught Jasian off-guard, causing him to blink rapidly for a moment. "What?" he inquired as he shook his head in disbelief.

"Apparently, the Lord of the Frostford tried to have someone assassinate the North King. Your father was there. He died protecting King Cyrus." Noticing the look of shock that formed on Jasian's face, Draven continued. "You'll be pleased to know that Cale Brock was hung the next morning for his treason. I believe that your cousin, Thasus, was responsible for dispensing justice to Lord Brock."

Jasian could not think. He could not focus. He lost all sense of reason. Normally, he may have asked why Thasus was in the North – why his *father* was there. But he had lost his brother, and now his father was gone. He tried to breathe, but the air started to leave the room. He tried to speak, but no words left his lips.

"I am truly sorry for your loss," Draven said. "I do hope that this does not linger on your mind during today's contests."

At that point, Jasian recovered from any sadness that he felt. Raising his eyes to stare at Draven, he saw that the Lord of Woodhaven showed no sign of satisfaction after the news that he had just delivered…but Jasian knew better. *He wants to break me*, he realized. *I won't give him that.*

"I just thought you should know," Draven finished saying before departing the corridor.

Waiting until Lord Darkwood was out of sight, Jasian sunk into the dirt floor and pounded his fist against the wall behind him. His scream rivaled the noise in the arena.

Less than an hour went by since Jasian received the terrible news. He found himself standing on the grass, expressionless, holding the same two swords that helped him achieve victory on the first day of the trial. His thoughts of regret, despair, and grief drowned out the crowd and their constant jeers. Jasian even ignored Draven Darkwood as he introduced the first opponent of the day. He could sense that the fighter standing across from him was approaching, but Jasian could only focus on his inner turmoil. Then, it dawned on him…He was now the Lord of Stoneshield. It was his duty to lead his people and help protect the Eastern capital, Angelia, as his father did.

At the same time of his realization, Jasian's opponent moved in close, as the match had begun. Jasian raised his eyes to gaze upon the man, and with one swift move, he sliced open the man's chest with both swords, ending the fight instantly. The sudden finish silenced the crowd to a whisper. Jasian took the opportunity to look up at the balcony where Draven sat. His eyes burning with hatred, Jasian simply stared at the Evolutionary until the announcement was made of the victory.

Minutes later, Jasian faced his second opponent. The man from Woodhaven wielded a spear with a jagged blade at the end. Never taking his eyes off of the dangerous fighter, Jasian blocked the spear continuously. Wanting to end the fight quickly, Jasian took his blades and brought them down on the spear, splitting the wooden pole in two. Closing in on his opponent, the Young Bear twisted around the man and plunged one sword into his back. The sound that rang through the arena was evidence enough of the fighter's painful death.

Awaiting the third and final opponent, Jasian stood patiently, his body stained with the blood of his adversaries. Though his rage and hatred lit the fire that helped him win the last two fights so quickly, Jasian started to envision his freedom. With the help of the other prisoner, he knew that they would soon be rid of Darkwood for good and be unshackled once more.

Draven stood and silenced the people, as he normally did before a new fight. "Jasian Bowlin, you have made it to your final contest – but you have already proved that you are worthy of freedom. I am a man of my word."

Jasian displayed confusion at first, but in his heart, he knew that it would not be so simple. The Lord of Darkwood's next choice of words confirmed those suspicions.

"But you are not the only prisoner that I have given my word to," Draven announced as he waved his hand.

The doors across from Jasian opened, and his mind began to race. The prisoner that had spoken of freedom and the death of Draven Darkwood walked slowly into the arena, holding a short sword, a shield, and nothing but a look of disappointment on his bearded face.

"After weeks of battle, this man has *also* proved his worth! I give you: Rhobu! A general in the army of Zenithor!" Darkwood shouted.

The new Lord of Stoneshield was caught by utter surprise. A part of him that knew the history of Areon wanted to condemn the man, if only because of where he came from. But Mika, too, was a former soldier of Zenithor – and was now Jasian's friend. Though, he wondered, *Where does this 'Rhobu' stand?*

"On my honor," Draven proclaimed as he put a hand to his chest, "*one* of you will gain your freedom today. Justice will be served to the other." A slow smile formed across his lips, much to the obvious vexation of the two combatants down below.

Chapter 23

THE POWER OF NIGHTFALL

Night had fallen and enveloped the city in darkness. Torches lit up what remained of any areas that were saturated with Woodhaven soldiers. The pair of intruders surmised that they were viewing the only true patrols within the city, as they were now aware of Jasian's trial and the crowd it would demand.

Peeking around the corner of the nearby pillar, Rudi pressed against the wood, unaware that the pillar was actually a tree that held up a portion of Woodhaven's north gate. Signaling to Ashra, he let his friend know that it was clear to move further into the city. The two of them snuck through the gate, making their way into a forked area devoid of any soldiers.

"We should split up," Ashra suggested.

265

Rudi's head turned so quick, his neck cracked. "Split up? Are you sure that's a good idea?"

"We'll cover more ground. We need to get to Jasian fast."

Rudi hesitated but eventually agreed. "Fine. We'll meet back here before the sun comes up." Ashra nodded and headed in the opposite direction of Rudi, leaving him to take the other path.

Minutes went by after they had gone separate ways when Rudi heard battle cries and deafening noises. *That can't be the trial,* he thought. He found that his instinct was correct as he stumbled across the sight of Woodhaven soldiers being cut down mercilessly by another army. Ducking behind a wall to avoid detection, Rudi breathed raggedly, not knowing what was going on. Looking in another direction, he spotted bright flames as they formed on their own, growing larger and larger with each blast. *A Fire Elemental,* he thought, as the inferno reminded him of his encounter with Oreus.

Attempting to steer clear of the unknown Sage, Rudi turned a corner, only to come face-to-face with a soldier dressed in black armor. Standing around the same height as Rudi, the man displayed the red shark fin of Zenithor on his chest. Before he could fully come to the realization that Woodhaven was being attacked, the soldier spoke to him.

"Who are you?"

"No one of consequence," Rudi replied. "I'm here to rescue someone – a captive of Lord Darkwood's. I want no trouble with you, Ser." Truthfully, Rudimere wanted nothing more than to test his limits against a man from Zenithor, but he was now in the middle of a battle, and he still wanted to remain concealed.

"Ha! You *do* know that House Palidor is an enemy of King Kelbain," the soldier said in a cocky manner, pointing to the young Palidor's armor and sigil. Turning to his men that had suddenly appeared, he said, "Take him."

Damn it. He made the mistake of forgetting that he still had the colors of his house on display. *So much for the element of surprise.* Walking toward the Zenithor soldiers without flinching, Rudi did not even bother to unsheathe his weapon. One soldier pulled out his own blade and swung it at Rudi's chest, watching as the sword was destroyed. Another soldier followed his companion and waved his steel weapon, only to encounter the same result. Now facing two unarmed men, Rudi took Vulcan from its scabbard and dispatched the enemies with ease.

Discerning the Palidor man's ability, the commanding soldier ordered the rest of his men, "Bring me his head!"

Preparing for a tougher battle against the three charging soldiers, Rudi moved into a defensive stance, holding Vulcan tightly with both hands. One man swung at his neck and missed, as Rudi ducked under the attack. Vulcan found its way into the man's belly instead. The other two Zenithorians tried to attack Rudi simultaneously, but both had not paid close enough attention to their fellow soldiers earlier. Their swords connected with Rudi and shattered instantly. Before the shocked expressions could set in, Rudimere impaled one of them and sliced the other's throat.

The commanding soldier of Zenithor drew his sword and slowly approached the man from Angelia. "May I have the pleasure of knowing your name before I kill you?"

"Hmph. Seeing as *you* are the one about to die – I am Rudimere Palidor, of Angelia."

"Ah, a prince!" he exclaimed with genuine surprise. "Well, Prince Rudimere, *I* am General Soros. It is unfortunate that you are here on this day," Soros said with false concern. "Woodhaven will finally fall to the might of Zenithor. Sadly, you will not be here to see our king's victory." The general swung with precision, narrowly missing Rudimere's head.

The East Prince wanted to stand still and let the man's weapon crash against him and break, but Soros chose his attacks carefully, only aiming for Rudimere's neck. *Have to fight back*, Rudi thought. *Take his weapon from him.* Parrying the next blow with Vulcan, Rudi brought his sword down upon Soros's arm, cutting it off at the elbow.

Soros dropped to his knees in agony as he held onto the bleeding stump. "You...cut through my armor...*clean through.*" Taking a moment to understand what had happened, Soros chuckled, despite the situation. "Ironforge weapon...the weapon of choice for most spoiled—"

Before he could utter another word, Rudimere plunged Vulcan into Soros's chest, killing him promptly. Standing over the dead general, Rudi had a fleeting thought: The more people that he killed, the easier it became to do so. It was an uncomfortable feeling, yet he knew that this was a time of war. There were always going to be casualties.

Lifting his eyes from Soros and pointing them down the hall, he was suddenly startled. A tall, unmoving man stood at the end of the corridor. His long hair was as dark as his armor. The mysterious man began walking toward him, his footsteps echoing over the noise of the battles that raged through the city.

"Impressive showing," the man praised Rudimere. "Soros was a seasoned veteran of the Sorcerer's War." Reacting to the young man's befuddled look, the man added, "He was much older than he looked."

"Who *are* you?" Rudi inquired.

"I am Kelbain," he said in a low, threatening voice.

Rudi was internally fearful at first, but his recent confidence due to his power overshadowed any doubts he may have had. Holding up Vulcan, ready for his next battle, Rudi locked his gaze with the West King.

"Oh, Prince Rudimere. Are you *that* eager to die?"

The East Prince's eyes widened. "How do you know my name?"

Kelbain's own eyes, red and terrifying, became slits. "I am beyond your comprehension, boy. I have knowledge that would make your world crumble." Continuing his approach, he noticed Rudimere take a step backward. "Does that frighten you? Does it pain you to know that, in any scenario, you have *no* chance of winning this fight?"

"You talk a lot," Rudi countered defiantly, "just like your brother." The West King stopped and flinched visibly enough for Rudi to see. "I fought Oreus," he pressed on. "At the Temple of Aman, I fought him, and I won." It may have been a bit of an exaggeration, as he could not have defeated Oreus without Mora's help, but Kelbain did not know that.

"Do you think *that* will affect the outcome of today's events? My brother was a pathetic and weak old man." Kelbain was growing furious at the mentions of Oreus.

"But he was a *true* Mystic," Rudi continued to goad the West King, "not a second-rate Sorcerer."

Inhaling sharply, Kelbain drew Hyperion from its scabbard. "I will end you," he remarked calmly before attacking the prince. Clashing blades with Rudimere, Kelbain towered over the young man, gaining the advantage with every swing of his sword. Quickly observing the design of Rudimere's weapon, Kelbain made a noise that was rife with cockiness. "My sword is Ironforge steel, just like yours. Hyperion will not break." Again and again, they crossed swords, sparks flying from the edges with each attack. Finally,

Kelbain grew weary of the duel and punched Rudimere in the jaw, sending the prince tumbling to the floor.

Cursing under his breath for not learning from his duel with Oreus, Rudi rose to his feet swiftly. As Kelbain's sword fell close to his neck, Rudi parried the swing, then kicked the king hard in his gut. Kelbain withdrew to recover, but before Rudi could capitalize, the West King pulled out a long spear and held it to Rudi's throat.

"*This* is Nightfall," Kelbain stated, discovering a look of shock on the face of the prince. "It is one of the Artifacts created by the Mystics." Curious that Rudimere's expression did not change, Kelbain tilted his head. "Ah, so you *do* know something about this. Would you like to know more?" he asked, right before using the tip of Nightfall to slash Rudimere's cheek.

Wincing from the wound – and stunned by the appearance of the Mystical Artifact – Rudi continued to hold his ground as he searched for an opportunity to fight back.

"You see, young Palidor, the Mystics came to Areon from another world. The place in which we currently stand, it is only *one* of the five realms. The Mystics came from the realm of Sule. They are the Sudae – not unlike the *Gods* that you pray to, from the realm of Volsi." The prince displayed a look of ignorance that seemed to irk Kelbain. "I know it's difficult for you to understand. You have a simple mind, after all. Nevertheless, Sule is a place that *does* exist. It is as real as you and me. You've all seen it," he remarked as he raised a hand to the sky. "The people of Areon refer to it as the *sun.*"

Ignoring the absurdity of Kelbain's words, Rudi attempted to swing Vulcan at the king, but was countered by Nightfall. The West King returned the attempt by slamming the butt of the spear into Rudi's belly, sending him to the ground again.

"Nightfall, like the other Artifacts, was crafted in the Ironforge of Rikter's Hollow. They're extensions of the Mystics who made them. So, you might say that they are pieces of the sun itself – shards, if you will. But that revolves around the birth of the Ironforge itself. You know of the crater, I'm sure. That's where my father and the other three Mystics appeared in this realm." Making sure that Rudimere remained on the floor, Kelbain knelt beside him and explained further. "At great risk to themselves, they came to Areon to share their power and knowledge – but the people of Areon were not grateful for their wisdom. A costly mistake," he said darkly.

Rudi made another attempt to fight Kelbain but was kicked so hard that he rolled down the corridor. With haste, he got to his feet and began to retreat to the other end of the hall – but Kelbain was in pursuit.

"My father was eventually betrayed by his own kind," Kelbain said in a defensive tone. "He had to do what was necessary to cleanse Areon of those who were unworthy of his benevolence."

"Enough!" Rudi yelled as he turned to face the West King. "Benevolence?! Your father murdered *thousands* during the Sorcerer's War! He was a monster!"

Kelbain stopped mid-stride. Narrowing his eyes, he said, "You are right, Prince Rudimere." Pulling Nightfall into view, he grasped onto the pole with both hands, holding it straight with the sharp end facing the sky. "But then again…" he remarked while the spear hummed with an unsettling noise. Power began to emanate from the Artifact, as it did when Kelbain first found it in the vault at Karthmere. Suddenly, his face began to contort, his arms and legs expanded, his chest felt as if it was on fire – all the while, Kelbain let out a bloodcurdling scream.

Rudi walked backward, terrified at what he was witnessing. Kelbain was using the Mystical Artifact to transform. He wondered how it was possible but was more concerned with leaving Woodhaven alive at that point. Though the next few moments were horrific, Rudi could not look away, as he was frozen in place. He watched as the West King's armor above the waist fell off, his chest puffing out into a muscular but hideous form. Kelbain's teeth grew to an enormous length and became razor-sharp. Rudi stood wide-eyed when the transformation had concluded as he gazed upon the gray-skinned, grotesque version of Kelbain. The West King seemed to now be a cross between his previous self and a giant, walking shark.

In a terrible and foul voice, Kelbain finished his thought. "We're *all* monsters," he growled before giving chase to the prince.

Run, his inner voice shouted. Rudimere, still in a state of shock, ran through the halls of Woodhaven, avoiding Kelbain at all costs. Turning around every now and then to get a better sense of his location, Rudi caught a glimpse of the new monstrous form of the West King and began running again. *How did Nightfall do such a thing?* he wondered. *No time to think about that now. Hide. Let him pass you by.* Finding a spot in the dark, behind a large pillar, Rudi waited. After a moment, he saw Kelbain start to walk slowly across from him, but the beast stopped. His nose – or what Rudi assumed was his nose – twitched as if he was smelling the area. Straight out of a bad dream, Kelbain turned to look directly at him and roared. The next thing Rudi knew, he was being dragged from the darkness by Kelbain's large arms, where he was then hoisted into the air. Without thinking twice, Rudi managed to retrieve Vulcan from his waist and stabbed Kelbain in his forearm. He was free, but the West King snarled with a terrible look in his black eyes. Before he could get far, Rudi was swept off his feet by Nightfall and knocked hard to the ground. Rising to his feet once more, Kelbain quickly grabbed him and sunk his teeth into Rudi's left shoulder, causing the prince to yelp loudly throughout the corridors.

As Kelbain held the prince tightly in his grasp, he felt Rudimere's useless attempt at freedom, as the man punched Kelbain in the face. With a low growl, Kelbain flung the prince into a nearby wall with tremendous force. Not allowing the young Palidor to get up again, he advanced on Rudimere with unbelievable speed. One blow to the prince's gut and one to his face was all it took to knock Palidor out. Kelbain stood triumphantly over the East Prince, smiling with his rows of blood-stained teeth, planning his next move.

Chapter 24

THE PRISONER'S SENTENCE

The dawn had just arrived. Thasus Palidor – wide awake due
to a lack of proper sleep – was pacing down the corridor outside of
his room. His long hair and full beard rustled in the wind that
traveled through the castle. The East Prince gathered his thoughts
regarding Kaya Gargan and her wrongful imprisonment. Though
he wanted to see her freed, he could not defy King Cyrus's wishes.
Strangely enough, he pondered, the King's state of mind was one
to be watched carefully. If Cyrus was sure that Oswall Gargan
would not attack, then there was no reason for any delay in keeping
his promise to aid the East against Kelbain. The entire situation left
Thasus confused, if not cautious. *The assassination attempt has changed
him,* Thasus thought, *and he may not be in his right mind…but I must*

speak to him once more. Before that, however, he decided to pay Kaya another visit. After all, he had already promised the woman that he *would* return to her cell again.

Without any further hesitation, Thasus made his way in the direction of the dungeons. Along the passages, the East Prince stumbled upon Whitecrest's new Royal Guard, led by Vyncent Reign. The men were standing about in their bright blue armor as they conversed in eager tones. Thasus breathed in sharply. *Finally,* he thought. It looked as though the Royal Guard were preparing to march – and if that were true, then perhaps King Cyrus was ready to head east.

"—be leaving soon enough," Vyncent finished saying to his men.

"Commander Reign," Thasus made his presence known as he addressed the man with authority. "What news? Has the king dispatched you to Angelia?"

Vyncent turned toward Thasus and scoffed. "It's actually *'Thane'* now," he attempted to correct the Prince regarding his new title. Quickly, he looked to one of his men. "Tell him."

The Royal Guardsman stepped between Vyncent and Thasus and cleared his throat. "The Thane of Whitecrest has been ordered by King Cyrus to gather the Royal Guard. We march west on the morrow."

Thasus was stunned. "West? I thought you'd be marching east. We came here to quell the rebellion. Cale Brock is dead. His army now fights for King Cyrus," Thasus pointed out. "It is over."

"It is *not* over," Reign snapped back. "The king believes Lord Gargan to be a considerable threat. We march on Rikter's Hollow at the king's command."

Thasus attempted to conceal his anger and frustration. *What turned his mind toward Rikter's Hollow?* Thasus wondered about Cyrus. He thought the purpose of Kaya's imprisonment was to keep Oswall at bay, but this was an unexpected chain of events. Then his eyes widened as he had a sudden realization. "What is to be done with Kaya Gargan?"

"*That* order just came from the king's mother a few moments ago. The Gargan woman is to be executed for treason."

The East Prince cursed under his breath as his mouth trembled with ferocity. "Tell me, *Thane*," Thasus began, "do you always follow Celia's orders? I wasn't aware that anyone other than King Cyrus could command the Royal Guard." The disdain in his voice was obvious.

Vyncent's eyes narrowed. "I take my orders from *all* members of House Norton."

"Does that include Queen Amasha?" Thasus replied quickly. "I'm sure the *queen* would take issue, now that her *sister* is about to be executed for a crime that she did not commit." *Tread carefully, Thasus*, he told himself.

"If you have concerns," Vyncent said slowly as he stood closer to Thasus, "you are more than welcome to take it up with Cyrus."

Thasus nodded. "Perhaps, I will." Before turning to leave, he noticed that the other Guardsmen stood at the ready if they needed to act. Even for him, those odds would *not* have been in his favor. It was time for him to think fast.

Finding himself in the next corridor, Thasus knew two things: He wanted to speak to Cyrus personally about the attack on Lord Gargan, and he needed to make sure that Kaya remained unharmed. But before all of that, Thasus made it a point to visit someone else – someone whose loyalty and trust could not be questioned.

After a few moments, Thasus arrived at the quarters of Ornell Balgon, the commander of Stoneshield's forces, and approached the old soldier with purpose. Taking the time to explain, Thasus informed Ornell of everything that had transpired with the North King as of late. He also mentioned his thoughts on Kaya Gargan's innocence, knowing that an honorable man such as Commander Balgon would take issue with the woman's predicament.

Ornell sighed, allowing the new information to settle before speaking. "What are my orders?" he asked, ready to obey his prince's command without hesitation.

Happy to have Balgon's support, Thasus put a hand on the man's shoulder. "You will remain here."

"My Prince?"

"Whatever the king's faults, we made a pact with the North. We agreed to help them bring peace to their region. If King Cyrus believes that will only occur with Oswall Gargan's defeat, then so be it. But Kaya will *not* suffer her end over false accusations."

"What will you do?" Commander Balgon inquired.

"I'm taking her," Thasus said simply. "Far from here." Ornell looked as if he wanted to object, but Thasus interrupted him. "I would not have you be a part of this, Commander. You and your men need to stay and assist the North King…it's what my uncle would have wanted," Thasus remarked with sadness.

"He would have stayed by your side," Ornell countered. "He had no love for Cyrus Norton."

"True," Thasus admitted, "but Uncle Marc saved his life from the assassin. It is your duty to see that his death was not in vain."

Ornell grunted. "As you wish, Prince Thasus. But I *do not* like it."

"I didn't expect you would," Thasus said with a rare smile, "but I know you'll bring honor to House Bowlin." With that, the two men grasped arms. "When the fighting is done here, we will welcome your return to the East."

"I ache to be free of the bitter cold," Ornell replied.

"Farewell, Commander Balgon. May the gods watch over you and the men of Stoneshield."

"Good fortune to *you*, Prince Thasus. I hope the gods are in a favorable mood today," Ornell added with caution.

Thasus parted with the old veteran, wishing to stay and fight by his side on the battlefield. But he had to make haste – King Cyrus was soon to be rid of Kaya. Originally, the East Prince was set to speak with Cyrus but began to consider that his friend was a lost cause. The king seemed only to heed the counsel of his mother, much to Thasus's dismay. *It's one thing to keep Kaya imprisoned,* Thasus thought, *and quite another to order her execution.* In that regard, he headed straight to the dungeons.

With luck, Thasus avoided any guards that may have wandered the halls of Whitecrest. As he descended into the dark, frigid underground of the Northern capital, Thasus spotted a single soldier guarding Kaya's cell. He could have attempted to talk the man into setting Kaya free, but he presumed that he was short on time. With one balled-up fist, the mighty Thasus knocked out the guard and took the man's key. After unlocking the door, Thasus hoisted a torch from the wall and knelt beside the sleeping prisoner.

"Kaya. Kaya, wake up."

The woman stirred, and her eyes suddenly jolted open upon seeing the man before her. "Thasus?"

"Hurry. We must go," he tried to explain in a rush.

Kaya sat up, confused. "What is happening? What do you mean?"

"I'm here to set you free," he replied as he unchained her hands and feet. As Kaya questioned him further, Thasus had no choice but to divulge what he knew. "You are to be executed, Kaya. The king's mother gave the order to the Royal Guard. I heard it from Vyncent Reign himself." Finally, Kaya stood up to face the East Prince. Her face was covered in dirt from sleeping on the floor, but Thasus could still identify the look of despair that had formed. He offered Kaya his hand. "I need to get you to safety before that happens."

Between thoughts, Kaya tried to figure out why Celia Norton would want her dead, but at the same time, she was extremely grateful to Thasus for saving her from such a fate. "Where will I go?" she asked, clearly fearful of her chances outside the walls of the city.

Thasus grew perturbed. He did not realize that Kaya thought she would be alone in her escape. The East Prince looked directly into her dark brown eyes. "We're leaving *together*."

Kaya fought the urge to shed a tear. The man from Angelia continued to surprise her. "Alright," she replied with a smirk, "where will *we* go?"

"Home," Thasus said. It had been some time since Thasus had accepted his father's task in rallying the Northern families toward a common cause. By this point, everyone in Areon had to have known that Kelbain was going to strike soon. Gathering allies, even in the North, *should* have been simple for Thasus…but the region proved to be full of stubborn and wild folk. *Nothing but tragedy here. Nothing but a petty civil war*, Thasus could not help but ponder.

However, the optimistic side of the man, small as it was, believed that Kaya was a welcome part of his journey throughout the North. "King Cyrus has no dominion over *my* kingdom," the East Prince stated. He then noted Kaya's understanding as the woman nodded, and together they set out from the dungeon of Whitecrest.

Moving quickly throughout the castle, Thasus led Kaya toward the front gate area. "There's a side entrance that also leads outside," Thasus explained. "Even *I'm* not so bold as to take on the number of soldiers at the gate." Not a moment after the words slipped from his mouth, Thasus and Kaya rounded a corner and found themselves standing in front of three Royal Guardsmen. The one in the middle removed his helmet, revealing the familiar visage of Vyncent Reign, his black, tidy hair unchanged from the headpiece.

"Lord Thasus," Vyncent remarked with false courtesy, "where do you think you're going with our prisoner?"

Shit, the Prince cursed. *Why didn't I Pathfind?* It was a costly mistake to sneak about the castle without using his Sage ability – but he was not about to let the error stop him and Kaya from fleeing. "I can't allow an innocent woman to be executed, Reign," Thasus replied. "Now, step aside."

The Thane of Whitecrest knew all too well the reputation of Thasus the Mighty. Still, he drew his sword and moved into a defensive stance. The other two guards mimicked their commander.

Thasus sighed and pulled Archangel from its scabbard. The sight of the greatsword caused Reign to tremble visibly, but the man continued to hold his ground.

"Stand down, East Prince," one of the guards addressed Thasus from Vyncent's side, "or I'll give you a scar that you *won't* walk away from."

Thasus and King Cyrus had their differences, that much was clear, but they were still friends at the end of the day. In that regard, Thasus had no intention of grievously injuring any soldiers of Whitecrest – none but the Royal Guard who just spoke.

"It would be *glorious* if you tried," the prince countered as his face turned to stone. Immediately, the guard rushed Thasus, swinging his sword in a frenzy. The East Prince blocked the violent attack with Archangel, then swung down at the guard's sword, breaking it with ease. Shock formed on the face of the poor man before Thasus bashed him with the hilt of his sword. Blood spewed from the man's nose, and he dropped to the floor with a thud. The other guard, formerly silent, shouted as he ran to the aid of his brother-in-arms. In one swift motion, Thasus swung his greatsword and knocked the guard's weapon out of his hands. While the man's eyes widened, Thasus seized the opportunity and pulled him closer before ramming his head into the guard's face, knocking him out cold. Turning his head from the guards on the ground, Thasus stared in Vyncent's direction, wondering when the Thane of Whitecrest would attack.

Vyncent quickly placed his sword on the floor. "That's an Ironforge weapon," he said almost breathlessly. "I wouldn't last any longer than my men." Noticing that the East Prince was slowly walking toward him, Vyncent dropped to his knees. "Please," he said, turning his head so his cheek faced Thasus, "make it look like I put up a fight."

Shaking his head with disrespect, Thasus sheathed his sword. "Your men have more honor than you," he said through his teeth before walking away. Though he decided to leave Reign untouched, Kaya did not share her companion's choice. The woman grabbed Vyncent by the hair and brought her knee up into the Thane's face. As the commander groaned on the cold floor, Thasus looked to Kaya with surprise.

She shrugged. "Can't have him alerting anyone else about us, right?" The prince smiled at her, and the two of them moved on to the next corridor.

They were getting closer to the side entrance that Thasus knew of. *Only three more rooms to cross*, Thasus thought. While he prepared to use his power to Pathfind outside the castle, he heard a noise and gazed at Kaya.

"I heard it too," she said.

Suddenly, a figure exited the shadows ahead and passed through the archway that Thasus and Kaya needed to go under. The man's white cloak shimmered in the light that shone through the windows, but his features were full of sorrow and anguish.

King Cyrus was deep in thought and did not seem to notice the two people in front of him.

"Your Grace?" Thasus called out to the man softly. He was cautious, especially after dealing with the king's Royal Guard, but he was also concerned about his friend. Cyrus looked disturbed and somewhat distressed.

Cyrus stopped walking and looked up at Thasus. After recently finding out about his son's torment at the hands of his mother, as well as the threats on the life of his new bride, the king sought out his mother. He had avoided a confrontation with her for two days but could not stay silent any longer. He needed the truth.

"Cyrus." Thasus attempted to gain the attention of the king once more but to no avail. Cyrus began to stare at the floor, seemingly preoccupied with more important thoughts. This angered Thasus, as he had questions of his own that needed answering. "Why?" he blurted out. "Why did you order Kaya to be executed? You and I already discussed her innocence. Why would your mother tell your Royal Guard to go through with such an act?" The words spurred the king to look up again – his face contorted into one of astonishment. Thasus raised his eyebrows. "You didn't know…" Cyrus shook his head with utter disappointment. The man looked truly lost.

Kaya put a hand on Thasus's shoulder. "What happens *now*?"

Sighing, Thasus knew that he had gone too far, and he needed to get Kaya away from Whitecrest. But he felt pity for Cyrus.

Though he would be leaving the city with the Gargan woman, he wanted to inform the king of important matters first. "We made a pact," Thasus stated for both Cyrus and Kaya's ears. Addressing the North King directly, he said, "Stoneshield's soldiers will remain here. I've already spoken to Commander Balgon on the matter. If you still desire their aid, you have it." Placing a hand in front of the fleeing prisoner, he added, "But Kaya and I are leaving the capital."

Taking a brief moment to recall the past, Cyrus remembered the last time that he had to make a similar choice regarding Thasus passing through Whitecrest. His answer remained the same as the first day that they met. "Go," he said, motioning Thasus and Kaya toward their destination.

Searching the king's eyes for any trace of betrayal, Thasus began to move with caution. Besides having the look of a broken man, Cyrus did not seem to be untruthful. Once satisfied that Cyrus's intent was genuine, Thasus nodded courteously and made his way with Kaya toward the exit. With that, the East Prince and his companion left the harsh chill of the Northern capital, heading down the path toward Hailstone Hold.

Using his Pathfinding ability now, Thasus gave Kaya specific instructions when it came time to move between buildings and avoid patrolling soldiers. If either of them were seen, it would draw much-unwanted attention and even more unwelcome questions about why a prince from the East was escorting a prisoner out of the North.

"How long will we need to slink around?" Kaya whispered.

"Not too long," Thasus replied. "Once we've passed the outer gate of Hailstone Hold, it's two days until we reach the Eastern border – where you'll be safe. Then, it's another two days to Angelia." Saying the words brought Thasus a measure of peace. To be home after such turmoil and tragedy that he experienced in the North…it would be joyous to see his city once more.

RING. RING. RING.

Bells, thundering atop the mountain, could be heard all throughout Hailstone Hold. As he continued to Pathfind, Thasus grabbed hold of Kaya and quickly backed against a wall under some cover, bringing her within an inch of his scarred face. A moment later, the sound of multiple footsteps echoed in the streets – thanks to Thasus's power, they had narrowly missed an encounter with Northern soldiers. To his surprise, even after the armor-clad group had gone, he and Kaya still clung to each other as if they remained in danger of being discovered.

Kaya was the first to speak. "Should we keep going?" she asked after clearing her throat awkwardly.

"Yes, I believe they've gone," Thasus answered, equally as embarrassed.

As they continued on, he almost chuckled under his breath. The last time he had been through Hailstone Hold, he enjoyed the company of a Northern woman in a warm bed. Now he was sneaking around town with another Northerner – cold, uncomfortable, and far from a pleasurable night in bed.

RING. RING. RING.

Thasus cursed. If the bells of Whitecrest were ringing, the cause was most likely his liberation of the prisoner. Since the king allowed them to leave, Thasus presumed that Vyncent Reign sounded the alarm…or Celia did. The king's mother was of a slithery nature, Thasus came to realize during his time in the capital. She had a strange hold over Cyrus and all of his decisions. It seemed, at times, that *she* was the true ruler of the North. Thasus had to remind himself that she *did* rule for years until Cyrus came of age and took the throne. *Perhaps she never wanted to give up the seat,* he pondered. That line of thinking did not help his and Kaya's situation. In the end, it did not matter who sounded the bells, but only that Thasus succeeded in getting Kaya to safety.

Coming to an abrupt halt, the East Prince held up a hand. "Wait," he said softly. In order to get a clear vision, he shut his eyes for a moment and saw the silhouettes of two men standing in front of the nearby wooden gate. It was around the corner from where he and Kaya stood…and it was the only way out. Opening his eyes, Thasus turned to Kaya. "*That* is our path." He motioned toward the edge of the wall, where Kaya then peeked around to find two guards standing in their way.

She sighed. "It's almost sunrise," she said with worry. "How are we to get past them in daylight?"

Thasus took her words to heart and tried to come up with a plan. Losing patience, he made a noise, sucking the air through his teeth. He took a deep breath, then stepped out into the open area in front of the gate.

"Good morning," he said casually. "If you would allow us to pass," Thasus gestured toward the wooden doors behind the guards, while Kaya followed his lead and stuck close behind him.

"Do you know how late it is? Besides, Hailstone Hold is on lockdown," the taller of the two stated.

"You know, when we became knights," the shorter one began to say to the other, "I never thought we'd end up on guard duty at the front gate – especially in the middle of the night."

"We're on *guard duty*, Brother, because you slept with the commander's wife," the tall one reminded the other.

"While that is most definitely true," the shorter one said, "in my defense, he was not the commander yet, was he? Reign got his fancy new position in the capital while we were left under the command of *that* fool." He shrugged. "Besides, she begged me to show her the view from the battlements. It wasn't *my* fault that she wanted to see more than that." The two brothers laughed heartily, even in their situation of displacement.

"Men," Thasus attempted to gain the guards' attention again, "I do not wish to harm you. Please allow us to pass."

The guards ended their conversation and stared in the stranger's direction. "If *you* are the reason that the bells are ringing, then we'll have to arrest you," the taller one said in a serious tone.

I don't want to kill these two idiots, Thasus thought. But he had no choice – he and Kaya needed to leave through the gate before more soldiers arrived. Stepping forward, Thasus unsheathed Archangel and grasped it firmly with both hands.

The shorter guard's eyes widened. "By the gods! Is that Ironforge steel?!" he remarked with wonderment, rather than fear.

"It *is*," Thasus said, beginning to believe the notion that his sword *was* made at the renowned forge of Rikter's Hollow. "If you don't want to be on the wrong end of it, then please move."

The taller guard stepped forward from his position. Cautiously, he studied Thasus's bearded face. "Are you from Angelia?" he inquired.

"Move," Thasus repeated, ignoring the question. Kaya, weaponless, cowered behind him.

The taller guard gazed at Thasus's chest, looking past the cloaked furs that concealed most of the sigil on the breastplate. "Gerad," he spoke carefully as he turned toward the shorter guard, "I think he's a *Palidor*."

Still amazed at the sight of the sword in front of him, Gerad replied softly, "Are you certain, Barrett?" His brother nodded slowly.

They know who I am. Someone must've sent word down the mountain, Thasus thought. Though, the scenario seemed unlikely. He and Kaya had moved swiftly – word could not have traveled that fast. As Thasus stood ready to defend himself, his expression turned to one of confusion. The two guards parted and pushed open the large wooden doors of the front gate. Still in shock, Thasus sheathed Archangel and led Kaya toward the open doors. Fully prepared to thank the two strange soldiers, Thasus looked closer at the faces beneath the helmets.

"You two…look *very* familiar."

The two men removed their headgear. The taller one, Barrett, had no hair, but he resembled the late Lord of Stoneshield, Marc Bowlin, in facial structure. Gerad, the shorter knight, had wavy hair and a long, pointed beard, both black in color. Thasus swore that he was seeing the ghost of Merroc standing before him.

"We should," Gerad replied with a grin, "we're your cousins."

Chapter 25

THE YOUNG BEAR

The two combatants stood a short distance from each other, the grass beneath their feet, both dismayed with the current situation. The Lord of Woodhaven forced Jasian Bowlin and General Rhobu to fight one another to obtain their freedom. It was still a question of whether or not Draven Darkwood would live up to his word.

"I do apologize for this, Bowlin," Rhobu said with sincerity as he raised his sword in one hand and shield in the other.

Jasian mimicked the general's action, moving into his own fighting position. "We can still leave," Jasian offered. "We can kill him and just leave." Even as the words poured from his mouth, he knew that the odds were always against them and their original plan – but he had held out hope anyway.

"If there is a chance of leaving this dreadful place alive, then I must take it," the general countered.

"Darkwood just changed the rules of Woodhaven's tradition," Jasian pointed out. "We were *not* supposed to fight each other. He wants us dead. Do you really believe that he will allow either of us to leave now?"

"That's a chance that I am willing to take," Rhobu said just before Lord Darkwood called for the battle to begin.

The crowd was even louder than before. It was apparent that the sight of two 'criminals' pitted against each other brought them much joy. As Jasian and Rhobu clashed swords with ferocity, the two men continued to attack and parry in a display of skillful swordplay. Time and again, the two of them battered each other's weapons until their own exhaustion drove them apart.

"You fight well," Rhobu complimented the young Lord of Stoneshield. "You would've been a perfect addition to my ranks. Perhaps I wouldn't have lost Woodhaven to that fool up there," he gestured toward the balcony in which Draven sat.

Jasian stood with a perplexed look. After piecing together what the general had mentioned, his expression changed to one of understanding. "You were the one that Kelbain left in charge here."

"I was the steward of Woodhaven," Rhobu said proudly. Grunting in frustration, he added, "But my garrison was too few. Draven took the city back." Rhobu went on the offensive once more.

The Young Bear defended himself and held the general at bay. "You and your men took Woodhaven from its people," he admitted. "Kelbain is evil. Do you not realize that?"

Suddenly, Rhobu leaned into the attack with his sword, and the blade connected with Jasian's arm, leaving a gash. After the young man yelped in pain, Rhobu looked at him and laughed. "Indeed, he is! The man *banished* his own brother for being Magor's true-blood son," he revealed as he circled the injured Bowlin.

Jasian was even more confused. *Kelbain has a brother? True-blood son of Magor?* Before he could think any further, Jasian was forced to defend against Rhobu's attacks again. Using both swords, he caught his opponent's steel and swatted it away. Though Rhobu held on to his sword, he was distracted long enough for Jasian to knock the shield from his other hand.

Rhobu recovered quickly, using his single blade to block the two short swords that came his way. Pushing Jasian back, the two men breathed heavily, exhausted from the fight. "I was there when it happened – the banishment," he continued to divulge. "His name was Oreus." The name seemed to cause him to wince as if bothered by a painful memory. "The other generals and I...we only went along with it after Kelbain promised us longevity…but we never forgot who the true heir of Magor was."

Jasian shook his head. "I care nothing about this. Magor, Kelbain, Draven, *you*," he said bitterly, "you're all the same. Nothing but greedy, power-hungry men." The remark spawned a look of anger that formed on the general's face. "We'll always be here to stop you," Jasian said defiantly.

Rhobu's angered face softened as he relaxed his sword-arm. "It's probably for the best," he said with a nod. "I was going to stab you in the back once we escaped." Without hesitation, Rhobu charged at Lord Bowlin.

Eyes widened, Jasian swiftly side-stepped the incoming attack, using one sword to smash away his enemy's blade. Leaping high into the air, the Young Bear brought down his other sword and plunged it into Rhobu's left shoulder, removing the sharp steel just as fast. The blood gushed out of the general's body like an erupting volcano. Shock set into Rhobu's eyes, never leaving them as the general fell like a hammer to the ground, his body lost in the thick grass.

Once again, Jasian Bowlin stood triumphant in the center of the arena, much to the chagrin of the Woodhaven citizens. Exhausted from the contest with Rhobu, he sighed as he pondered the next series of events. He wondered if Draven would actually allow him to leave but knew the truth – Jasian fully expected to be killed, despite his best efforts. While he knew in his heart that his death may have been Draven's plan all along, he would never have given up without a fight.

Suddenly, the crowd began to cheer loudly, shaking the floors around the arena. Jasian looked to the balcony, wondering what the commotion was, though he found no one seated on the high terrace. Realizing the meaning of Draven's absence, he turned around to find the Lord of Woodhaven standing in front of the doors that led to the arena's inner corridor. Darkwood was poised to enter the circular field of battle, shirtless and armed with Mika's axe. Jasian simply inhaled and thought, *At last.* It was a moment that he imagined since their previous encounter – since his embarrassing defeat in The Great Wood. *I won't make the same mistake this time,* he thought as he reminded himself to aim for Draven's neck. Between his time in the dark dungeons of Woodhaven and the days of training for his trial, Jasian dreamed of removing Darkwood's head plenty of times – and now he had his chance.

The Lord of Woodhaven sauntered into the middle of the arena, raising his axe high for the crowd to see, prompting them to shout with excitement. Turning to face Jasian, Draven smiled darkly. "I commend you for defeating Rhobu, Lord Bowlin. His continued success in the arena was becoming problematic. I started to think that he'd *never* lose," he said with a chuckle.

"My victory over him didn't count," Jasian stated, realizing that Draven had only used him to get rid of the general from

Zenithor. "Were you to be my final opponent this whole time, or are you only attempting to save yourself the shame of releasing a prisoner?"

Draven's eyes narrowed. "You were not expected to make it this far. It's time that I correct the errors of the warriors before me." Darkwood grasped his axe with both hands and brought the weapon to the ground, holding it in place. "You stand no chance of winning, Lord Bowlin. I am an Evolutionary, and you are *nothing*. Admit defeat now, and I will make it a quick death."

Staring at his brother's murderer, Jasian nodded with acceptance. Looking to the swords in his hands, he twirled them in order to get a better grip while also testing the arm that Rhobu had slashed. Feeling up to the task, Jasian maneuvered into a fighting stance.

"So be it," Draven said with a shrug. The Evolutionary attacked Jasian with the full force of his double-sided axe. To his annoyance, the young Bowlin avoided all of his attacks, as he ducked, jumped back, and side-stepped every swing. "Stand still!" he yelled in frustration. Another moment or two went by while Jasian evaded the axe, until finally, Draven connected with one of Jasian's swords, obliterating it.

Jasian would not let himself lose focus. Though he had one sword remaining, he threw his unarmed fist at Draven's hairless face, sending the Evolutionary reeling backward. Not expecting to injure the man, Jasian was shocked to find the state that the Lord of Woodhaven was in. Draven stood back up, blood trickling down his lips and rage in his eyes. The Young Bear felt a swell of reassurance. *He can* be *hurt!*

Out of nowhere, the crowd in the arena began to panic. Screams were heard, almost as loud as the sounds of steel clashing against steel. As Jasian and Draven surveyed the stands, they witnessed multiple Zenithor soldiers making their way in and cutting down any Woodhaven citizens that they came across.

"No!" Draven shouted at the top of his lungs. He watched as his soldiers tried to fight back, but they were clearly outnumbered. Seething with anger, the Lord of Woodhaven clenched his fists. "Kelbain," he said through his teeth.

From the nearest seats, a lonesome soldier yelled, "Lord Darkwood! What do we do?!"

"Hold them back by any means necessary! I will *not* lose Woodhaven to that dishonorable pretender!" Draven cried out. The soldier of Woodhaven nodded hesitantly and ran toward the ongoing battle.

Jasian paid almost no mind to the chaos around him. He remained focused on Draven Darkwood. Catching the man's attention once more, Jasian gripped his last sword and prepared to continue the fight.

Lord Darkwood tilted his head curiously, then threw his axe to the ground. "No weapons, Young Bear," he suggested. "Your sword is of no use anyway." Spitting out the blood that still dripped from his mouth, Draven said, "Come. Finish what you've begun."

Glad to oblige, Jasian tossed his weapon to the grass and strode toward Draven with purpose. Throwing the first punch, Jasian's speed allowed him to connect once more, but Draven recovered and returned the hit. Jasian stumbled for a moment, but his heart pounded with anticipation, as he believed that he could now defeat the Evolutionary. Before he could enjoy the thought for too long, Draven followed up with another blow to Jasian's face and a kick to the gut. Jasian dropped to the floor and coughed from the pain.

"Years as a mercenary," Darkwood explained, "I traveled all throughout Areon – even south to the island of Skal. You see, there's more gold to be made in a fight with no weapons." Following his words, Draven waited for Jasian to stand before battering his face again. Adding insult to the attack, Darkwood circled around Jasian and kicked him in the back of the knee.

Jasian shouted in pain and fell down once more. While on his back – his face a red mess – he struggled to view his surroundings. He could scarcely see numerous battles still taking place amongst the stands in the arena. Suddenly, he felt Draven sit atop him.

"It was thrilling," the Lord of Woodhaven continued. "I'd sail over to Forsa, have a woman before going back to Skal the next day and do it all over again." Wrapping his hands lightly around Jasian's throat, he spoke so the Young Bear could hear him. "I've killed with swords, axes, arrows – everything that you can imagine – but the best kills were just like *this*, when I could see the light disappear from their eyes."

Jasian spit in the face of Lord Darkwood. "You're still just a murderer. Nothing more." Draven's grip tightened around his neck, slowly robbing him of life. As he choked and braced for death, Jasian thought to himself, *I failed you, Merroc...I couldn't keep my promise and return to you, Ashra...*

The Lord of Woodhaven suddenly loosened his grip, causing Jasian to gasp for air. Recuperating from the edge of death, Lord Bowlin lifted his head and found a startling sight: Mika's axe was buried deep in Draven's back – the man himself remained atop Jasian for a moment before he tumbled to the ground, writhing in anguish. Once Darkwood fell, Jasian strained his eyes through the blood and sweat to see a figure standing there. Curly blonde hair flowed with the incoming winds, and a gentle face stared back at Jasian with concern and joy. "Ashra?"

Rushing to Jasian's side, the woman from Triton cradled his body in hers, tears streaming down her cheeks. "I've got you," she said, trying not to let his injuries affect her.

Through his bloodied mouth and bruised cheeks, Jasian smiled. "I'm glad to see you," he said. Their reunion was cut short, however. Out of the corner of his eye, Jasian noticed Draven's limp figure begin to move as the man crawled slowly through the grass with the axe still embedded in his back. "Help me," Jasian asked

Ashra. She obliged and grasped his arm, assisting him to his feet. The Lord of Stoneshield stepped toward Draven, bent down, and forcibly removed Mika's axe. Darkwood grunted harshly. "Get up," he said to Draven in a cold tone.

The Lord of Woodhaven, still in a dire amount of pain, used his hands to push himself up from the ground and to his knees. He began to chuckle softly. "I am at your mercy, Lord Bowlin. That axe…it can still harm me, even after I healed the last time…" He locked eyes with both Jasian and Ashra. "So, this is it. Go on then, my Lord. Avenge your brother, but do it quickly. The West King is not known for his mercy."

Gripping the axe hard, Jasian prepared to end the murderer's life. Staring at Darkwood, he was surprised to feel a sense of pity, as he found a hint of sadness in his green eyes. Before he could act, the Lord of Woodhaven spoke again.

"I only wanted this place to be different than all of the rest," he stated as he observed the devastation of his home. Turning back toward Jasian, he said, "Don't let him win this war, Young Bear. Areon will be nothing but *ashes* when he's through with it."

Stunned by Draven's final words, Jasian nodded and pulled Mika's axe back, ready to swing. Draven simply gazed at his city with a half-smile as his head quickly left his body. The Evolutionary was no more. Indeed, as Mika had told Jasian, it only took one good swing.

With Darkwood's death, Jasian had fulfilled his promise to Merroc. Dropping the axe, he turned to Ashra, and the two of them embraced in a long-lasting kiss. Once the moment passed, he smiled. "You came for me."

Ashra placed her hands on his cheeks. "I love you, Jasian. I'll always be by your side – even if that means rescuing you from a madman every now and then."

Smiling even wider, Jasian replied, "I love you too. Come," he said as he took Ashra by the hand, "we must leave."

"Yes, we *must*," she confirmed, "but first, we need to find Rudi."

Immediately, Jasian formed a look of confusion. "Wait…Rudi's here too?!"

"I'll explain once we start moving!" she shouted over the rising sounds of destruction that rocked throughout Woodhaven. "And don't forget the axe," she was sure to point out, as Jasian was oblivious to the importance of Harbinger. Dragging Jasian back through the way she came in, Ashra was met with more questions than she could count.

Chapter 26

THE DAY OF RECKONING

The hour grew late. It was the time of night when the winds surrounding Whitecrest would blow throughout the castle, whistling in the corridors louder than some could speak. This was especially noticeable in the King's bedchamber when the door to the balcony was open.

King Cyrus stood in the middle of the room, staring at the crown set upon the wooden chest in front of him. Thinking of all that had happened in just the last few days, Cyrus contemplated the entirety of his time as North King. He wondered what he would be remembered for. Would it be for his role in uniting the North? Saving the life of Thasus the Mighty after the battle with the Fenrok? His survival against the assassin from the Frostford, and his subsequent execution of Lord Brock? Scoffing after that last thought, he whispered, "A lie…" Taking another look at his golden crown, he began to feel unworthy. *I should have told him.*

Earlier that day, Cyrus struggled with the idea of telling Thasus the truth about what happened to Marc Bowlin. Then, when he saw the prince attempting to flee with Kaya Gargan, he wanted to reveal everything at that moment…but he was afraid. If Thasus would not decide to kill him, then one of the men from Stoneshield surely would if they ever found out – and Cyrus was not ready to die. His son needed him now…

Faintly, he could hear footsteps ascending the staircase outside his chamber door. Cyrus exhaled shakily as he prepared to confront the cause of his recent distress regarding his son. He watched as his mother opened the door forcefully, walking through with purpose. Her silver hair and blue dress whipped around violently as a gust of wind suddenly passed through the room.

"Cyrus," Celia addressed her son while holding her hair in place, "why have you summoned me here? Your men still search the city for Palidor and the prisoner."

While secretly hoping that Thasus and Kaya made it out of Whitecrest unharmed, Cyrus continued to gaze upon his crown. "How did you do it?" he asked vaguely. "All those years that you ruled the North, you did so with no issue."

The king's mother looked confused but answered, "So have *you*. In the 16 years that you've been king, you've done beautifully."

Cyrus was silent for a moment. *Have I?* he wondered. Shifting his eyes toward the ground, he sighed. "This is where it happened," Cyrus spoke again indistinctly. He did not turn to look at his mother but could imagine the expression she displayed. "This is where Marc died."

Celia seemed to wince at the mention of the misdeed. "Why are we still discussing this, Cyrus? The man is gone." Her voice carried a cold, heartless tone. "Is *this* why you called me here? To discuss the past?"

Glaring at his mother with intensity, Cyrus replied, "That and *much* more." Turning his back on Celia, the King walked toward the open door of the balcony, stopping at the threshold. "I know that you threatened my wife," he stated bluntly.

Celia did not bother to hide her transgression. "Oh, come now, Cyrus. If I hadn't put some fear in her, she would've betrayed you."

"And Saul?" he asked, rounding on Celia. "What of *him?*" His mother attempted to feign surprise at the mention of her grandson, but Cyrus pressed the issue. "What have you been doing to him?!"

Celia approached her son cautiously. "I'm not sure what that woman told you, but she and I will have words again, I promise—"

"You will have words with *me* now," Cyrus said darkly.

Celia's eyes widened. "I don't care for your tone, Cyrus. You will apologize to me at once," she insisted.

The North King shook his head. "What have you done to Saul? What sort of *fear* did you put into *him*?"

"These accusations, Cyrus…How dare you! I am your mother!"

"I AM YOUR *KING!*" Cyrus shouted. Noticing the shock on her face and the silence that followed, he continued. "You will tell me. *Now.*"

"What would you like to know?" she asked almost casually, dropping the act.

"It has not escaped my eyes that Saul is terrified of you. I need to know *why.*"

Celia formed a half-smile. "It's escaped you for quite some time. Saul needs a…*special* sort of attention."

"What do you mean?" Cyrus inquired, almost afraid of the answer.

"He's an Evolutionary," Celia revealed.

Cyrus's mouth dropped. His stomach was spinning, and his mind was running in too many directions to focus properly. He was not concerned with Saul being a Sage, but was worried about the life that his son would have. "What have you done?" It was the only complete thought that he could muster, and he aimed it directly at his mother.

"I've done *nothing,*" Celia countered. "He's had this power since he was very young." Her son began to open his mouth to speak, but she interrupted him. "I'm a Sensor, Cyrus," she stated, though Cyrus already knew that information. "I have *always* known about Saul's ability. Just as I've known of the East Prince's Pathfinding ability since the night of the feast – the same night that you killed Marc. Soon after your son was born, and your wife took her last breath, I stood outside the room and felt the power radiate from Saul."

Cyrus could not help but flinch at the mention of his first wife, but he continued to question his mother in his search for the truth. "Why does Saul fear you, Mother?"

Celia scoffed. "The boy is weak-minded. *But*," she began to say as she held a finger pointed high, "he grows stronger every day. At this point, he should be immune to almost everything."

The king pursed his lips. His eyes were filled with anger and utter disgust. "You tortured him…you tortured my son."

"I *helped* him," she corrected Cyrus. "He will be the most powerful Sage in all of Areon." Celia seemed to stand taller as she spoke – proud of what she had done to her grandson. "Sages are a large part of this world, son. Having one more in our family will ensure our survival." She had left the North King speechless. "In truth, I had hoped that *you* would be a Sage…I went so far as to scour the North for a Kindler, just to see if he could unearth a power hidden within you." Celia shook her head in disappointment, her silver hair shining in the moonlight that found its way into the room. "He failed. So, I had him disposed of. Without a Sage power, I knew that you'd always be vulnerable,

Cyrus. It is why I kept you so close all these years – to protect you from all sorts of distractions."

It all started to make sense for Cyrus, though his mother's last remark left him curious. "*What* distractions?"

Celia waved him off. "I tire of this, Cyrus. I have told you more than I ever cared to." She walked away from her son and onto the balcony to enjoy the night air.

Following his mother, Cyrus stood beside her and looked out toward the snowy mountainside. Not bothering to gaze in Celia's direction, he spoke softly. "Tell me."

With a hint of hesitation, Celia turned to look at her son. Sighing, she said, "Cassie was a nice enough woman. But a future queen, she was *not*. I tried to get her to leave." As she continued, her son finally glared at her, patiently waiting to hear the rest. "It didn't matter what I offered her: land, gold, another man. She wouldn't leave your side. Then, she was going to have your child…" Celia shook her head as if she had relived a bad memory. "Your wife and child would've kept you from becoming the greatest king in all of Areon. I *had* to make certain that you were protected. So, I poisoned her…in an attempt to kill them both, I poisoned your wife."

Cyrus was blank in the face, holding in all of his anger and vengeful feelings. As he did so, he continued to hang on his mother's every word.

"That was why Cassie did not survive childbirth. I questioned why your son lived, but as I said earlier, I discovered his power shortly after. It was then that I knew…I *knew* that the gods had delivered a savior to our family," she spoke with her eyes closed for an instant, holding her hands out in respect of the Gods of Volsi. "With *your* lack of power and the incident with your father, we were finally blessed."

Swallowing silently, Cyrus asked, "And what about my father?"

"Well," Celia began with a soft chuckle, "between *him*, Marc, and those two little…*mistakes* of mine, it was up to me to fix all of it. I was going to throw them over the edge…right here," she said as she took a glimpse over the edge of the balcony, "but your father had already convinced me to send the twins down to Hailstone Hold. I thought it ended there. I found out that he wrote a letter to Marc, informing him of his bastards. He almost destroyed us, Cyrus. *Ruined* us." Sighing again while her son merely stared at her, she said, "Your father lost sight of what was best for us. Much to my regret, I had to be rid of him." With a small, unapologetic laugh, Celia resumed her confession. "Fate, it seems, has brought us right back to where I—"

He had enough. It was too much to bear. Cyrus grabbed hold of his mother's glistening locks and pulled violently. "FATHER?! MY WIFE?? *SAUL?!*" Cyrus shouted in his mother's face, letting all of his pent-up emotions out in a moment of terrible rage.

"All for *you*, Cyrus," Celia said quietly, ignoring the pain that her son was inflicting upon her. "For *us*."

Tears began to fall down Cyrus's face as he looked into his mother's eyes. He loosened his grip on her hair and pulled her in close in a loving embrace, the water streaming down his cheeks with purpose.

For the first time in a long time, Celia felt at peace. Unburdening herself of all the lies from the past was a freeing experience – and she was happy that her son still welcomed her with open arms. Suddenly, the air from beneath her feet rose high as Cyrus began to lift her up.

"Cyrus…let go of me, Cyrus…Son…LET GO!"

With no more hesitation, King Cyrus launched his mother over the side of the balcony and watched as she plummeted to the hard ground below, her screams echoing between the mountain and the castle. Though it was a long fall, he was thankful that it was quicker than he thought it would be.

Moments went by before Cyrus looked to his hands in a shocked state, as he caught a glimpse of silver hair between his fingers. Collapsing to the floor, he sat against the railing and let out a yell that rivaled the strong winds high in the tower of Whitecrest.

Chapter 27

THE SHADOW SANCTUM

The Prince of Angelia scoured the temple with caution. The Sanctum was devoid of life, making it eerily quiet. While the moonlight continued to fill the room he was in, he noticed that the light began to fade the further he traveled inward. It was disconcerting to think that the lack of a simple torch could keep him from obtaining the Mystical Artifact.

As the light began to dissipate, Andemar tried to hurry along, rather than stop to admire the depths of the temple – but as he walked down the long corridor, he noticed symbols on the high walls above. Unlike the runes outside the Sanctum, the markings inside resembled the sun. He stared curiously at first but paid it no further mind.

The deeper he ventured into the Sanctum, the more it seemed like the walls were closing in. Andemar was beginning to think about his family back home and how they would feel if they knew the trials that he had faced so far. *Maryn and Ginny would be worried sick*, he thought. *Anden would pretend he wasn't, but the boy would eventually give in to his despair.* A frown suddenly crept onto Andemar's face. He missed his wife and children terribly and wished nothing more than to be with them again soon. But in his heart, he knew that his quest would make them proud.

Steeling himself and moving on, Andemar came across a room that appeared to be the last one in the temple. Against the back wall, there was an altar of sorts that contained a dusty, old sword plunged into the stone. Narrowing his eyes, he said aloud, "This cannot be it." Walking up to the altar, the prince brushed off the dust as best he could. The blade was certainly ancient and may have had the makings of a Mystical Artifact, but something inside him was telling him otherwise.

"Andemar."

Startled, the East Prince unsheathed Thanatos and turned around to discover the origin of the voice. "Who said that? Who's there?"

"Andemar," the voice repeated. "Are you worthy?"

It sounds…familiar, Andemar thought as he held up his sword, ready to defend himself. Suddenly, he noticed that the moonlight was fading faster. "Show yourself!" he shouted to the growing darkness.

A shadow began to move from the back of the room, detaching itself from the stone wall and stepping into the small amount of light that was left.

Andemar's jaw dropped. Lowering his guard, he gazed upon the apparition before him. Where there was once a long beard, there was nothing. Where there was once a hunched-over old man, there was a younger man that stood up straight, strong-looking and healthy. Andemar thought that he was dreaming. Eyes widened, he spoke to the spirit.

"Horus?"

"What you see before you is merely a memory," the apparition explained. "A shadow of my former self. The man you know as 'Horus' is my true self, though I'm afraid I had to adopt the façade you have met so often. My real name is Garis. I am one of the Sudae from the realm of Sule. The people of *your* realm call us Mystics."

Completely in disbelief, Andemar looked around the room suspiciously, almost searching for another surprise that would catch him off-guard. "You're Garis? The Eastern Mystic? *That* Garis?"

"As I've said," Garis confirmed. "Now, you must prove your worth."

"Hold on," Andemar demanded. "We're not finished talking." It was rare for him to get angry, and he had not felt that way since he learned of all the lies that his father had told him over the years. If Horus was truly Garis, then he needed to know more. "How is it that you know of my previous meetings with Horus if you've been *here* all this time?"

"I share all thoughts and knowledge with my true self," Garis said. "It is an advanced version of what Sages call 'Pathfinding'. I was left here many years ago to protect Stormbringer."

Realization dawned on Andemar. "The Artifact..."

"Yes. It was the weapon that I had created in the Ironforge centuries ago. For a long time, I had no use for it, so I kept it hidden here in my temple. 'Horus' – my true self – sent me here to watch over the weapon, after this place was sealed, only for me to present it to the most worthy."

Ignoring the shadow's attempt to move past his questions again, Andemar asked, "Where were you during the Sorcerer's War? Lord Varian's father found Stormbringer back then but was afraid that the power would fall into the wrong hands. It was the Varians who sealed the entrance, as well as the Artifact. They have protected the secret ever since then."

"I am still grateful for their efforts," Garis admitted. "The weapon could have fallen into the hands of the enemy, leading to an age of eternal darkness. As for my absence...After Magor began his war on Areon, Rikter disappeared. Aman was already dead," he spoke of the other Mystics. "*I* was alone and, therefore, no match for Magor's power. So I hid away in Angelia, far from the major battles in the war." Seeing the look of disappointment on Andemar's face, Garis defended himself. "I do not ask for your forgiveness, young Palidor. Know that I would have faced Magor if I thought it would have made a difference. As his power grew, mine faded. That is why I poured most of my strength into Stormbringer," Garis revealed.

"What do you mean?" Andemar inquired.

"I can see things from all moments in time – past, present, and future. The one who wields the sword could do the same. In addition, the skill of 'Pathfinding' allows me to search for anything that I can imagine. Holding the sword will not only allow you to mimic that ability, but Stormbringer will take you to the place that you envision…instantly."

Andemar hung on every word as his curiosity piqued. Garis explained the basic abilities of a Watcher and a Pathfinder, but, in short, he seemed to indicate that Stormbringer enhanced those powers. Andemar had not considered that the Artifact would contain the powers of a Sage. If he was truly the one to wield the weapon, then he needed to be sure that he was ready for the power that came with it.

"I will ask you again, young prince," Garis interrupted Andemar's thoughts. "Are you worthy?"

"If you have knowledge of everything Horus and I have discussed," Andemar pointed out, "wouldn't you already know if I was?" Even as he asked the question, Andemar let a sliver of doubt creep into his mind. *What if Horus was wrong?*

"Let us find out," Garis said. The Mystic stepped further into the light – what was left of it at that point. "What do you desire?"

Andemar thought it was a strange question. "Desire? How does that prove if I'm worthy?"

"Stormbringer shall be wielded by someone pure of heart," Garis seemed to recite. "What is your desire?"

Thinking about it for a moment, Andemar then answered, "I wish to protect those I love. At all costs."

The shadow of Garis narrowed his eyes. "What is your *desire*?" he asked again.

Searching deep within himself, the prince still had his doubts about everything: the journey, the Artifact, his destiny…and he needed to be honest with Garis if he wanted to save the people of Areon. "I wish to know what my *true* destiny is."

"So, you *still* doubt yourself?"

Hesitating at first, Andemar raised his chin and replied, "Yes."

A smile formed on the face of the shadow. "Andemar Palidor, you *are* worthy." Waving his hand, the wall behind the stone altar began to crumble as it opened up to reveal another room.

"But…how?" Andemar attempted to find the right words.

"If you struggle to know your destiny," Garis explained, "then that just makes you human. A man who would walk in here fully confident – fully *sure* – that he was the one to wield Stormbringer…would not be worthy at all."

Garis was right, Andemar thought. Even after Horus, his mother, and Lord Varian had all told him that he was destined to be the one to save Areon, he never believed it completely. *Now*, as he spoke to Garis, and as he peered into the newly opened, well-lit room, he *knew* it to be true.

Noting the expression of understanding on Andemar's face, Garis continued. "I sent you here with a purpose, Andemar. Now, we must see that same purpose fulfilled."

Stepping through the gap in the wall, Andemar turned back for a moment and saw that the moonlight had finally disappeared, leaving the rest of the Sanctum in darkness. The room that he had set foot in was large, with high ceilings, and carried a blinding tower of light in the center. But Andemar quickly realized that it was no ordinary light that he surveyed, but one born from magic. Approaching the pillar of blue luminescence, he then saw what was inside: a sword, suspended in mid-air, wreathed in never-ending lightning.

"Stormbringer," Garis informed the prince. "It waits for you."

Andemar took slow steps toward the Artifact, noting the stone circle around the bottom of the glowing column as he drew closer. There, he could see small objects with markings – runes, he surmised.

"They form a protection spell," Garis said of the rune stones. "It is how the Varians sealed the Artifact in place. You, alone, can claim it."

"How?" Andemar inquired with genuine concern.

"As my true self told you: You are not a Sage. The sword's power will not be as overwhelming as it would have been with your brothers or your father."

Not satisfied with the Mystic's answer, Andemar asked, "And the protection spell? What will happen when I reach for the sword?"

"You are the *one*," Garis emphasized. "The sword belonged to *me* once, and now it shall be yours. Believe in yourself, and you will be able to retrieve Stormbringer."

Turning his gaze toward the floating Artifact, Andemar approached as close as he could get to the light without crossing the runes. Staring at the brilliant flashes of lightning that surrounded the blade, he exhaled sharply and plunged his hand into the gleaming heart of the pillar. Immediately, he felt the effects of the spell – it was as if he was being torn apart from his fingertips to his elbow. Pushing through the pain, he somehow felt the strength of will to overcome the magical barrier. Reaching further, the agony intensified, and he was forced to pull his hand from the light. Taking a moment to let his aching arm settle, he steeled his nerves and threw his right hand back into the barrier. Andemar winced from the familiar pain – it was excruciating but manageable. Finally, he slipped his fingers over the handle, feeling the lightning course through his body at the same time. It was a new sort of pain, but it quickly faded as he began to pull the sword from its magical prison. Suddenly, he felt the extent of the protection spell as it seemed to fight him for supremacy over Stormbringer. As he pulled, the light tugged in the opposite direction. *I've come this far,* he told himself. *I won't give up.* The power of the sword fought the might of the runes. Lightning bolts swam inside the barrier wildly while Andemar continued to pull. As he felt the mix of power and restraint throughout the light, Andemar let out a visceral scream that shook the room…and he freed Stormbringer.

Holding the powerful Artifact, the prince stood in awe. Wordlessly, he turned to Garis, who expressed looks of respect and relief. Not a moment later, Andemar felt something within the sword…something calling to him. Glancing into the blade itself, he could see a vision. Struggling to make it out at first, he cleared his mind and suddenly became fearful.

"Rudimere?" he wondered with confusion.

"It is the present that you see," Garis told him.

Andemar closed his eyes and shook his head, unwilling to believe what he saw. "He was in chains…imprisoned. I saw…I saw someone else standing over him. A man dressed in black armor, with the sigil of Zenithor on his chest."

"Look again, Andemar."

Nodding, Andemar stared into the blade and paid more attention to the details of the surroundings. "Trees…made into structures…a city." Widening his eyes, he figured out the vision. "Woodhaven! My brother is imprisoned in Woodhaven!"

"Yes," Garis agreed. "It is Kelbain who holds him there."

"Kelbain?"

The shadow of Garis closed his eyes to concentrate. "I can see them – as clearly as I can see you *now*. You must go, Andemar. If Kelbain is there, you can end this new war before it is too late."

He's right, Andemar thought to himself. *Areon must be saved. My family…my children await my return.* Taking a deep breath, he held the sword tightly in his hands. He started to focus, almost as if he knew what needed to be done next. Remembering what Garis said about using the sword to travel, Andemar thought of Woodhaven…thought of the room where Kelbain held Rudi captive. Stormbringer started to hum with power. Lightning surrounded the sword, as well as Andemar.

Not a moment later, a thunderous bolt dropped from the sky and into the temple, enveloping the East Prince and whisking him away in the blink of an eye, leaving the shadow of Garis behind.

Chapter 28

RAGNAROK

In the time that it took to let out a single breath, Andemar had left the Shadow Sanctum and appeared in Woodhaven. At first, he was not sure if he was dreaming, but the instant travel from one place to the other took a toll on his body – apparently, there was a small price to pay for using Stormbringer in such a manner.

Breathing heavily and wincing in pain, the prince slowly realized that he was standing in the same room he envisioned at the temple. Observing his surroundings with caution, he tried to find his brother without drawing any attention. He could faintly hear the sounds of a battle but did not have time to investigate while Rudi's life was in danger. Still holding Stormbringer, and with Thanatos

firmly secure in his scabbard, Andemar was ready to defend himself
if needed.

Suddenly, he heard a loud noise, which he quickly discovered
to be the running footsteps of armored boots heading in his
direction. Sticking to the shadows on the wall, he narrowly avoided
the two soldiers that ran past. Glimpsing the sigil on their chest
plates, he confirmed that they were servants of Kelbain.

"It came from over here," the man told his companion.

"Well, there's nothing here *now*," the woman replied. "A 'bolt
of lightning'. Ha!" The soldier mocked her fellow Zenithorian until
his face turned red with embarrassment.

"I swear!" he pleaded. "By the Mystics, there was lightning
inside the city!"

"Sure, sure. Can we get moving already? The king seeks to
burn this place to the ground, and I don't intend to be here when it
happens," the woman said as she and the other soldier trailed away.

After they had gone, Andemar continued his search.
Eventually, he came across a large room with no roof. Inside, there
stood 10 or 12 pillars, all made of wood and covered in vines. As
Andemar surveyed the rest of the room, he noticed a set of stairs in
the back corner but paid more attention to the figure to his right.
Chained between two of the pillars, the man still had his armor on
and his weapon on the floor beside him, though he could do
nothing to free himself.

Rudi! The prince ran to his brother's side, fully intent on breaking the bonds that held the young Palidor imprisoned. "Rudi! Rudi!" Andemar shouted in a quieted voice. "You must wake!"

Stirring from a forced sleep, Rudimere lifted his head and found his older brother staring at him. "Andemar?" he wondered in a weakened tone.

"I'm here, Brother." Andemar moved Rudi's hair from his face to show him that he did not imagine things. "It's me."

Rudi sighed with pure happiness. "Andemar…It *is* you."

"We're getting out of here." The older Palidor looked at the chains to find a way to open them but only found two locks with no key in sight.

"How did you get here?" Rudi asked as his brother attempted to free him.

Andemar casually pointed to the sword that he had placed on the ground nearby. "With *that*," he replied. "It's a Mystical Artifact – Stormbringer."

Rudi seemed to wake up faster at the mention of the weapon. "Mystical…How did you—"

"I'll explain later," Andemar interrupted. "We need to get out of here." Still, he shook the chains in an attempt to break them loose somehow. Then, he finally realized that he could use either of his swords to free his brother. Snatching Stormbringer from the ground, he told Rudi, "Hold still."

"Leaving so soon?" a voice called out to him.

Stopping mid-swing, Andemar turned his head and found the tall, black-armored man from the vision: Kelbain.

"West King," Andemar said as he feigned a courteous bow.

"Prince…Andemar," Kelbain responded with a smile.

Andemar's brows furrowed. "You know me?"

"It was fate that brought us all here tonight."

"And it is the night that your rule comes to an end," Andemar stated defiantly. "Areon will no longer suffer while Sages like you roam free."

Kelbain scoffed loudly. "Roam free? I am more than a simple Sage, young Palidor. I am the West King – the greatest Sorcerer since the days of my father – and tonight, you will see just how much power I possess."

Andemar pulled Stormbringer into view and locked eyes with the son of the Demon Sorcerer. While he stared into the red slits across the room, Kelbain reached around his back and drew a long spear with an edged blade at the end.

Rudi's expression turned fearful. "Watch out!" he shouted to his brother in an attempt to warn him of the opposing Artifact's power.

Without delay, Andemar charged at Kelbain. As he swung his sword downward at the West King, Stormbringer and Nightfall collided, causing a wave of power that shook the pillars throughout the room. At the same time, Stormbringer had shown its true self – the same way that it did in the Shadow Sanctum – and produced an endless swarm of lightning that encased the sword. Catching Kelbain off-guard, Andemar attacked with pure efficiency and knocked Nightfall to the ground.

Kelbain's eyes burned with anger. He responded to losing his weapon by conjuring balls of flames from his hands and quickly tossing them in Andemar's direction.

Instinctively, the East Prince defended himself with Stormbringer, only to find out that the flames disappeared as they touched the sword. Shock crept along his face, but he was interrupted by his opponent's stubborn attempt at using his Fire Elemental ability. The West King summoned even more flames, manipulating them into a wave of deadly heat. Andemar watched as Kelbain pushed the wall of fire toward him – but using Stormbringer once more, he broke through the flames unscathed.

Kelbain made a noise of frustration but had little time to react as Andemar charged at him again. Still without Nightfall, Kelbain unsheathed Hyperion from its scabbard and used the weapon from the Ironforge to parry the incoming attack. Before he knew it, he was sent tumbling backward, only after glimpsing Hyperion's destruction at the hands of the Mystical Artifact.

Andemar stood over the fallen West King, pointing Stormbringer at his chest. "It is done, Kelbain."

The Lord of Zenithor looked to his broken sword on the ground – the sword that once belonged to his father – and became furious. Then, spotting Nightfall nearby, Kelbain calmed himself and replied in kind. "No. It is *not* done." Quickly switching his powers, Kelbain summoned a large gust of wind and threw Andemar to the floor. Using two elements in succession caused the West King a great deal of agony, but he managed to stumble over to Nightfall and retrieved it. Twisting his body around, he found Andemar within inches from his face, but he was ready this time. Wielding Nightfall, Kelbain clashed with Stormbringer once more – the weapons echoed off of each other, humming with great power. Staring into Andemar's eyes as they connected Artifacts, Kelbain flicked his wrist and utilized yet another element at his disposal.

Andemar cocked his head fast, looking to the ground below, as he watched the dirt come to wrap itself around his feet. Before he could figure out what was happening, Kelbain knocked Stormbringer from his hands. He reached for his own Ironforge weapon, Thanatos, but Kelbain anticipated the move by summoning vines from the nearby pillars to bind Andemar's hands. Seconds later, Andemar found himself stretched between two towers of wood, held up by the vines, while his feet were rooted to the floor by dirt.

Collapsing from the pain that he felt, Kelbain took a moment to remain on his hands and knees before trying to rise. "No one," he began to say while he caught his breath, "has ever forced me to use that many elements in a single battle. In all of my 76 years in this world…not once." Struggling to stand, the West King finally made his way to where he had imprisoned Andemar. The East Prince squirmed to get free, as did his brother just a few feet away. Kelbain drew closer to Andemar and nodded. "You really *are* the one."

"Let him go!" Rudimere shouted.

Turning toward the younger Palidor, Kelbain said, "Not to worry, Rudimere. It will all be over for you both soon enough." Pacing between the brothers, Kelbain continued to explain. "While I *am* a great Sorcerer, I could never compare to the great Magor. I've led many people to believe that I declared war because I want to rule Areon. But this is not true at all. I could *never* rule – Areon is not *mine* to do so. That honor belongs to Magor himself."

Andemar and Rudi looked to each other, wide-eyed. The more that Kelbain spoke of the Demon Sorcerer, the more they truly became concerned.

"My father's blood runs through your veins," Kelbain divulged to the Palidors. "You...are the key to his rebirth." Slowly turning his head toward Andemar, Kelbain finally revealed the truth. "*That* is why you are here."

Andemar pulled at the vines that held his arms up, but could not break free. *He speaks as if he knew I was coming...* Andemar pondered. Then, it suddenly became clearer as he watched the West King pull out a small weapon from his belt. *A dagger*, he thought to himself. *Black in color...Gold edges...Strange markings...I've seen this before.*

"Behold: my father's Artifact. The same dagger that pierced Victor Palidor and blessed you all with the blood of a Sudae – the blood of my father, Magor. And now," he said with a shudder, "the instrument of his return."

Rudi and Andemar exchanged glances. While Rudi breathed hard, his face covered in fear, Andemar closed his eyes briefly and opened them again with a begrudging look of acceptance. The older Palidor then turned to find Kelbain standing over him.

The West King placed one hand on the Palidor's right shoulder and held up his father's dagger in the other hand. "Do not be afraid."

Andemar could see Maryn…Anden…Ginny…and his unborn child, all at that moment. A single tear rolled down his cheek as his breaths became uneven.

"This is the will of Ragnarok," Kelbain stated as he looked between the dagger and Andemar…before thrusting the Artifact through the white breastplate and into the heart of the Palidor.

With every bit of voice that he had, Rudi screamed. His brother, still held up by the unforgiving vines, slumped over after taking his last breath…right before his body began to convulse. Rudi shook his head, unable to comprehend what was happening. To his horror, he watched as Andemar's corpse filled with life. The veins in his brother's neck momentarily turned red, as if his blood began to show on the outside before returning to normal again. From there, Andemar's blue eyes turned to a reddish hue, as a small light flickered within. Rudi *knew* what it all meant, but could only lower his head in despair.

Kelbain merely stood back in awe of his accomplishment. With the ritual complete, he aimed to release Andemar's body from the vines. Out of nowhere, he felt immediate pain in his gut, and he grunted loudly. He looked down and found an arrow sticking out of his belly, and within seconds another one found its way into the left side of his chest, close to his heart. Kelbain gasped for air as he noticed the archer with curly blonde hair run into the room, accompanied by another companion.

"Rudi! Rudi!"

The broken man looked up weakly. "Ash?"

"We have to get you out of here," Ashra said, almost on the brink of tears. She had just seen Andemar's death at Kelbain's hand before unloading two arrows into the murderer's body. "Jasian, use the axe."

Rudi turned his head to see his cousin, battered and bruised, standing next to Ashra. "Jasian...you are alive..."

"Just barely," Jasian replied as he used Harbinger to cut the chains off of Rudi's arms. "Let's hurry." Before he could get Rudi to his feet, however, Jasian pushed his cousin and Ashra to the side and held up the axe to defend them both. A blast of fire came hurdling their way by the injured West King.

Picking his head up from the floor, Rudimere scowled at Kelbain, wishing for the man's quick death. Then, out of the corner of his eye, he saw the Artifact that his brother had brought to Woodhaven. Stormbringer laid on the ground right where Kelbain had knocked it from Andemar's hands. "We need that sword," he said softly to Jasian and Ashra.

Jasian looked to the spot that Rudi spoke of and nodded. "I'll hold him back," he said, referring to Kelbain.

"Jasian, wait!"

Injured or not, he ignored Ashra's plea and headed toward the West King. By the time he had reached Kelbain, the Zenithorian had retrieved a long, ancient-looking spear. Without hesitation, Jasian swung his axe at Kelbain, which the king parried with his spear. The contact between weapons caused a booming noise within the room that made everything else shake uncontrollably.

"How perfect," Kelbain struggled to say with both arrows still inside him, "you've brought us Harbinger. Now, all *four* of the Artifacts are within his grasp."

At that point, Rudimere joined the fight, wielding Stormbringer. Not bothering to listen to what was said, Rudi attacked viciously. Kelbain, though gravely injured, fought back against both Rudi *and* Jasian.

The West King used his power to hurl sharpened vines in their direction, hoping to ward them off until his father awoke. When he finally pushed them back far enough, he fell to the ground without warning, incapacitated from his wounds.

Rudi pushed forward, blinded by his quest for vengeance. "Now *you* die," he told Kelbain.

"Rudi! Jasian!" Ashra yelled in terror from the back of the room as she stood next to the staircase.

Jasian turned around and noticed that Ashra was not looking at *them*. Shifting his gaze, he found out why she was so afraid. "Rudi…" he said cautiously, "We must go…"

"But, we have him!" Rudi replied angrily.

"Rudi…" Jasian repeated with widened eyes.

The prince turned to face what he had feared most. His brother stood before them all, apparently alive…but it was *not* Andemar that stared at them with that dark, evil grin…it was Magor. The Demon Sorcerer had returned.

"We must leave *now!*" Ashra shouted again.

Backing away slowly, Rudi stared at his brother's empty husk and saw nothing but darkness. At the same time, he saw that Kelbain had recovered and pulled the arrows from his body. While the West King still seemed to be dangerously near-death, he held Nightfall close and started to change. Refusing to fight that monstrous creature again, Rudi put a hand on Jasian's chest, motioning his cousin to move toward the staircase.

"What *is* this magic?" Jasian commented as he witnessed a portion of Kelbain's transformation.

"No time," Rudi responded. "Go."

By the time he and Jasian reached Ashra's location, Rudi realized that Ashra held his sword, Vulcan.

"I found it where we freed you," Ashra remarked. "I have *mine* already. Sheathe Vulcan for now and use the damn lightning-sword if you need to."

Not knowing what she meant at first, Rudimere looked down at the sword that he carried and saw that the blade was covered in a blue and white whirlwind of lightning. As if by instinct, Rudi then turned to look back at his enemies. While the beastly form of Kelbain walked toward them slowly, Magor stood in place and stared at Rudi with a smile. Wanting to kill them both, it took every bit of willpower for Rudi to follow his companions down the stairs and toward safety.

At the bottom of the staircase, the three of them ran...They ran to escape Woodhaven and the horrors they had encountered within. Surprisingly, they did not stumble across any soldiers from Zenithor, though Rudi knew why. If Kelbain was expecting Andemar to appear, then he would not have wanted any of his men to harm Andemar at all. *How did he know? How?!* Rudi tried not to think about such things, but his brother was dead...and Magor lived in his body. He needed answers.

While the trio continued to run, they were starting to feel a strange sensation. The city around them started to feel warmer as the minutes went by.

"What's going on?" Ashra wondered aloud.

Suddenly, they saw trees catch fire. The pillars of wood and vines that lined up against the walls of the corridor began to burn. As all three of them turned around, they watched as Magor set Woodhaven ablaze.

"He's destroying the city..." Jasian said with an utterly shocked expression.

Rudi's eyes became slits. "Hurry," he told them as they started to run once more.

Rudimere, Jasian, and Ashra ran for their lives, attempting to escape the clutches of the Demon Sorcerer, but were suddenly stopped. A curtain of flames fell down in front of them, blocking their way out, as Magor had brought down the wooden gate with ease. Turning to face their enemy, the three of them embraced the dire situation.

"If I am going to die today," Ashra said as she drew her weapon, "It will be with a sword in my hand." Looking to Jasian with a hint of sadness, she thought only of what sort of life they could have had together. Jasian seemed to mimic the thought as he nodded to her silently and held Harbinger in a fighting stance.

Magor closed in on them slowly, his son not far behind. Before they could act, they were suddenly distracted by a small battle that had broken through a nearby doorway. A group of Woodhaven citizens was fighting back against Kelbain's soldiers.

The Demon Sorcerer turned to the monster beside him. "Go. Leave none alive."

"But, Father…" Kelbain replied in a subhuman voice. He traded looks between Magor and the three that stood before them.

"I will deal with them myself," Magor said. "Now, go."

Rudimere stood between Jasian and Ashra, unable to comprehend what he was witnessing: The grotesque form of Kelbain had made his way over to the other battle, where he was last seen to be tearing a man's head off with his jaws before spitting it out to the ground. As for Magor, though he now inhabited Andemar's body, the sorcerer also had Andemar's *voice*. It was deeply unsettling…but Rudi started to wonder…

"Don't kill him," Rudi said abruptly.

Ashra jerked her head toward her friend. "What?! Rudi—"

"Andemar could still be in there!"

"That is *not* your brother!" Ashra shouted at Rudi. "He's gone!"

"She's right, you know," Magor suddenly interjected, gaining the attention of the three people that defied him. "Your brother is no more. I am all there is. *I* am eternal."

Rudi inhaled sharply, as the words caused him to shiver. He knew that his brother was dead, but could not let go of the possibility that he was still there…even in spirit. "Andemar, please," Rudi tried to speak to Magor, believing that he would find his brother somehow. "Be free of him. Please!"

"You are a fool," Magor said harshly. "There is nothing that can be done." Narrowing his blood-red eyes as he stared at

Rudimere, Magor stated, "He will not be the only Palidor to die on this night." Holding out his hands, he summoned the elements of fire and ice in preparation for the upcoming battle.

"Stay behind me," Jasian whispered to Ashra, knowing now that the Artifacts could deflect such powers.

The Demon Sorcerer flung balls of flames toward the unknown man and woman, while he tossed daggers of ice in the direction of the young Palidor. To his annoyance, they used Stormbringer and Harbinger to shield themselves from his attacks. "You cannot hold out forever," he said calmly over the sound of the elements that he continued to aim at them. With a flick of his left wrist, Magor altered the direction of his sharpened ice and fooled Rudimere into thinking that they were being aimed at his back – but the sorcerer forced *one* dagger toward the Palidor's front. In the blink of an eye, the ice slashed Rudi's throat and sent him tumbling to the ground as he grasped his neck.

Jasian's eyes widened in horror. "Rudi!" he shouted. Without pause, the Lord of Stoneshield turned his attention to the enemy. Managing to push through the fire with his axe, Jasian reached Magor with little effort. He then kicked his cousin's body in the gut and pulled Harbinger back, ready to swing. *Forgive me, Andemar,* he thought as he brought his axe in for the kill. But somehow, he was stopped. As he gripped Harbinger, he tried to push through again but felt something invisible holding him in place.

With one hand in mid-air, Magor looked up into the eyes of Harbinger's wielder. "*This* is true power, mortal." Using his ability, he threw the man across the room, toward the fallen front gate.

"No!" Ashra cried out. She had only been a few feet behind Jasian when he was in front of Magor. Acting quickly, she charged with her simple sword. But the Demon Sorcerer held her in place, just as Oreus had done at the Temple of Aman.

Using his power, Magor pulled the blonde woman closer to him until he could feel her breath upon his face. "Such beauty," he said as he studied her for a moment. "You have a certain fire deep within you, young one." Suddenly, to his surprise, the woman spat in his face.

"Go to Mistif, you bastard," she uttered through her teeth.

Wiping his face slowly, Magor glared at the one that disrespected him so blatantly. "I have a *different* sort of fire. Where I come from, the inferno that surrounds my world burns long and without apology." Still holding her in place, Magor placed his left hand on her cheek. "To be touched by such a thing...it would be *most* painful."

Ashra let out a blood-curdling scream. Fire seared her flesh, though she saw no flames in the moment – it was all beneath her skin. She tried to move away from the sorcerer's hand, but she could not. When she finally began to pass out from the pain, Magor tossed her into the same area as Jasian.

Staring at the two on the floor, the Demon Sorcerer shook his head. "You could have had a quick death. But now," he remarked as he conjured a scorching fire in both of his hands, "you will suffer for your insolence." Aiming at his foes, Magor launched two large waves of fire toward them. But something happened that he was not expecting: A figure seemed to jump into the path of his chosen element.

As the smoke cleared, the mysterious figure revealed itself to be Rudimere, unharmed from the flames due to his Evolutionary ability. He stared at Magor, contempt spread across his face, with his neck wound beginning to heal. He was now immune to *ice*, in addition to fire.

"No…" Magor whispered into the night, fear clutching his voice, as Woodhaven continued to crumble around him. Realizing that Rudimere was an Evolutionary, Magor sought to kill the Palidor with haste. "Not *this* time," he commented.

Watching as the Demon Sorcerer walked toward him, Rudi was ready for the fight of his life. But then he took a moment to turn and gaze at Ashra and Jasian. While Ashra was unconscious and badly burned, Jasian did his best to hold her as he stared back at Rudi with a shocked expression. Clearly, Rudi had almost forgotten that his cousin was unaware of his power. But beyond all of that, he realized that he needed to get Ashra and Jasian to safety at all costs. *The gate is destroyed…it's a pile of burning wood now. How are we supposed to get out of this place?* Then his eyes grew large – he remembered what his brother said about Stormbringer, and how the sword had somehow allowed him to get to Woodhaven. He thought of Mora and the day that they had parted – and suddenly, as he looked at the blade in his hands, he *saw* Mora, standing in celebration with the people of Summerhold. *We need to leave,* he thought as he stared at the sword. *We need to get to Summerhold.*

As if he knew what was about to happen, Magor unsheathed Andemar's sword, Thanatos, and began to walk toward Rudimere even faster.

Stormbringer crackled to life, and the blade became surrounded in lightning as it had done so earlier. Thinking fast, Rudi made his way over to Ashra and Jasian. Seeing that Jasian was still cradling Ashra, he made sure that they all stayed connected. "Hold onto me," he told his cousin.

Before they knew it, a giant bolt of lightning crashed down upon them, hurtling them into the night sky and out of Woodhaven. They could hear the faint shouting of an angry sorcerer as they departed.

***

With a thunderous crash, Rudi, Ashra, and Jasian arrived in the throne room of Summerhold. Jasian was the first to rise, but the trip had awoken Ashra as well. Rudi, however, remained kneeling on the floor with a look of defeat.

339

"Rudi!" a voice called out from nearby. The man ran toward the group, overjoyed. "Jasian! They found you!" Suddenly, he stopped directly in front of the group, his smile faded, and he addressed the clear injury upon his friend's face. "Ash!" Paxton said with a tone of surprise. "What happened?!"

Ashra started to speak but had trouble forming the right words to describe the experience at Woodhaven. She merely turned to Jasian and sobbed in his arms.

By the time Paxton turned to Rudi to get some answers, he had found his friend, and brother, in a state of everlasting anguish.

Chapter 29

ETERNALLY IN VOLSI

The city was quiet – quieter than it should have been. Just days ago, the people of Summerhold, under King Wilfred's leadership, defended their homes from the army of Karthmere. Tragically, the king, his queen, and the chancellor of the city all lost their lives, along with scores of men and women who fought hard during the siege. In the days that followed the battle, more devastation arrived on Summerhold's doorstep. Prince Andemar Palidor, of Angelia, was dead. By the use of dark, unknown magic, his body was used as a vessel for the return of Magor, the Mystic of the West. While Andemar's loss was mourned, some were more concerned with the threat of the Demon Sorcerer...

In the cold, dank crypts beneath the great hall, Saris Orthane stared at the grave markers for her mother and father, wishing that she could have done more to protect them. It had only been days since their deaths, and she knew that they would soon have proper statues to honor their spirits, but Saris grieved as any daughter would. In the past, members of House Orthane visited the tombs of their ancestors from time-to-time, though they had no reason to do so in a long while. The recent events at the Temple of Aman – and the tragedy during the siege – gave them a new reason to pay their respects down in the depths of the dark catacombs.

Hearing the faint sound of footsteps, Saris stood in place as she knew who was coming to stand by her side.

"Sorry I'm late," Paxton said with sincerity.

"No apologies are necessary," Saris replied. "This is their resting place now. They'll be here for quite a while."

Paxton nodded solemnly. "It was good of the entire city to attend the funeral. Your parents would have been happy, I think."

Saris smiled weakly. "My father spent most of his life trying to live up to his own father's name: the great Gilder Orthane." She then chuckled softly. "While Gilder passed away in his sleep, my father died in battle. It was a warrior's death," she said proudly. "Indeed, he *would* be happy." An expression of unease suddenly found its way onto her face. "Paxton…we received a letter from the Northern capital of Whitecrest. Your friend, Jasian…His father was murdered."

"I know," Pax said with regret. "Tomis told me before I came to see you."

Seeking comfort, Saris wrapped her arms around Paxton in a loving embrace. "So much death...all around us," she remarked, her face mostly buried in Paxton's chest. She leaned back and asked, "Do you think Rudi will be alright? What happened to his brother was..."

Paxton took a moment, wondering how *he* was doing, knowing that a man that was like a brother to him for most of his life was gone. "I don't know about Rudi," he replied, "but I wish that I was there that night." His lips started to quiver. "Andemar was a good man – one of the best."

Saris nodded with a half-smile. Changing topics, she sighed. "Let us leave death behind," she said as she glanced around the crypt, "and make our way to the throne room."

As the two of them began to walk out of the darkness, Paxton said, "I *do* worry about Rudi. Perhaps now that he's back here, he can spend time with Mora and find some happiness again."

Saris tilted her head slightly. "She has enough troubles now," she responded, trying not to sound cold. "She has a kingdom to rule."

"Of course," Paxton said, hoping that he did not sound silly a moment ago. "She will do well – especially with Tomis at her side as the new chancellor." Suddenly, he noticed Saris's face as it formed a look of concern. "Do you regret stepping down?" Paxton asked.

As if pulled from a daze, Saris shook her head. "Oh no, that's not it at all. I'm *glad* that she took her rightful place on the throne. I never wanted it in the first place." Saris thought of the moment that Mora came back after the fall of the Convergence. She hoped, more than anything, that Mora would remember her duty to her family and retake her place as the first in line…though neither of them ever thought the decision would come into play so soon. "I'm just worried about her. This is her first court as the Queen," Saris reminded Paxton. "All eyes will be on *her* today. I know Mora. She is probably terrified that she'll forget something. Let's give her all the support that she needs."

***

Jasian sat patiently beside the woman he loved. As he gazed upon her, unable to avoid the blackened mark of Magor's hand on her cheek, Jasian internally swore that he would never let anything happen to her again. However, he could have kicked himself as he knew that Ashra would never allow him to speak of such a promise. She was a fierce fighter who never let any obstacles get in her way. *She'll be alright,* Jasian thought. Holding her hand within his, he shed a tear while looking into her closed eyes.

"I love you, Ash…I love you."

Turning his head quickly, Jasian caught a glimpse of someone walking in his direction. Standing up to meet the man, he smiled and breathed shakily.

"Hello, my friend," Mika greeted Jasian.

Jasian began to smile wider, immediately overwhelmed with relief that they both survived up until that point. "Mika," he replied before the two of them hugged. It was hard to believe that they had not seen each other since The Great Wood.

"How is she?" Mika asked.

"She will recover," Jasian replied, though it was with a hint of sadness, "but she will bear that mark for the rest of her life."

"Ashra is strong, Jasian. *You* must be as well."

Jasian sighed. "You're right...You're right."

After a moment, Mika shifted uncomfortably. Attempting to find the right words, he said the only other thing that was on his mind. "Did you kill him?"

Jasian turned to look into his friend's eyes – he knew how much the answer meant to Mika. Slowly, Jasian nodded. "With Ashra's help," he confirmed. "She saved my life. I couldn't have done it without her," Jasian said gratefully as he looked to her again.

Letting out a huge breath, Mika smiled as his eyes shot upward. He silently shared the news with his mother and father, certain that they were finally at peace...just as *he* was.

Another moment later, one of the healers that served the Orthanes walked into the room. Jasian asked if there was anything else they could do for Ashra but was told that they did everything they could. It was up to *her* to wake.

Allowing Ashra to rest as needed, Jasian and Mika headed to the throne room, anticipating Queen Mora's first official court.

***

She stood in front of the people in the throne room, nervous and afraid. It was not those in attendance that she feared, but her own strengths and weaknesses – and what she feared most was her ability to rule as well as her parents did for so long.

"Do not be despair, Mora."

Locking eyes with her brother, Tomis – who stood at her side as the new chancellor – she thought of her response so that he would be the only one to hear.

"I just want to make them proud," she said in her mind. *"Thank you for helping me, Brother."* She reached out her hand to grasp his for a short moment as they smiled at each other in understanding.

Turning to face the people in the room, she took note of all that shared in the occasion. Along with all of the city's nobles, she spotted her sister, Saris, and Ser Paxton Korba standing side-by-side. Suddenly, she was surveying the entirety of the hall in search of Rudimere...but he was not there. Mora's heart was filled with sadness, but she understood that Rudi wanted to be alone after his brother's death. Moving along the large group of people, she found Mika Gainhart and the Lord of Stoneshield, Jasian Bowlin. Lastly, with as much forgiveness as she could muster, she had allowed the Captain of the Viper Legion, Loreena Stenwulf, to attend court. Mora knew enough to keep an eye on her, but as Stenwulf had betrayed Harlan Wallis during the siege, Mora felt that the woman deserved some recognition for that act.

"Thank you all for joining me today," Mora addressed the people. "This moment marks the start of a new era for Summerhold, as well as the whole Southern region. You chose me as your queen, and for that, I will repay you all with the kindness and honesty that you deserve." Her face began to turn sour as she spoke again. "With that being said…I would be careless if I did not address the latest tragedy to befall Areon. As most of you know, one of the princes of the East, Andemar Palidor, lost his life at Woodhaven. Though the fate of his spirit remains unresolved, I have no doubt that the gods have welcomed him into Volsi."

Amongst the crowd, Paxton lowered his head sorrowfully. He truly hoped that Andemar found his way into the Hall of Legends, where the prince was certain to meet with his grandfather, Victor, once more. The thought brought a smile to Paxton's face, as he knew just how close the two Palidors were.

Queen Mora lifted the golden goblet that stood on the arm of her throne and turned to her brother. Tomis then filled the cup with red wine. "May Andemar find mead and merriment in the Hall of Legends," she announced the traditional words loudly. "And may he forever rest in the arms of the gods." Lifting her cup for all to see, she exclaimed, "Eternally in Volsi!" The crowd repeated her words in unison.

After the tribute, Paxton looked around the room once more, hoping to find Rudimere, but sighed when he could not spot his friend anywhere.

Placing her cup down, the queen addressed the people in attendance again. "On to other matters," she said before looking to Tomis.

The new chancellor was befuddled at first but quickly remembered that he was responsible for making declarations during court. "Captain Loreena Stenwulf, please step forward."

The woman from Karthmere was surprised to hear her name called within the great hall. Stepping in front of the throne, she kneeled before Mora. "My Queen."

"Your name carries weight in Karthmere, Captain. The Stenwulfs are one of the oldest families in the South," Mora stated.

"Yes, my Queen," Loreena replied courteously. "It is with your generosity that the name still lives on, as *I* am the last Stenwulf."

Mora nodded, knowing that fact already. "During the siege, when your lord asked you to fulfill your role as Witness and partake in Second Combat...you refused. You recognized the dishonor that Harlan Wallis displayed during the duel, and you stood your ground. I find that quite admirable," the queen said with sincerity. "Therefore, until I can find any reason to have another person take the seat, *you* will watch over your home with the same honor and respect that is expected of you." Catching the shock on Loreena's face, Mora spoke up again. "Loreena Stenwulf, I name you the Steward of Karthmere."

Throughout the hall, multiple gasps were heard, but they were all silenced when Tomis placed his hands in the air and lowered them, signaling the crowd to hush.

"You honor me, my Queen," Loreena said humbly. "I gladly accept."

Queen Mora bowed her head slightly, giving the new steward permission to rise and make way for the next matter to be addressed.

"Mika Gainhart. Please step forward." Tomis announced.

After a moment, Mika walked to the center of the room, still favoring his back from his encounter with the Lekuzza. Getting sliced from behind by a large talon was no simple thing to heal from.

Watching as Mika descended to one knee, Mora smiled. "For your bravery and leadership during the siege of our city, I intend to grant you a knighthood."

Mika's eyes met Mora's instantly. "M-My Queen?"

Mora stood and addressed the head of her household guard. "Captain St. Clare, your sword, please." After Valentyne drew her blade and handed it to Mora, the queen approached Mika. "I command you to protect those who need protection," she said as she laid the flat end of the sword on one of his shoulders. Moving to his other shoulder, she said, "I charge you to defend the crowns." The queen stepped back to allow the man some space in that moment. "Arise, Ser Mika Gainhart, Knight of Areon."

A rare thing occurred as he stood up – a tear slid down Mika's cheek. It was a day that he would always remember. Draven Darkwood was dead, his parents were avenged, and he was knighted by the South Queen of Areon. *If only I had an apple*, he thought to himself, wishing that he had such delectable fruit to celebrate with.

Once Mora sat on her throne again, she turned to Tomis once more and smiled widely.

"Ser Paxton Korba, please step forward." Tomis declared.

Not unlike the others, Paxton displayed a stunned look on his face but quickly rearranged his features before kneeling in the center of the great hall. "Queen Mora," he said with a bow.

"Ser Paxton, you showed distinct valor and fearlessness when you challenged Harlan Wallis to Single Combat. With one phrase, you attempted to end the siege single-handedly. I think I speak for all of us when I say thank you." Paxton bowed his head low with respect. "For your efforts against that dishonorable Water Elemental, I name you: Paxton Frostbane."

"FROSTBANE!" the people in the hall shouted together after the queen made the announcement.

"That is not all, Ser Paxton," Mora divulged. "I wanted to grant you a knighthood as well, but it seems that you are already a knight. If there is anything that you would ask of me, you shall have it."

Paxton thought long and hard but knew exactly what he was going to ask. "With your permission, my Queen," he said nervously, "I'd like to ask for your sister's hand in marriage."

The request drew a collective shock from everyone in attendance, including Saris. Mora smiled and countered, "Why not ask her yourself?"

Paxton remained on his one knee and turned toward Saris, who had already walked toward him with large, watery eyes. "I love you, Saris Orthane. It would be my greatest honor in this life if you would marry me."

Starting to lose her composure, Saris gave in to her emotions. "Yes!" she shouted right before hugging her future husband. She kissed him passionately, much to the delight of the crowd in the hall, who cheered for them during one of the happiest instances of their lives.

Later, after the great hall had cleared out, Paxton made his way to Rudi's room to determine why he had not attended court.

Entering his friend's bedchamber, Paxton felt a knot in his stomach as he stared at the contents of the room. The two most noticeable objects were situated on the feather bed — both in plain sight, for anyone to find. The most obvious was the Mystical Artifact, Stormbringer. Paxton had only seen it the night that Rudi and the others appeared in Summerhold but could never mistake the sword for any other in the world. Lying next to Stormbringer was a piece of parchment, which Paxton correctly assumed to contain a letter from Rudi. Paxton picked up the item and read its message. Disappointment set in as he could only focus on certain parts of the letter. Rudi left Stormbringer for anyone who wished to wield it — he also left the city with no possessions except for his own sword, Vulcan.

Finishing the letter, Paxton lowered the hand that held the parchment and shook his head. His friend never once mentioned where he was going. "Rudi...you damned fool," he whispered.

EPILOGUE

LADY OF THE SKY HALL

Evermount. The Sky Hall. The seat of Lord Drudorn Varian. Centuries ago, it was the throne of the Evermount Empire. Now…it was occupied by Lucille Varian.

The Lady of Evermount contemplated much in the past few days. Her encounter with Andemar Palidor over a week earlier ended up more casual than she had intended. While she had plans to speak with the prince in detail, she did not expect that he would demand to speak only with Drudorn.

Hmph. Royalty. The disdain that she had for the man stemmed from her own past dealings with kings and queens, though not many would be able to comprehend how that was possible. Nevertheless, Lucille heard recent rumblings of the prince's demise, as well as the scorching of Woodhaven. Curious about the validity of the rumors, the Lady of Evermount waited for confirmation from the chancellor.

As if miraculously summoned to her side, Theodore Graves entered the hall, swiftly approaching the woman at the back. "Lady Lucille," the hollow-eyed man greeted her. "I bring news."

"Go on," she commanded him.

"The rumors you heard were true, my Lady. Prince Andemar is dead. Woodhaven is nothing but ashes. The flames even spread to The Great Wood, and the forest has burned for days. But there is…ah…something else. It couldn't be true…" he said with hesitation behind his voice.

Lucille narrowed her eyes. "Speak," she said threateningly.

"It seems that…well…the Demon Sorcerer has returned. Magor is *alive*."

The Lady of Evermount expressed disbelief as she stood up and paced around her chair, while her long yellow dress flowed behind her. "It can't be," she muttered. Coming to a halt, she twisted her body and glared at Chancellor Graves. "Your words are false," she accused. "I would have been told."

"Oh, but it *is* true," a voice said from the darkness.

Lucille and Theodore turned to discover the source of the interruption, finding a middle-aged-looking man with short, grayish-brown hair. He was staring at them with ashen eyes that seemed to pierce through the blackened corner of the room.

Stepping out to reveal himself, the man spoke once more. "And you are being told *now*."

"Garis!" Lucille said, surprised at the Sudae's appearance. "We've not seen you in some time."

"I am no longer required to hide in the shadows," Garis said with a smile. "The plan has been fulfilled."

Her eyes lit up as if she had been in the presence of Magor already. "I-I can hardly believe it. Kelbain has spoken of this day for so long," she said in a whisper.

"Let's not forget that the spawn of Magor could not have achieved this feat without me," Garis said spitefully. "I realize you have had your loyalty to Kelbain for many years, but you would be wise to let go of that attachment and serve *another* master."

"Of course," Lucille quickly agreed. "Magor's return is a gift. I am looking forward to meeting him."

Garis smiled and placed a hand on her face. "You played your part well. I am thankful that you were able to get my letter to Kelbain so swiftly."

"It was my duty," Lucille stated with pride. "Getting him to Woodhaven was of paramount importance."

"Yes…" Garis remarked nonchalantly. "I found it tiresome trying to get the young Palidor to the same destination. Convincing him to grab Stormbringer was even more tedious." Suddenly, he found himself laughing. "I had to tell him that I was just a 'memory' of Garis – or Horus, as *he* knew me."

Lucille and Chancellor Graves joined in the jest until the Lady of Evermount made a sarcastic comment. "Pretending to be someone you're not…That must have been difficult."

Garis smirked. "*You* should know all about that."

Lucille's body began to shift in plain sight. Her blonde hair turned dark, her skin became pale, and her eyes now looked to be the color of the sun.

"Ugh! I cannot stand that awful form," she said with disgust.

"It's good to see the *real* you, Lamia," Garis said. "It is long overdue that *all* of us step out of the shadows." Turning to the chancellor, whom he had ignored up until that point, Garis spoke in a belittling tone. "Be a good servant and make sure that Lord Varian has not succumbed to your poison yet."

Fearfully, the chancellor replied, "At once, Garis."

After Graves left the great hall, the Sudae turned to Lamia and smiled wickedly.

"Everything that I have foreseen…*everything*…is coming to pass."

SHARDS OF THE SUN

APPENDIX A

SAGES

Sages – Individuals in Areon with extraordinary abilities. They are divided into 4 different classes: Illusionist, Foreseer, Evolutionary, and Sorcerer. These classes also have sub-classes. **NOTE: Sages do not always have all abilities in a class**. They are as follows:

Illusionist: Changer, Reader

> ➤ *Changer*: One with the ability to shapeshift into any person
> ➤ *Reader*: One who can speak to, control, and read the minds of others

Foreseer: Watcher, Pathfinder, Sensor

> ➤ *Watcher*: One with the ability to see the future (not always accurate)
> ➤ *Pathfinder*: One with the ability to locate an object or individual
> ➤ *Sensor*: One who is able to sense Sage abilities in another

Evolutionary:

> ➤ *Evolutionary*: One with the ability to develop a resistance or immunity to whatever they were injured by or exposed to.

Sorcerer: Elemental, Kindler, {Sorcery}

> ➤ *Elemental*: One with the ability to control the elements, such as fire, earth, water, or wind (extremely **RARE** to be able to control more than one element)
> ➤ *Kindler*: One with the ability to activate latent Sage abilities in another
> ➤ *{Sorcery}* The ability to move objects with one's mind (NOTE: Only Magor and his son, Oreus, are known to exhibit this ability)
> ➤ *Longevity*: Having a longer lifespan than a normal human (NOTE: This is not entirely a Sage ability, and has only

been known to be *gifted* through a Kindling by Magor or Kelbain)

SHARDS OF THE SUN

APPENDIX B

THE RULING HOUSES AND LORDS OF AREON

(as of this novel's start)

The East – Ruling from the grand city of Angelia, the Palidors have held dominion over the Eastern region of Areon for centuries.

In a time nearly forgotten, when the realm of Areon had no true ruler to speak of, one man started a campaign that would change the world forever. Vulcan Palidor, the man who built Angelia from the ground up, marched on the Eastern lands in a bid to save the people from a tyrannical ruler. Many battles were fought, but once the cities of Evermount and Triton had fallen under his leadership, Vulcan had his stonemasons build a fortified city between the mountains that led to the 'White Jewel' of Angelia. He named the new city: Stoneshield.

Vulcan had established the first true kingdom, and so the people declared him their East King.

Many years passed after his bold conquest, but Vulcan's reputation as a just and fair ruler grew to new heights – and the Lords of Stoneshield, Evermount, and Triton gladly swore fealty to their King for all time.

HOUSE PALIDOR
OF ANGELIA

- [VICTOR PALIDOR], Former East King of Areon and Hero of the Sorcerer's War, died of natural causes
    - VANDAL PALIDOR, ♚ East King of Areon and Lord of Angelia, son of Victor
    - SERENA PALIDOR (née BOWLIN), ♛ East Queen of Areon and Lady of Angelia, wife of Vandal
        - THASUS PALIDOR, East Prince of Areon, first born son of Vandal and Serena, called THASUS THE MIGHTY
        - ANDEMAR PALIDOR, East Prince of Areon, master-at-arms of Angelia, second born son of Vandal and Serena
        - MARYN PALIDOR (née KELLI), wife of Andemar
            - ANDEN PALIDOR, first born son of Andemar and Maryn
            - GINESIA PALIDOR, first born daughter of Andemar and Maryn, called GINNY
        - RUDIMERE PALIDOR, East Prince of Areon, third born son of Vandal and Serena, called RUDI

- SER PAXTON KORBA, Knight of Angelia, originally from Triton
- HORUS, an eccentric Foreseer with his own shop in Angelia

House Sigil: White horse on a blue field

HOUSE ARGON
OF TRITON

- ABACUS ARGON, Lord of Triton and Hero of the Sorcerer's War, called ABE
    - ASHRA ARGON, first born daughter of Abacus

House Sigil: A merman, with a lower torso and fin of green, holding a gold trident on a blue field

HOUSE BOWLIN
OF STONESHIELD

- [MARC BOWLIN], Former Lord of Stoneshield, Serena's older brother, murdered in the tower of Whitecrest by Cyrus Norton
- HANA BOWLIN (née VARIAN), wife of Marc, Drudorn's younger cousin
    - [MERROC BOWLIN], first born son of Marc and Hana, nephew of King Vandal and Queen Serena, murdered at Squall's End by Draven Darkwood
    - JASIAN BOWLIN, Lord of Stoneshield, second born son of Marc and Hana, nephew of King Vandal and Queen Serena

- ORNELL BALGON, Commander of Stoneshield's army

House Sigil: Black bear in front of a white castle on a blue field

HOUSE VARIAN
OF EVERMOUNT

- DRUDORN VARIAN, Lord of Evermount, Hana's older cousin
- LUCILLE VARIAN, Lady of Evermount, second wife of Drudorn
    - RANDAR VARIAN, first born son of Drudorn and his first wife, called RANDAR THE REPULSIVE, the half-wit
    - DORIAN VARIAN, second born son of Drudorn and his first wife

- THEODORE GRAVES, Chancellor of Evermount

House Sigil: Gold phoenix on a blue field, with gold flames surrounding the outer edges

The West – Zenithor – a castle, a keep, a small city in its own right, the place has become the only remnant of what was once a vast stretch of land. All other villages and cities were decimated in the conflict known as the Sorcerer's War, save for Woodhaven, and the wastelands that formed took on the name of the Deadlands. Taken over by Magor, the 'Demon Sorcerer', hundreds of years in the past, Zenithor stands the only true power of the West.

Magor was the primary enemy of the people of Areon during the war. While his son, Kelbain, was defeated at Woodhaven by the South King, Gilder Orthane, Magor's army made a last stand outside Zenithor. The Sorcerer himself remained inside the fortress, waiting for those who would seek him out. He was met by a band of heroes, which consisted of Lord Abacus Argon, of Triton, Lord Maven Brock, of Whitecrest, Nia Silverthorne, of Hailstone Hold, Lucius Karver, from the island of Atley, and their commander, East King Victor Palidor. Though Nia and Lucius lost their lives to the dark Sage, the other three prevailed when Maven took Magor's head.

Kelbain, a 16-year-old boy at the time, was pardoned and given leave to live out his days at Zenithor. But, the 'boy' grew to be a vengeful man, continuing a small civil war on his own with the sanctuary city of Woodhaven, as there was no West King to be named while the two houses warred on.

It should also be noted that Kelbain, like his father, declined to take a surname, believing himself to be above those he meant to rule. Magor's most faithful followers, such as the family of Dirce and Lamia, renounced their own surnames in order to prove their loyalty.

FORTRESS OF ZENITHOR

- [MAGOR], Former West King of Areon, called THE DEMON SORCERER, one of The Four Mystics that arrived in Areon centuries ago
    - KELBAIN, ♔ West King of Areon and Lord of Zenithor, son of Magor
    - [DIRCE], Kelbain's betrothed, murdered at Squall's End by Merroc Bowlin
        - [ZANE], Former West Prince of Areon, son of Kelbain, Dirce's secret lover, killed in Single Combat by Kelbain
    - Generals of Zenithor army:
        - LAMIA, Dirce's older sister
        - SOROS, co-steward of Zenithor
        - MALOS, co-steward of Zenithor
        - RHOBU, former steward of Woodhaven

- MIKA GAINHART, Former Zenithor soldier, originally from the small village of Redberry, traveling warrior, called THE SAGESLAYER, wields the family heirloom of House Brock

House Sigil: Red shark fin on a black field

HOUSE DARKWOOD OF WOODHAVEN

- DRAVEN DARKWOOD, Lord of Woodhaven, former Justice of the people, former mercenary

House Sigil: Dark green tree on a black field, silver stars above the tree symbolizing the night sky

The North – The one region in Areon where the people do not believe in having a sigil, the North is in a constant state of winter and is comprised of some of the proudest people in all the land. However, as it was in the West, the entirety of the North was ruled by its King up until the end of the Sorcerer's War.

The animosity between the Northern houses has been present for a long time, ever since the fall of Magor. While the North King, Maven Brock, was swinging his axe to destroy Magor, his seat at Whitecrest was stolen by the Nortons, a lower house that had its start at Hailstone Hold, and Rikter's Hollow was taken by the powerful Gargan warriors. Once Maven had returned to the North, he and his army fought first to take back Whitecrest, but were unsuccessful, as they were pushed back to the Frostford. By that time, after suffering losses in the war, as well as against the Nortons, the Brocks hadn't bothered to attack the Gargans at Rikter's Hollow, instead choosing to recover in their new home at the Frostford.

With the Nortons solidifying their rule over the North, and with the Gargans holding the Brocks' ancestral home and the Ironforge – an important resource to all of Areon – Maven Brock and his people were left with a bittersweet taste in their mouths after having played an integral role in saving the realm of Areon.

HOUSE NORTON
OF WHITECREST

- [MARCEL NORTON], Former North King of Areon, died after falling from the tower of Whitecrest
- CELIA NORTON, Former North Queen of Areon, wife of Marcel, ruled the North until Cyrus came of age
    - CYRUS NORTON, ♚ North King of Areon and Lord of Whitecrest, son of Marcel and Celia
    - AMASHA GARGAN, Cyrus's betrothed, fourth born daughter of Oswall Gargan
    - [CASSIE NORTON] (née CORA), Former North Queen of Areon, wife of Cyrus, died during childbirth
        - SAUL NORTON, North Prince of Areon, son of Cyrus and Cassie
- VYNCENT REIGN, Commander of Hailstone Hold

HOUSE BROCK
OF THE FROSTFORD

- [MAVEN BROCK], Former North King of Areon, Former Lord of the Frostford, Hero of the Sorcerer's War, called THE DEMON'S BANE, died at age 88 fighting the FENROK
    - [BALDRIC BROCK], Former Lord of the Frostford, son of Maven, killed in Single Combat against Mika Gainhart
        - CALE BROCK, Lord of the Frostford, son of Baldric
        - KAYA BROCK (née GARGAN), Lady of the Frostford, wife of Cale, second born daughter of Oswall Gargan

HOUSE GARGAN
OF RIKTER'S HOLLOW

- OSWALL GARGAN, Lord of Rikter's Hollow
    - GRENNA GARGAN, first born daughter of Oswall

- JORGA GARGAN, third born daughter of Oswall, called
THE JUGGERNAUT

The South – The 'Land of Riches'. If the North was known for its rigid and stern folk, the South was the opposite in the sense that its citizens were found to be ever joyful, due to their wealthy and lavish lifestyles.

The Orthanes of Summerhold have ruled the South since the days before Vulcan Palidor conquered the East. The Southerners were always content with what they had, though they enjoyed the thrill of competition. Whether it was a tournament of knights from Summerhold and Karthmere, a battle of wits between the merchants of the Silk Isles, or a comparison of one's ownership of gold, the South mostly kept their pleasure and entertainment to themselves...until the Great Trade War.

Trading goods between their own locations was accepted for many years, but when their borders opened up to the kingdom to the east, as well as to the once peaceful lands of the west, disputes and arguments escalated quickly. Years went by without a proper resolution to the conflict, but with the arrival of the strange beings that later came to be known as the Mystics, everything changed. Ports were built, commerce was established, and a new era of peace began in Areon.

Centuries later, the Sorcerer's War came and went, and the South grew to be less of a jubilant place. The Lord of Karthmere, Samus Weyland, was killed and usurped by his friend and Captain of the Castle Guard, Rayburn Duke, ushering in a dark time for the region, as Duke also sought to take the throne from South King Wilfred Orthane. The shipping of goods from the Silk Isles to the rest of Areon still commenced, though some of the Isles preferred to operate on their own terms. While the Lord of the Silk Isles sat in luxury amongst his peers on Atley, dangerous sport was held on Skal, Forsa became the epicenter of debauchery, and Fura's weapon and trinket shops were the focus of pirates who sought to obtain treasures by unnecessary force. Only the island of Lon stood untouched and fully protected, as its vast amount of farms and breweries were of utmost importance to the people of Areon.

HOUSE ORTHANE
OF SUMMERHOLD

- [GILDER ORTHANE], Former South King of Areon, Hero of the Sorcerer's War, died at age 82 of natural causes
  - WILFRED ORTHANE, ♟ South King of Areon and Lord of Summerhold, son of Gilder
  - KAYLA ORTHANE [née DUKE], ♛ South Queen of Areon and Lady of Summerhold, wife of Wilfred
    - MORA ORTHANE, first born daughter of Willard and Kayla, former Priestess of the Convergence, Crown Princess and heir to the Southern throne of Areon
    - SARIS ORTHANE, second born daughter of Willard and Kayla
    - [WILLARD ORTHANE], first born son of Willard and Kayla, killed by Saris Orthane at the Temple of Aman
    - TOMIS ORTHANE, second born son of Willard and Kayla, former Initiate of the Convergence

- VALENTYNE ST. CLARE, Captain of the House Guard of Summerhold

House Sigil: Blue raven on a red and gold field split diagonally

HOUSE STILLWELL
OF THE SILK ISLES

- BEN STILLWELL, Lord of the Silk Isles, ruling from the island of Atley

House Sigil: Bright golden satchel on a red field

HOUSE WALLIS
OF KARTHMERE

- [RAYBURN DUKE], former Lord of Karthmere, Kayla's older brother, buried alive by West King Kelbain
    - [DALTON DUKE], son of Rayburn, killed by Harlan Wallis

- HARLAN WALLIS, Lord of Karthmere, former Captain of the Viper Legion

- LOREENA STENWULF, member of the Viper Legion

House Sigil: Green serpent on a black field

R.T. Cole

COMING SOON:

CHAINS OF VENGEANCE

BOOK FOUR OF

THE REALM OF AREON

R.T. Cole

.

ABOUT THE AUTHOR

R.T. Cole is an author of fiction, and is currently working on *Chains of Vengeance*, the fourth installment of The Realm of Areon epic fantasy series. He lives in Northern New Jersey with his wife and son.

When he's not writing his next novel, he's binge-watching TV shows, relaxing in front of a movie, or playing video games.

https://linktr.ee/Officialrtcole

R.T. Cole

1/26/2021

Made in the USA
Middletown, DE
16 January 2021

31600556R00229